IT'S DANGEROUS TO BE DIFFERENT

Lorna Hayes had seen a lot of people come and go in this big city—the worldlings, the hip people, the ones who could grab without giving. It was something one had to learn and accept, because everyone wore two faces.

But this girl was different. There was something weird about this Susan Miller, for all her youth and good looks and honest eyes. And when Susan came home after her first day of work with a big, tough-looking character following her, Lorna smelled trouble.

But there was a lot that Susan, with her innocence, and Lorna, for all her sophistication, didn't see. That tough-looking character, Peterson, saw it—the whole mess. And it looked to him like little Miss Miller was unwittingly getting herself mixed up in murder. Maybe her own.

D1564089

Turn this book over for second complete novel

THE
ONE-FACED
GIRL

by

CHARLOTTE ARMSTRONG

ACE BOOKS, INC.
1120 Avenue of the Americas
New York 36, N.Y.

CHAPTER I

THE LANDLADY felt it. Something about this girl gave her a touch of the fidgits. But the landlady was not going to turn a tenant away without a more tangible reason, and this girl had the first week's rent in her hand. It wasn't her looks. She was young, healthy, neat and clean, and her manner was not furtive. She looked one in the eye. The landlady took the money and looked away.

Lorna Hayes, who lived in the other front room, heard voices and peeked through her cracked door to see who was moving in. Lorna had been a bachelor career-girl for a long, long time. She took note of the new tenant's face, figure, clothing—and something else about her—who could say what? Lora closed her door with a little shrug.

But that evening, when the girl knocked and asked for advice there was no reason to refuse it.

"I'm Susan Miller," the girl said. "I thought you could help me. Would you please?"

"Hi, Susan," said Lorna with easy good nature. "I'm Lorna Hayes. What can I do for you?"

"I want to know how to put make-up on my eyes," the girl said. She didn't seem embarrassed or shy, which was odd. "*You* do, I see," she continued, eyeing Lorna's eyes. "I bought a lot of stuff at the drugstore."

Lorna was intrigued. "Well, there's nothing so hard about it. Sure, I'll show you. Why not?" So she crossed over to the girl's room. It was just like her own. Dresser, chair, bed dis-

5

guised as a divan, a narrow door to a tiny bathroom. On the dresser the girl had spread her purchases.

"Are you . . . uh . . . looking for some special kind of job here?" asked Lorna. It was crossing her mind that this could be one of the poor little moths drawn to the flame of Hollywood, dreaming of glamour and fame.

"I have a job," the girl said. "I'm going to work tomorrow, at the Shank Development Company. I am to be a file clerk."

She had a pleasant voice, not harsh, not shrill. Something about her, however, was abrasive to the nerves. Lorna batted her own mascaraed lashes and caught sight of her own blue eyelids, her thin black brows, her tinted hair, and the lizard texture of her aging flesh. Perhaps it was the pair of phenomenally clear gray eyes set in so fair a young face that offended. *Jealous, eh?* Lorna twitted herself.

"Sit down," she said to the girl cordially, "and we'll see what we can do. You want to look sophisticated? Is that it?"

"Maybe," said Susan Miller. "I notice that all the women are wearing paint around their eyes. I'd rather not be conspicuous."

Lorna was seeing the texture of this skin close-up now, and it made her sigh. She picked up an eyebrow pencil. "Where do you come from?" she asked, "that you never fooled around with this stuff before?"

"I come from the mountains. My Dad is a forester."

Lorna began to stroke the fair brows with the darkening pencil. "The mountains, eh? Why aren't you all weather-beaten and country-looking?"

"I don't know," said Susan. "My mother is. I must be too young."

"You make *me* feel a hundred years old," said Lorna in burst of good-natured honesty. "Now, see, you smear this shadow up from the lashes. You try it."

The girl worked seriously. "It feels sticky."

"Oh, well, we women don't mind a little suffering to make ourselves attractive. Whoops . . . shade it off. That's right. Now, you take the eye-liner—"

When all was done, the girl sat looking at herself solemnly. Then she burst into howls of laughter.

"It's too much," Lorna admitted. She swallowed down a

6

bitter taste. "It's O.K. on some people." To look like a painted old harridan suited Lorna. Perhaps it was the outer sign of an inner spirit. At her age, it was even gallant. But the heavily decorated eyes on this girl looked so wrong as to be mad! Ridiculous! Lorna showed her how to get it off.

"Well," the girl sighed, "that doesn't work." Her gray gaze came swivelling around. "But I surely do thank you. I'm glad we have met. I don't know anyone else in this whole city."

"You don't know me," said Lorna lightly.

"Why, yes, I do." The girl smiled. She had pretty teeth. When she smiled her eyes shone.

Lorna drew in a breath. "Maybe you'd better be a little bit careful about picking people up," she said casually. "The woods are full of wolves around here."

The gray eyes sobered and met Lorna's eyes with an impact, like a head-on collision. "Thank you. I think you are very good and kind to advise me."

Lorna was startled and a little frightened. A shiver ran on her spine. Her own gaze slid away.

"But *I* know how to tell the good guys from the bad guys," said the girl, and Lorna looked at her again and she was smiling, almost mischievously.

"The bad guys ride the black horses, eh?" said Lorna sharply.

The girl laughed. "No, but it's easy," she said with a happy lilt. "The good guys are . . . well . . . the best way I can put it—they are merciful."

She didn't seem to think she had said anything odd. She bent to touch her eyelid with the cleaning tissue.

Lorna sat down on the divan-bed and bit her own mouth. What on earth kind of girl *was* this? She said, in a moment, "If you want to be inconspicuous, you'd better not go around saying things like *that*. You give me the old-fashioned willies. Watch out for the wolves, hear." Lorna found herself quite concerned. "You are pretty young. All right. So I sound like your old maiden aunt, or something, but you don't seem to me to be . . . well—"

The girl was watching her with grave respect. "Scared enough?" she inquired.

Lorna sighed. "Could be."

The girl tipped her head thoughtfully. "I'm scared *enough*, I think. When you say 'wolves' you mean men, I guess. A kind of man?"

"A predatory kind of man," snapped Lorna, astonishing herself. "A male flirt, let's say, whose intentions are not too terribly honorable.

The girl said, "I see."

"Excuse me," said Lorna with exasperation. "You say you come from the mountains. Haven't you ever been around with a bunch of kids your own age? I mean, in school, for instance?"

"We're a large family," Susan said. "I have three sisters and three brothers. The seven of us had our own school. My father and my mother both used to be teachers. They are qualified. Of course, *I've been to college*."

Lorna, who had been holding her breath, let it go. "I'm glad to hear that."

"For half a term," the girl went on. "But it didn't work. So I went home."

"What do you mean, it didn't work?"

"It wasn't profitable," said Susan. "The courses weren't hard enough to be any fun, and they went so slowly. It didn't work socially, either. I couldn't *talk* to the other students. They didn't want anything to do with me." The gray gaze was level. "There must be something about me."

Lorna was rather touched. "Must have been tough," she murmured.

"So I told Dad he had better send my brothers off before they were spoiled for it. Two of them are in college now. It is expensive."

"Just a minute," said Lorna. "You were brought up on this mountain? Out of this world? Tell me, didn't you even have television?"

The girl said, "Why certainly we had television. And books and magazines. It's not out of this world! I suppose it's isolated. We used to go down to the nearest little town on Sundays, though. For church, you know."

Lorna felt her eyes closing in a gesture of despair. She

8

fored them open. "And now your father and mother let you come down here, all on your own?"

"But I am twenty. I should earn some money. I intend to work hard and get ahead. There's another thing, too. I should be meeting some young men. I'll want to get married."

Lorna said, "Litte sister, you are making my hair curl! Now, you come tell Lorna all about everything you don't understand. *I've* been around, the Lord knows. I've struggled twenty years in this jungle. Looks like I'm electing myself your Auntie Lorna."

The girl said, with a glow in her eyes, "You *are* good. I told you I could tell."

Lorna Hayes took a handful of her hennaed hair. "People don't say things like that," she cried. "They don't even use that word that way."

"I know they don't," said Susan Miller agreeably. "Isn't that odd?"

CHAPTER II

ON THE fourth floor of a substantial building in Hollywood, the next morning, Miss Hagerty, head of the office force at Shank Development, was too busy to notice much about the new clerk. Miss Hagerty was so constantly panting to keep up with the record-keeping here that it would have been hard for her to state just what it was that Shank developed. A great many small businesses seemed to be involved, and money whizzed out and then in, and she breasted the paper seas.

The new girl looked neat in sensible blue. Something about her made Miss Hagerty say to herself 'Beaver, eager,' and let it go at that. In her distracted fashion she gave instructions. The girl went swiftly about her tasks.

When the clock on the wall had moved to five-thirty, there was the usual slam of desk drawers and slap of typewriters into their wells, and the dozen females, none of whom had done more than glance at the new one, began to flow towards the way out. Miss Hagerty slapped finis to a day's work with the rest. When she gave her customary last look around, she did not even see the crouching figure, almost on its knees between the desks, of the girl who was rooting about in the lowest drawer of a tall file cabinet. It never entered Miss Hagerty's head to imagine that all of her staff had not dropped work as soon as it was legitimate to do so, or even sooner. Miss Hagerty walked down the long room to the corner office and peered in. "Goodnight, Mr. Shank," she cooed with proper deference. "Shall I leave the lights, sir?"

The big boss said, in his kindly way, "Please do. I'll tend to them. Good night, Miss Hagerty."

So she went her way.

Mr. Shank got up and closed the door to his private sanctum. It had another door, directly to the corridor. This one he unlocked. Then he went to tip his window blinds.

In the big outer office a dusty quiet settled. There was nobody there but Susan Miller, who kept running her fingers over the manila folders, absorbed in spotting those that had been misplaced. She paid no heed to the murmuring of voices somewhere, a little later.

The voices were shut into Shank's private office. Shank, himself, a middle-aged man with the contours of a robin, a pink face, and pure white hair, sat behind his desk. In the red-leather visitor's chair sat a small dark-haired, thin-faced man whose name was Kirby. In a third chair, apart, there was a man with a crew-cut head, a nose that had been broken at least once, who lounged there with his strong legs sprawled and his big hands clasped across his middle, and his eyelids drooping.

Mr. Shank said to the thin one, "Tell you the reason I asked you to drop by, Kirby. But first, are you sure you want me to talk in front of this man?"

Kirby said, "Where I go, Peterson goes."

"What is he, your gunman?" asked Shank with distaste. "Is this necessary?"

The thin man spread his thin lips. "No guns. You could say he gives a little man like me a feeling of security. Make a muscle, Peterson."

The muscular one did not move. He seemed to recognize an old joke.

"Go ahead, talk. He takes no interest," said Kirby to Shank. "What's on your mind?"

Shank said, sweetly, "I'm sure you must have been reading in the papers that I may be about to go into politics."

The thin man commented with a movement of one shoulder. He had force, this little man, and his attitude was dominant, and slightly contemptuous.

"It's pretty much the wife's idea," Shank went on. "She would like to see me in public service. For the sake of the prestige, and all that. I don't mind admitting that the idea appeals to me, too. It occurs to me, Kirby, that *you* might get some ideas that wouldn't appeal to me at all."

Kirby's thin dark brows rose. "Ideas, Mr. Shank?"

"You've been . . . uh . . . 'fronting' for me," said Shank, "for . . . twelve years now, isn't it? We got along nicely. I don't complain, and neither should you. We've both done well out of the Kit-Kat Clubs. Very well indeed. Now, however, you might begin to think that *if* I go into politics and *if* I do get the nomination, then I'd be in a position where, less then ever, I would want this . . . uh . . . private arrangement of ours to get out and be known." Shank leaned back and looked indulgent. "Don't tell me you haven't thought of that, Kirby. Was it in your mind to hold me up for a bigger cut of the profits?"

Kirby said brightly, "Keep talking, Mr. Shank."

Shank said, "Oh, I've got nothing much to *say*. I've got something to *show* you." Sucking in his belly, he opened the flat middle desk-drawer and took out a piece of paper.

"That's a thermofax copy," he said. "The original is where I've put it. Not here. So don't . . . uh . . . exercise your muscle." Shank's eyes flitted to the third man, who did not stir.

Kirby raked Shank's face with a sharp stare. Then he took the sheet of paper, bent his pale face to it, and flung up his

11

head angrily, almost immediately. "What are you going to do with this?"

"Nothing," said Shank blandly. "I've had it for some time. I've done nothing, have I? I simply think that the time has come to show you what I am holding. It . . . uh . . . gives me a feeling of security to have this document," Shank turned on cold emphasis, "that can get you into prison for the rest of your life, any hour, of any day, that I choose."

Kirby said, without excitement, but coldly in his turn, "Now is the hour?"

"No, no," said Shank, beaming with friendship. "I don't want you in prison. I want you running my Kit-Kat clubs for me and making us both a lot of money. This is only in case you were . . . uh . . . getting ideas."

Kirby said, "Who else knows about this letter?"

"Not a soul. I made that thermofax copy myself."

"I'm supposed to believe that?" Kirby's teeth showed. His contempt had curdled into rage, but he kept cold.

"I think so," said Shank smoothly. "What else can you do? Nothing changes. I've had this a while. I show it to you now, simply to clear up the present situation. I wanted you to understand."

"I understand, Councilman," said Kirby nastily.

"Go ahead. Destroy the copy," said Shank indulgently. "Relieve your frustrations."

Kirby's thin hands began to tear the sheet of paper into tiny bits while Kirby's dark eyes watched Shank.

"If I've got a little yen," Shank said, "to be a public servant and get my name in the papers and so on, why, I can see how this gives you leverage. Voters frown on gambling profits, eh? So, I take the precaution of showing you what leverage *I've* got. Pressure against pressure, eh? That's the way the world wags, my friend. So now we understand each other? Right?"

"Right," said Kirby. He stood up. The big man in the other chair came to attention and took up a position two paces to the rear of his master.

Shank, perceiving that he had made his point, rose and showed them out through the main office, turning off lights as they went. He tested the self-locking door behind him.

Then the three of them strode along the corridor. Shank said, his voice reverberating in the dusty silence of after-hours, "I'll grant you this, Kirby. The Kit-Kat clubs give me an excellent return. Excellent. And if you keep on working for me and being the good boy, why, I am a reasonable fella and we *could* cut the melon a trifle heavier on your side."

Kirby said venomously, "We could?"

"Oh, you cultivate the vine," said Shank genially. "I concede as much. You are well paid to do it. However, I—"

They turned the corner. A young girl in blue standing beside the elevator looked up and said cheerfully, "I've pushed the down button."

The three men came to a stop that rocked them to their heels. Not one of them spoke. Shank's lips were open. Kirby's were tight. The big man was alert. Silence and emptiness fell dustily around them. It sang with tension, but the girl did not seem to sense this. She was placidly watching the indicator. The elevator's door slid open.

She stepped in. Shank made a quick horizontal motion of his hand. He stepped in. Kirby followed. The big man came last. Susan Miller flicked a glance around their faces. Kirby's head jerked and, at once, she pushed the button for the main floor and they all sank downward.

They let her walk out first. She said, "Thank you." Then she said in a friendly fashion, "Goodnight, Mr. Shank." She walked away, past the deserted newsstand, and pushed out through the big glass doors.

Shank snapped out of his paralysis and whirled around. "What did I *say?* What did she hear me say?" he demanded.

Kirby said, "Who is she?"

"I don't know," said Shank, "but she knows who I am."

Kirby whipped out a command. "Peterson, go after her. Watch what she does. Find out who she is. Call me here."

The big one said nothing, but went shambling obediently towards the street. Kirby turned back to the elevator. "Get in," he ordered. He had the force. He was in command.

Shank said, "Now wait . . . now wait. What's he going to do?" Shank's little eyes rolled with alarm. He deplored his own indiscretion. He was afraid. But he was also afraid of

Kirby, since he knew some of Kirby's ways. Mr. Shank had no stomach for violence.

Kirby said, "He'll do what I told him to do. Come on. Back upstairs. She must work on your floor—whoever she is."

"Never saw the girl in my life." Shank mopped his face.

Kirby said, "She knows you. If she picked up any information just now, you'd rather she hadn't—we'll have to fix that, won't we?" The dark eyes blazed contempt.

Shank quivered. "No, wait. Maybe it didn't matter. What did I *say*?" His memory at the moment was blank.

"It's whether she caught on," said Kirby as if he explained to a child, "and what she is going to do about it."

Shank shuffled into the elevator.

It was a little late for going home from work. The streets were rather empty. The girl walked to the corner and waited for the bus. Back against the buildings, in the shadows, the man with the broken nose slouched behind. The bus came and she got on. He swung fast across the sidewalk to get on also.

The girl walked briskly with crisp heel taps. About two blocks farther on, in the light from the windows of a drugstore, she stopped and turned and said to the man, in her clear voice, "Are you following me?"

The man with the broken nose was startled. He took a step backwards. "I beg your pardon, Miss," he mumbled.

"If you are not," she said, "I beg *your* pardon. But if you are, I would like to know why."

The man's eyes turned under the drooping lids. "I'm afraid I don't understand," he muttered.

"You don't understand?" the girl said, tipping her head. He could see her face very well in the drugstore's radiance, and he seemed to wince. "Well, then," she said slowly and still clearly, "goodnight."

She turned her back to him and walked on. The man with the broken nose muttered a word or two to himself. In a moment he crossed the street and began to make strides, carefully seeking shadows.

The girl flew up the steps to the stoop, used her key quickly and nipped through the door. She ran up one flight, hurried along the upper hall, unlocked her own door. She flipped the light on and went to the window and drew down her blind. She hesitated. She moved again.

Lorna Hayes heard her knocking and went quickly. The girl said, "A man followed me. Turn off your light, please. Let me see."

Surprised, and reluctant to believe, Lorna accepted the flip of her light switch and groped with the girl a way to Lorna's front window.

"See?" whispered Susan. "Over there. He *did* follow me."

"Across the street?" There was a lamp across the street shedding light between tree-shadows. A tall man stood there, looking up at this house. He began to cross over.

"What is he doing?" breathed Susan. "He's down at the door. Is he going to ring the bell?"

"No. There . . . he is going away now. Looks like he was checking the address." Lorna creaked to her feet.

The girl said in the dark, "What shall I do?"

Lorna said, "Why, there's nothing to *do*, honey. He's gone." She groped back to the light switch. Susan Miller pulled down Lorna's blind. Still kneeling, she looked up. "You think he is a wolf?"

Lorna smiled. "Or an interested male. Don't you?"

"No, I don't. Because when I stopped and asked him if he was following me he *pretended* he didn't understand."

Lorna sputtered, "Ss-stopped—"

"But he must have understood," the girl insisted. "I was speaking plain English. And he kept on following."

"You asked?" gasped Lorna.

"Yes, and the thing that puzzles me . . . if he is just interested, then why didn't he—? There I was. And I had turned around to speak to him, and if he had simply wanted to make my acquaintance—"

"Since when did he follow you?" asked Lorna, bewildered.

"Oh, he was in the building with my employer. I mean Mr. Shank, the head of the company."

"I don't get this," confessed Lorna.

"Well, I was late because somebody had left one of the

15

files in a *state*. When I was waiting for the elevator these three men came out."

"The man who followed you was in your building, with your boss?"

"Yes, he was. Shall I tell the police about it?"

"The— Now wait a minute."

The girl said, "Don't you think it is strange that he lied to me? And kept on following?"

Lorna sighed. "Look, honey, the man hasn't done anything. He's gone, isn't he? Sometimes, it's best not to . . . well, mix in something you really don't understand. I mean, especially if he was with your boss. Your boss knows him then, doesn't he?"

"Of course. He must." The girl was thoughtful.

"Well, then, I really don't think you should stir up the police. What could they do? Why, they might go to your boss, don't you see? And that could be embarrassing. I'd just lie low, honey. Of course, if he ever does it again and annoys you—"

"It does annoy me," the girl said, "not to understand."

Lorna said, "Sweetie, it's a big old crazy world you're in, now that you're down off the mountain. You can't expect to understand always. Probably it's just one of those things," she soothed.

Susan frowned. "One of what things?"

Lorna felt as if she were fighting smoke. She couldn't get a grasp on whatever it was she was trying to reach. She said sharply, "Skip it. That's my advice. Just don't stick your neck out."

Then the girl baffled her, worse than ever. "Thank you," said Susan gravely.

"Oh, come on, relax," said Lorna crossly. "I was fixing to make supper on the hot-plate and I've got an extra chop. How about it? I want to hear about your hard day at the office."

"It wasn't hard," the girl said absently. She rose. "I've got the worst of it untangled. Thank you. I'd like to stay for supper."

Lorna could feel a tingle on her spine. Something about this girl was too . . . too *something*. "Well, take your shoes

16

off," she said flippantly. Then suddenly, "Did I hear you say you worked late? Did your superintendent know it?"

"I don't know," said Susan.

"Look, child," said Lorna. "You are being paid for so many hours, and when the bell rings—"

"That's rather silly," said Susan Miller. "Why would they pay me unless it is to get my work done?"

Lorna looked into the fair face and thought, *She's impossible*. She said amiably, "I guess they'd rather not, at that. Sit down. Make yourself at home. Believe me, you can't help. There isn't room."

When she looked over her shoulder in a moment, the girl was in the chair, taking her shoes off. *Maybe she is literal-minded*, thought Lorna. *Maybe that's what it is*.

The girl wiggled her toes. She began to laugh. "He was so huge, you know," giggled Susan Miller. "and he's had his nose broken and he looks *tough*. But when I turned around he looked so scared—it was funny. Like a great big ugly bulldog, being scared of a m-mouse."

Baby, you scare *me*, thought Lorna Hayes.

CHAPTER III

DOWN ON the streets, the young man with the broken nose walked swiftly until he came to an outdoor phonebooth into which he swung himself. He dialed.

A voice said, "Detective Bureau, Captain Walters speaking."

"Peterson here," said the man in the booth.

"Go ahead, Pete."

"Shank called Kirby into his office tonight," said the man with the broken nose, in a brisk monotone. Shank's got a document. Looked like a letter. Kirby is afraid of it. Shank says it can send Kirby to prison for life."

"Where is it?" said the voice with interest.

"Don't know. Shank's got the original somewhere, not his office. He showed Kirby a copy which Kirby destroyed. Shank owns the Kit-Kat clubs, all right.

"We know that," said Captain Walters. "Can you prove it?"

"I can testify," said the man with the broken nose. "Shall I come in?"

He was ignored. "Find out where that document is and get it, if you can. Any chance?"

The man in the booth said, with resignation, "There could be. Kirby doesn't like it, one little bit. If he makes any attempt to get the letter he'll use me, probably. I am his muscle, he says."

"Don't sound so unhappy, Pete," said the Captain, changing to the voice of the man who had know Pete's father very well, who had taken him to ball-games when he was seven years old, who had been a courtesy uncle, once upon a time, when Pete was a lad. "Muscles are what you get for playing football," said his uncle. "You got in there very nice, young Pete. Very nice. We'll have to use you undercover for a while yet. You know that."

The man in the booth said, in a disgusted voice, "Oh, sure I know. One more thing—there is this girl. Shank thought his building was deserted and he talked too much in the corridor. There was this girl and they are worried about what she might have overheard. Sent me to follow her. Might be best the department keep an eye on her."

"Name?" said the captain wearily, recognizing a nuisance.

"Either Susan Miller or Lorna Hayes. Young. *Very* young. Sort of half-way between blonde and brunette. Good figure. About five-four."

"Good looking babe," said the captain, teasingly official.

"Yes, sir," said the man in the booth stolidly.

He could still feel the shock on his nerves when that girl had turned around and accused him of the truth. She was a strange one. But good-looking. He had to admit it. "Lives on Susquehanna Street, number 408. Roominghouse," he continued into the phone. "Works in Shank's own office, or so I guess, because she called his name. I'll do what I can to convince them she didn't notice . . . no sweat. But this Kirby, about him you couldn't tell. So watch it, will you . . . uh . . . sir?"

"We'll watch it," the captain said. "Mind your business. Which is to get Shank. Tell you this, though, Pete. You get us any document that can put Kirby away, I'll take you off the undercover job. That's a promise."

"Can but try," said Peterson gloomily.

He hung up and leaned in the booth, chewing his cheek. John Peterson thought of himself as a police officer, upholder of law and order, and proud of it. He was ambitious. He was going up in his profession. He detested this undercover job. But he had been trained two thousand miles away and now, coming new to this territory, it was only sensible that he be used as a spy. It would last only as long as he was new and not known in the wrong circles. It was an apprenticeship only, but he wished it were over. If he was good at it, if he had gotten in there very nice, as the captain said, this was a triumph of disciplined brain over natural disposition. He grimaced. He dialed again.

When the phone rang in Shank's private office Shank himself grabbed it up. "Yes?"

"She went right home, Mr. Shank," said Peterson, and his voice was different, thicker, with a 'dese and dose' flavor to it. Peterson observed sadly how good he was at this distasteful business.

"Get her name?"

"Either Miller or Hayes."

"Susan Miller," said Shank. "We found a Susan Miller on the new employees list. But she went right home, you say?" Shank asked.

"Aw, she knows from nothing," said Peterson, trying to sound disgusted. "Just went home, like everybody else. Let her alone, I'd say."

Kirby's waspish voice answered this. "Let her alone, *you'd* say? No ideas in her head?"

"Uh uh. Nothing on her mind. Listen, boss, she's looking

in the store windows, no hurry, nothing. Sometimes you can make trouble where there wasn't going to be any."

Kirby said sourly, "I don't pay you to philosophize. Get over to the club. I'll bring the car." Kirby hung up.

John Peterson ran a finger along the bridge of his nose that had been smashed by an All-American tackle one glorious day, and he thought to himself, Kirby's nervous. Shank's got him fit to be tied with that letter. He'd just as soon take it out on somebody. They'd *better* watch out for the girl. He wiggled his big shoulders. Why did the stupid chick have to call Shank by his name! He felt worried, not because he thought the girl was stupid, but because there was something about her not average—not reliably average.

Kirby said to Shank, "It's your neck on the gambling club deal. This gets to the general public and you get no nomination."

"I'm covered," bleated Shank. "No proof exists."

"Proof," said Kirby scornfully. "You get a cute little girl talking. Rumor starts. Who needs proof? Especially in politics. How does my neck stand? What happens to me if your position changes? What about that letter?"

Shank, his wits addled by worry, said, "That letter's in my s-safe place." He stumbled a little and recovered. "Nothing happens to you," he declaimed, giving Kirby his frightened attention, "until, shall we say, something violent happens to my person. Then the letter goes to my lawyer, automatically and fast." His little eyes were baleful.

Kirby took a step backward.

"I hear you have your methods, Kirby," Shank said, red-faced and earnest, "and I don't believe that I would care for them. So I protect myself. Now, I say to you, let the girl alone. Violence won't help here. You can't keep her quiet, your way. You'd only get yourself in so deep—"

"Oh, I don't know," Kirby changed to a drawl so suddenly as to shock, "I've got a little fellow, works for me occasionally, who's very clever. You'd be surprised to know the number of mechanical things that can . . . well, go wrong real suddenly. Like blow up? And nobody around. Except, of course, whoever it might be that you'd rather not have around any more."

Shank croaked "I say no."

Kirby enjoyed his fright. Kirby said saucily, with a cock of his head, "I don't think you're thinking clearly, Councilman."

"I say no," repeated Shank, "and I've got the letter, you remember?"

Kirby shrugged. "As you say," he said, "for now."

The night went over. The sun came up. The wheels of another working day began to turn. Sales would be made, bargains struck, records kept, and problems tackled. The hired help arrived at Shank Development. There, as elsewhere, the big bosses came in a little later.

A little later, in another office, not a mile away—an office whose dominant feature was a huge muddy oil painting in an ornate frame—Kirby brooded in a soft chair. He was there early, for him. It was not yet noon.

Peterson, the muscle, said to him, "So if the letter is in a safe, like you think it is, Mr. Kirby, I happen to know a little bit about safes."

"Handy, aren't you?" snarled Kirby. "You think I'm figuring on house-breaking or safe-cracking?" The thin man seemed to think these crimes were beneath him. Then his eyes lost flash. He brooded. "Shank says to me—you heard him—pressure against pressure, he says. That's the way the world wags. The pompous old—" Kirby's voice declined to murmurous profanity.

Peterson said doggedly, "But if it's in the safe—"

"Cut it out, will you?" said Kirby irritably. "I'm only guessing where it is. I'm guessing he's got it in a safe at his house. All I'm going on is a slip of the tongue. Keep quiet. Let me think. What I want is a way to pressure that letter out of Shank's safe, or wherever it is." Kirby began a soft snapping of his fingers.

Peterson kept quiet.

CHAPTER IV

AT A quarter-to-twelve noon, this day, Susan Miller got the nod to go to lunch. She fished her bag out of the lower drawer where she had put it. She walked down the long room. Instead of turning right, she turned left. Nobody stopped her from tapping lightly on the glass of the door to Shank's private office.

"Yes?"

Susan turned the doorknob, pushed, and went in.

Mr. Shank was standing beside his water cooler, with a paper cup in his hand. He looked rather startled to see her. He said "Yes?"

"Mr. Shank, I'm Susan Miller."

Shank threw the paper cup away and smoothed his hair. He moved around to sit behind the desk in a position of power. He turned on a certain purring quality. "Yes, Miss Miller?" He had small, pale eyes and they were wary.

"I'd like your advice, sir," the girl said.

"Well, now, what can the trouble be? Won't you sit down, Miss . . . uh . . . Miller?"

Shank busied himself with courtesy. He was quaking.

"Do you remember the man who was with you last evening? I don't mean the thin dark one, but the bigger, the younger man?"

She was perched on his visitor's chair, now, young body erect, young face grave. Shank didn't know what to think. He cleared his throat and said "Yes?" for the third time.

"You see, sir, the younger one followed me all the way home last night. And I am not sure what I ought to do. I thought you could help me because, of course, you know who he is."

Shank said, "I . . . uh . . . as a matter of fact he simply came with the other man. I . . . uh—"

"With Mr. Kirby?" said Susan brightly.

Her employer simply stared at her.

"It worries me, sir," Susan went on, "because I can't understand why he did what he did. Ought I to tell the police?"

Shank was lifted right out of his chair. He surged to his feet.

"Because it was strange," the girl was saying, "and perhaps the police would *like* to know."

He said, "To *know*? I don't quite— To . . . uh . . . know?" He was badly rattled.

"Yet I don't want to embarrass anyone," she said.

"Embarrass anyone," said Shank slowly, feeling suddenly much steadier, now that he thought he could see exactly what she was getting at. "Embarrass how, Miss Miller?" He sat down and looked sly.

"Since you know him, sir, I thought you might be able to tell me what kind of man he is. You see, if it was . . . well . . . just a young man's kind of thing that he did, then I would understand."

"I see," said Shank. He did not see. He was flustered again. The girl's attitude was thoroughly respectful. Could this rigamarole she was giving him be real?

"So I thought you could tell me about him," she repeated.

"Well, now, as a matter of fact," he bumbled, "I barely know this man Kirby."

"But he works for you."

She said this and sat there, perfectly calm. Shank's nerves twanged. He said rather sharply, "I am not sure that I understand you."

Susan said, "Then I haven't made it clear. I am from out of town. I don't know people in this city. I don't know any young men, at all. So, if this man wanted to make my acquaintance, I thought I ought to ask you whether he is . . . oh, heaven's to Betsy—" Susan broke into smiles. "You know what I mean. Is he of good repute?"

"Of good repute?" Shank repeated in a daze. He had not

heard a young girl use this phrase in his entire experience of life.

"Because if he isn't," she went on, "or if he followed me for some other reason, then I am not sure that I shouldn't tell the police about him. What do you think, sir?"

Now Shank licked his lips and pulled his wits together. He drew on an avuncular air. He'd go along with the gag. (A young girl asking her elders for advice!) He'd have to go along.

"I am glad you came to me, my dear," he said solemnly. "You *are* young, aren't you? And alone? You say you have no friends here in this city? No family?"

"Not here," she said.

"Well, now, suppose you let me make a few inquiries," purred Shank. "Just let me handle it. I think you are quite right to be wondering. However, as a snap judgment, I would say that since you are a very attractive young lady, the chances are that he would like to make your acquaintance."

Susan said slowly, "Thank you, Mr. Shank." The flattery didn't seem to affect her.

"You mustn't worry about it. You let me make a little check." Shank rose to come around his desk and suggest her departure. He couldn't look at her much longer. "Are you on your way to lunch now?" he asked.

"In a few minutes, sir. As soon as I fix my hair."

"Have a nice lunch," Shank said. "I am glad that you came directly to me in this matter. Just leave it in my hands."

"Yes. Thank you, sir." The faintest ripple of a frown was on her fair forehead. But she left his office gracefully.

Shank mopped. He hurried to his phone and dialed on his private line.

"Kirby? Listen. Do something about that girl. You know which one. She's on her way to lunch in a couple of minutes. *Do* something."

"What's up?" asked Kirby without excitement.

"She heard a hell of a lot. She knows your name. She knows you work for me. Saw your man following her last

24

night. She doesn't exactly come out with it, but she's talking copper. So do something!"

"My way?"

"*Any* way," said Shank in his state of nerves.

The line closed in his ear and Shank sat down and mopped. *He* didn't know how to deal with this girl. She baffled him. Was she as innocent as she sounded, or was she incredibly subtle for one so young, or what? Or what? He shivered.

On the other end, Kirby said to Peterson. "Got to go after the girl. My car. You drive."

Peterson came to heel obediently. *Now what?* he thought. Kirby answered the thought. "Shank's panicking. Better take her out to the desert. I've got a shack. I'll show you on the map. Take her out there and keep her until I can organize something."

"O.K., Boss," said Peterson without expression.

"Or," said Kirby when they had leaped into his car and Peterson was whipping it away from the curb, "you're a handy man. Maybe you know a good way to keep her quiet permanently."

"I might," said Peterson calmly.

"Shank's office," Kirby directed. He sounded pleased. "And pour it on. You'll have to pick her up. How can you work that?"

"I think I can work it," said Peterson confidently.

Peterson poured it on and came zipping down the street to swoop to the curb. It was a green curb, but this was no time to worry about such trifles. Kirby slipped out of the car, fast, and drifted across the wide sidewalk. He plucked a newspaper out of a wire rack and placed himself against the building wall as if to read it there.

As for Peterson, he got out of the car more deliberately and stood beside it, watching the outpouring people as they were filtered through the revolving door. He had a job to do and he had to do it. He felt confident that he would do it— although he would not go as far with it as Kirby expected.

The girl came out almost at once, and Peterson moved, at once, towards her.

"Miss Miller?"

She stopped walking and looked up at him. "Yes?" People detoured around the two of them. John Peterson felt strangely alone with her, as if on an island. "I'd like to talk to you," he said, using his own voice. He had a warm and flexible voice. It could persuade. It often had.

"I'd like to ask *you* a question, too," the girl said.

He had never seen eyes like hers in his life, and now, in the light of day, they were certainly disconcerting. "Then won't you please come have a bite of lunch somewhere?" he said politely. "I have my car here."

"You lied to me last night," the girl said. "It was just a statement. She did not move her feet one inch.

"Yes, I owe you an apology. I want to explain."

"All right," she said cheerfully.

"Good." He gave her his most boyish smile. He touched her forearm very gently. She let herself take three steps beside him.

"You know *my* name. I don't know yours," she said.

"Peterson. John Peterson." His hand became a bit more urgent. He bent to open the car door.

"How do you do?" said Susan Miller. She stood quite still.

"Please get in, Miss Miller." Through the back of his head he *felt* Kirby watching.

"Why, no," said Susan. "I won't get in, Mr. Peterson."

He looked down into those eyes and he knew a stone wall when he saw it. Another way then. He said, sotto, "Believe me, it's the best thing *for* you. I'm trying—"

"I would like," she said, paying no attention to this muttering, "to hear why you lied to me. And why you followed me at all. And why, if you wanted to make my acquaintance, you didn't say so last night."

"I say so now," he burst out. "Please?"

"Why?"

"Why *what?*" He was beginning to feel exasperated.

"Why do you want to get acquainted?"

"Isn't that obvious?" said Peterson with what he knew was a sickly smirk. His mind was divided. He sensed Kirby and he was playing too many parts at once. He didn't know how close behind them Kirby might be, right now. Or whether Kirby could hear.

Then the girl said, in ringing tones that Kirby couldn't miss, "There isn't *anything* about this that's obvious to *me*."

"Please listen," he muttered.

"I'll listen," she said. "*Of course*, I said I would." She was smiling. What kind of girl was this?

"Then get into the car, please?"

"No," she said.

So he moved closer and his hand on her arm tightened. "I'm afraid you have no choice. You'll have to do as I say."

She said clearly, "Why, that isn't true at all. I don't have to do what you say."

Peterson felt ready to blow his top. He said, "Will you stop this nonsense, and let me—"

"You're the one who is talking nonsense," the girl said in her maddeningly reasonable fashion. "I told you that I would not get into your car. I do have a choice, and that is what I choose."

"Shall I put you in?"

"How will you do that?" she inquired. "You are bigger than I am, true. But you can't put me into that car by force, because I won't go quietly, and there are lots of people all around us."

She was right. That was the devil of it. He clinched his jaw. He said, risking it, "Listen, will you *please*. I'm trying to tell you that you are in danger."

"I think that's possible," said Susan Miller judiciously, "so I would rather be careful. Good-bye, Mr. Peterson." She stepped back and her forearm moved to loosen itself from his grasp.

His hand tightened.

She said, loudly, "This man is trying to put me into his car, and I don't want to go."

The currents of foot traffic on the side walk began to eddy. People were slowing down to listen.

He said furiously, "Be *quiet!*"

"Not at all," the girl said. "I think I will scream."

He took his hand away as if from fire. He said, "I only want to talk to you."

"That could have been arranged," she said calmly, "without all this nonsense." She was rubbing her forearm where he had held it, but she did not run away. "What's the matter with you?" she asked. "What *is it* you want to talk about?"

He stood there, helpless.

A woman with a head full of metal curlers had pushed close to the girl. "It's O.K. miss," she said. "I just sent my kid up to the corner to get the cop. You don't needa worry. He ain't going to get away with a thing!"

Peterson looked at her delighted malicious face. Then he looked at the girl, whose clear eyes examined him, whose brow wore a small puzzled frown.

"You don't do as I ask, then?" he said to the girl quietly.

The nosy woman said, "She sure won't, Buster."

Peterson shifted his head and caught the figure of Kirby in an eye-corner. Kirby was signalling. His signal meant *drop it*.

"Who do you think you are, anyway?" the nosy woman was blustering. She was beginning to have an audience and she enjoyed this.

"I'm not touching her," said Peterson defensively. "She won't let me talk to her. O.K.?"

He shrugged and took a step away and, of all things, the girl herself stepped after him. "But I will let you talk to me," Susan said. "I told you—"

"Don't you do it," said the nosy woman, keeping up with them. "He's prolly one of them psychos. Prolly he wants to kidnap you. Prolly he wants to kill you."

John Peterson looked helplessly at the girl and she looked back, just as helpless in a way as he. Her mouth twitched and a little mischief crept into her eyes. "Do you?" she asked him.

He looked a fathom deep into those gray eyes. "That you will never know," he said politely. "Will you, Miss Miller?"

Peterson wound swiftly through the little ring of on-lookers that had collected. As he neared the wall, Kirby moved so that they would be shoulder to shoulder. Kirby said, without moving his lips, "Get out of sight."

Peterson was feeling defeated and worried and guilty of anger. "No fault of mine," he growled. In another second he realized, with a pang of alarm, that he had just used the

28

wrong voice to utter the wrong choice of words. But Kirby, scuttling along beside him, seemed to take no notice.

Susan stood where he had left her. The nosy woman was still enjoying herself. "That's showing him and the likes of him. Here comes the cop. Now you'll see him run!"

The crowd murmured, its members asking each other what this was all about. Through them came pushing the dignified figure of Mr. Shank himself.

"Miss Miller, are you all right?"

"Why, yes, Mr. Shank."

"I saw from my window." Shank was breathing heavily.

"His name is Peterson," she said.

"Where'd he go?" the woman demanded. "Here comes the cop. Somebody oughta chase that psycho. Put him away."

Shank said to her politely, "Excuse us, please?" His hand came to Susan's elbow. "Miss Miller," he murmured, "you don't want an ugly scene on the street, do you, my dear?"

"No, sir," she agreed.

So he led her toward the building entrance. As they went he said into her ear, "Let me suggest . . . I have a close friend rather high up in the police department. Wouldn't it be better to report this thing to *him?* I think advice from a real authority— Now, my car's around in the parking lot. Suppose we—you wouldn't care to see this incident in the newspapers, I'm sure."

"No, I wouldn't," Susan said.

"Now, then, if we just turn into the building and go through to the back before this . . . uh . . . cop appears. Frankly, I *don't* think a scene is necessary."

The girl said, "Mr. Shank, couldn't you reach this Mr. Peterson through Mr. Kirby?"

"Through the door," Shank urged. "And quickly, please."

But she looked up the street. "Where did he go?"

Shank said, "I feel somewhat responsible. I want to do all I can to protect you. But I do *not* want a scene. Not on the sidewalk in front of my offices, nor my picture in the paper."

"Oh, I'm sorry," said Susan quickly. She went through the revolving door.

Shank let her go on through. He was looking up the street

to his right. Kirby was watching and Shank made signals with his hands.

Peterson was inside the corner drugstore, seeming to be inspecting an array of magazines. Kirby came inside and said, without seeming to speak to him, "Shank's house. Bring the car when you can."

"Sorry, boss," muttered Peterson.

"It's O.K. Shank's got her."

Kirby drifted out of sight beyond some loaded counters. Peterson saw the upper part of a glass door to the cross-street wag and catch light. Kirby was taking this calmly enough. Why wouldn't he? Shank had the girl.

Peterson shifted to be able to see down the street to where the nosy woman was haranguing the cop and the cop was taking note of the car's licenses. Peterson thought he had better wait.

Couldn't wait! He was still annoyed with that girl and, moreover, afraid for her. Shank was taking her to his house. Kirby, no doubt, was going there. He, Peterson, had better do something. Could not wait. Far at the back, he spotted some phone booths.

He went quickly back to the row of booths and chose a dark one at the end. When he closed the door the light came on. In the next booth there was no light. It's door was not completely shut. The man in there had his back to the door, his head bent low. Peterson had not seen him turn around and duck his head. Peterson, besides being a police officer doing his duty, was also both an angry and frightened young man.

He said into Captain Walter's ear, "Peterson here. Shank's got the girl. Where were *you?*" This was not the way he ought to speak, reporting.

"What do you mean, Shank's got the girl?"

"He's panicking. *I* just missed the job of doing her in." Peterson's voice betrayed his agitation. "If she hadn't been such a little—" he stuttered to a stop.

"*Where* has he got her?"

"His house. Or on the way. Green Chrysler. Pick him up?"

"On what charge?" asked the Captain grimly. "Now, Pete—"

"Get over to Shank's house, then," cried Peterson recklessly.

"Cool off, Pete," the captain said in kindness and forbearance. "Make some sense."

"All right. Listen. Kirby thinks the letter is in Shank's house in his safe. Go after *that*, then." Peterson could feel his career slipping out from under him. "I've *got* to go after the girl!"

"Go where?" snapped the captain.

"Shank's house," yelped Peterson.

The captain said sharply, "Under cover?"

"*Yes*, under-cover. For one reason. Maybe I still get the job of doing her in. Somebody's going to get that job, and I'd a little rather it was me."

"Just a minute," said the captain coldly. "You have an assignment."

"I've got to do something about that idiot girl," shouted Peterson. "What else can I do?"

"You are sure the letter is there?" asked the captain quietly. He would waste no more time on this lad's emotion, and none at all on his own.

"No. I'm not. I'm sure of nothing. But I have to get there."

"Now wait, Pete," the policeman slipped into worried uncleship.

But Peterson had hung up.

Captain Walters brought his orderly intelligence to bear on the situation. Did any law give him the power to look into Shank's safe in Shank's house? He didn't think so, but he had better check. Then he'd go himself. He made this resolve because his experienced and prophetic bones were warning him that the project of 'getting Shank' was about to degenerate into chaos. Because of some girl.

As for Peterson, he raced back between the drugstore's displays and burst out upon the sidewalk. He'd get the car. Brush off the cop. He saw that the cop had gone. So he went racing.

In the booth next to the one Peterson had used, Kirby was tight in the dark corner. He had started out that side door, changed his mind. Luckily. Kirby grinned. Luck was for the using. He neither trembled nor rejoiced. Kirby dialed and his thin hand was steady.

"Eddie?" He spoke low, but for all that, crisply. "Pick up one of your little inventions and meet me at Shank's house. Trouble, yeah. Also, a gun. You hear me? And also the way to get into a safe, just in case. Right. I'll meet you two houses north. I'll be on foot. No, he's not with me." Then Kirby sent his drawl over the wire. "What do you think, Eddie? Peterson is a cop."

CHAPTER V

DRIVING along, Shank kept his tongue loose and his tone dripping with soothing kindness. The girl, he was glad to see, sat docilely in his car. She did not seem suspicious. Possibly she had no guile after all. She did not inquire about the route he was taking. When he swung into his own driveway, she roused a little.

"My place," he told her. "Come in a minute."

"Oh? But I thought we were going to the police station."

"Oh, no, no. The friend I spoke of isn't *there*," said Shank. "Also, he is quite a busy man. Now, come in, please do, while I make a phone call. Find out where we can meet him— make the appointment."

Shank was out of the car, holding the door for her. She hesitated, and he said, just a trifle impatiently, "I agreed to help you."

Susan Miller slipped across the seat then and under the wheel and out. So he took her to his front door and used his key. "My wife won't be at home, I am sorry to say. This is one of her Club days. Well, now . . . come in."

He led her into his foyer and then into the huge living room, seeing its elegance with pride, as he aways did. "Sit down. Relax. Now, I'll phone my friend, in just one minute. You haven't had your lunch, have you, my dear? Nor I. Would you care for a small glass of sherry?"

She said, "No, thank you, Mr. Shank." She wasn't looking at the furniture but at him, and he had to turn away.

"Will you forgive me if I do?" he said from the handy little bar. "This is really excellent." He poured wine. "Are you sure? No? Well, then—"

He was stalling. Kirby would come soon.

The girl said, "Mr. Shank, I really don't understand."

Shank began to believe this. There she sat in the green chair. Just a girl, a young girl, with no friends in the city. Shank discovered that he wasn't afraid of her, at the moment. Maybe he could handle her himself. He sat down facing her, and he said in his most benevolent purr, "Perhaps I understand better than you think. Now, I doubt, my dear, that you know a great deal about . . . uh . . . business."

"I don't suppose I know very much about it," the girl said agreeably.

"Sometimes," said Shank, "there are business reasons— Last evening, for instance. Now, you surprised us. My point is this: very often there need to be secret meetings, between business men, and *that* may be what you don't understand. We . . . uh . . . would not meet in secret if we did not want the secret kept. Do you see?" She nodded. "So I will say this to you," Shank beamed. "If you will guarantee to mention last night's meeting to no one—neither whom you saw or anything you may have overheard—why, in return for this favor, you will receive five hundred dollars. Does that sound interesting?"

"Yes, it does," she said quietly, in a moment.

"There, I knew that if you and I could just have a little talk." Shank sipped his wine.

"Is this what Mr. Peterson wanted to talk to me about?" she asked.

"Perhaps," said Shank with his most charming grimace.

"And you knew all about it?"

33

"Perhaps," he repeated. "As I say, it is simply a business matter. Very profitable to you."

"You could have told me this before," she said gravely. "You could have asked me, as a gentleman to a lady, not to speak of it."

"I do ask you, my dear," beamed Shank. "I ask you now."

"Why did you pretend you were going to make inquiries?" the girl said with relentless calm. "And then, that you were taking me to some police person? Those were lies, weren't they?"

Shank bridled. "I am afraid, Miss Miller," he said stiffly, "that you don't quite realize you are in no position to call me names."

She said thoughtfully, "As well as I can see, they certainly were deceptions. And now you are offering me a bribe?"

"No, no," said Shank. "Not at all. It is just that I will be grateful."

"If you had asked me, as a favor, and I had done the favor, you could have been grateful," Susan said, "and that would have been enough." Her eyes flashed. "I don't think I want to stay here." She rose.

Shank said, "I can't let you go, you see, until you give me your word."

Then this girl looked at him, and her sight was clearer than his own. "How *can* you take my word?" she said in that maddening way, thoughtful. "You don't believe in keeping one's word. At least you don't do it, yourself. That means you can't trust anybody."

Shank turned red. He struggled to his feet. He said, "You may be right. I can't afford to take your word. I'll have to try something else, will I not?" He was grinning at her rather nastily.

The doorbell pinged; the door opened; there was a rush of feet, and the young man with the broken nose stood in the archway.

"Ah, there," said Shank with relief.

"I'll take over," said Peterson brusquely. "That's O.K." he said to the girl. "Come along, now."

"So that you can apologize?" she said with a flash of temper.

"Not here," Peterson came close to her.

"That's right," said Shank. "Not here. I've been trying to make her see reason. But I wouldn't trust her." His wattles shook indignantly.

"She won't do any harm," said Peterson. "Nothing to worry about. Leave it to me." He took the girl's arm. She resisted. He pulled and she stumbled forward and then Kirby's voice was drawling, "What's this?"

Peterson looked around at the thin little man. He heard his own voice thicken in self-protection. "It's O.K., boss. I got her. I'll handle it, like you said."

Kirby lifted his hand. "A minute."

Peterson, noticing the glitter in the dark eye, began to sweat. He carried no gun. Kirby took some strange pride in this, and Kirby was an observing man. So Peterson stood there in his muscles. Physically, he could sweep these two aside, but it would blow his cover. He could stall. There might be a better way.

Shank was sweating and mopping. He both needed and feared Kirby and Kirby's methods. He floundered. "I offered her five hundred. She wouldn't listen. How about a thousand, Miss?"

Peterson groaned to himself. Too late. The girl did not move nor speak.

"You don't want this kind of trouble, Miss," Shank pleaded. "What does it matter to *you?* Promise, that's all I—"

She folded her lower lip over the upper and looked at him. Shank's voice stopped.

"My way," said Kirby languidly. "Isn't that right, Peterson?"

"Right," said Peterson. He could feel, under his hand, a tremor beginning in the girl's arm. But she said nothing.

Kirby took a few steps toward her. It was like—Peterson's insides quivered—like an irresistable force approaching an immovable body. He said, "Why don't I just get going with her, boss? I got your car outside."

"So I saw," said Kirby carelessly.

"Or I could use Mr. Shank's car." Peterson was throwing bones between dogs, trying to create diversion and delay. Walters would be sending somebody.

Shank bleated at once, "Not *my* car."

Kirby raked him with a contemptuous glance. "You think you can handle it, do you, Peterson?" he asked carelessly.

"Sure thing."

Get her out of here, Peterson was thinking. *That's* what I've got to do.

"Maybe I better handle it myself." Kirby's eyes were hidden. "Here and now."

Shank yelped. "Not *here.*"

Kirby shrugged. "My car, then," he said with the contempt twisting his mouth. "I don't mind." Then he seemed to flame. "I'd like to sock her in her stupid little puss. She's got it coming." His eyes burned.

The girl lifted her chin. Peterson could feel the tremor stop. Courage was coming up in her like the mercury in a thermometer. He thought to himself, No, no, don't do that. Cringe a little bit. Satisfy him.

Kirby said, "She made a monkey out of *you,* Peterson." Now the dark eyes blazed on him.

"Yeah, she did," growled Peterson.

"So now you'll take her out to the shack," said Kirby, shifting in his sudden way to his drawl. "You know how to get there. Take you an hour-and-a-half. Drive slow and careful. Keep her quiet. You get that?"

"I got it, boss." Peterson thanked heaven that he had it, but he kept relief out of his voice.

"And when you get her out there, you'll put her good and quiet, eh?"

"Right."

Kirby's grin was full of malice. "A pleasure, eh?"

"Right," said Peterson. He yanked at the girl's arm. They would have to go around Kirby to get through the arch and into the foyer and out of the front door. But it was best to get out.

"One minute," Kirby said. "Before you go. Hit her. For me."

Peterson's head jerked.

"Hit her, I said." The eyes blazed. "Sock her a good one. Go ahead. Slap her down. *You* do it. I don't want to dirty my hands."

Shank said, "Now, now, no need for this sort of—"

But Kirby snarled, "*I* got a need. *Peterson's* got a need. Isn't that right, Peterson? She made a monkey out of him—middle of the sidewalk." Kirby's mouth was nasty. "He needs to relieve his frustrations, wouldn't you say, Councilman? So go ahead, Peterson. Sock her."

The man with the broken nose stood still.

Kirby said softly, "I'm giving you a job. You got the guts to do it, I wonder? *Any* of it?"

The doorbell pinged and Shank leaped within his clothing and Kirby said smoothly, "That will be a couple of my boys. I thought I might need them. The question is—who is going to do this job?"

"A pleasure," said Peterson. He widened his mouth in a big smile. He let go of the girl with one hand and raised the other and he slapped her and slapped her hard. So hard that Susan Miller went flying and fell against the couch, arms flailing, and tumbled bumpety-bump to the floor.

Peterson did not look at her. He looked at Kirby, keeping cheerful. "Do I get the job?" he asked, "or shall I hit her again?"

Shank began to squeal, "No, no, not here. Not here. Now, listen—" He made noise. The girl, and it was uncanny, made no noise.

Two men had come into the hall behind Kirby. One had a bald pate and a ruffle of hair around the back of his head. The other had a mottled face. The mottled one now stepped even with Kirby. He said nothing. There could have been the flicker of an eye.

Shank kept on squealing, "I'm sorry. Now, I'm very sorry, but I can't have this sort of thing in my house."

Kirby's mouth twisted. "O.K." he said, "Elsewhere."

"Another thing," Shank was frantic. "I want this understood. Now, I don't know anything about this. It's nothing to do with me. Kirby is in charge. The rest of you are working for Kirby. Now you remember that. And I don't want to know what you intend to do—you *understand* that?" Shank looked from face to face.

"He understands," said Kirby easily. "Peterson does what I tell him to do." Kirby's head jerked an order and a release.

Peterson felt relief enough to melt his bones. He strode to where the girl was lying. She had one hand to the side of her face. He met her eyes. He thought they were terrible, but he met them. He leaned and lifted her to her feet, without gentleness.

"You may have to hog-tie her," Kirby said mildly.

Peterson looked around the room, once. Then he ripped off his own necktie. He went down on one knee and whipped the tie around her ankles and tied them together, working fast, tying tight without mercy. The girl wobbled. She put her hand on his shoulder to keep herself from falling over. She had not yet cried out.

This was very odd. Shank, who was at his bar, felt it and looked fearfully around. Even Kirby seemed to feel that this was odd. The small man shifted his weight and said, "Want to tap her? Keep her from screaming?"

Peterson said, "I'll see she don't scream." He put his left arm around her from behind, in a mugging position. His right hand held her right hand tight to her hip and he lifted her, in a bum's rush, out of that house.

In Shank's driveway Kirby's car stood behind Shank's. He wrestled the girl to Kirby's car and he put her inside. He got in and shoved her away against the opposite locked door.

Kirby's men had followed them out. The bald one was looking up and down the quiet street. The mottled one said to Peterson, "Boss says take the Freeway. Fast, but not too fast. Me and Al are going to trail you out of town. She gives trouble, don't worry about a thing. We'll be right behind you." The mottled one grinned. "See what the boss let me bring?" Peterson saw.

He grunted, "O.K., Eddie." He started the car, backed out into the street. The two men were hurrying toward a third car, parked along the curb. Peterson was yards away now. But he could feel Kirby in that house, sense that Kirby was watching. So with his big left hand he shoved the girl's head down on the seat. He lifted his hand high and made a chopping motion. His foot pressed and the car jumped. He saw the third car making a U-turn to follow. He glanced down. The girl was looking up and he had a curious view of her face, upside down.

He said to her, "Just keep quiet and stay down. I'll get you out of this. I am a police officer."

Inside the house, Shank was pouring himself something stronger than sherry.

Kirby said, "Get that letter out of your safe and be quick."

"What? What?"

"The cops are on their way. I don't take *that* chance. So hurry."

"I don't believe it. How do you know?" Shank's little eyes flickered.

"Because Peterson is a cop," said Kirby calmly.

Shank goggled. "Now wait . . . wait! A cop! You let him get away and the girl, too!"

"That I did," said Kirby. "Far, far away. My car is booby-trapped. Told you I had a clever little man. Eddie can work fast. What did you think I was doing? Playing games? I was giving Eddie time, and keeping Peterson's mind off the window."

Shank collapsed into a chair.

"The car goes up in one hour." Kirby was calm and informative. "They should be pretty well out of town by then. So up he goes, and the girl with him. Simple?"

Shank felt saliva slipping out of his mouth. "But he won't go where you sent him," Shank choked. "If he is a cop, he'll go right to the cops! You've—"

"My boys will see to that," said Kirby complacently. "If he goes out of line, they take over. Eddie's carrying a gun and Peterson knows it. What he *doesn't* know is that he's riding with a time bomb. The boys will stay on his tail until she's about ready to blow. Leaves nothing to worry about."

"Don't tell me these things," moaned Shank.

"Then get the letter," snapped Kirby.

Shank did not move. A picture of the spot he was in was shaping in his mind, like a print coming up on the paper in a pan of chemical.

Kirby chose to accelerate the process. "When the cops show, you can tell them what you like. Explain the Kit-Kat clubs?"

Shank stared up at him.

"And in case you are feeling humane, you can also tell

them about the bomb in my car. If you do, you can *also* explain how you fingered the girl—for murder. You realize the motive is all yours? And that I work for you? Don't you, Councilman?"

Shank was a bowl of jelly.

"This is called pressure, Mr. Shank," said Kirby sweetly. "You are familiar with pressure? So get me the letter. *Now*."

Shank said, "I'll get it." He got up and shambled into his den where the safe was.

Kirby put a match to the piece of paper, dropped it on the cold hearth and watched it burn. Shank pushed his safe shut and mopped his neck.

"Pull yourself together," said Kirby, not unkindly. "Everything is simple enough, now. If Peterson and some girl get blown to bits on some country road, what's that got to do with you? Nobody can prove she was ever in your house. There they come."

Shank winced.

"Of course *I'm* here," Kirby continued to watch the bit of flame that had eaten all but a last corner. "It wouldn't look good for me to be seen trying to get away."

Out of doors, a car door slammed, and then another. The sound was plain. Kirby calmly put his foot on the ashes and ground them under his sole. "No problem," he said to Shank. "I got the rumor you're thinking of running for office. I came to sound you out about one thing or another. You can be old Joe-pro-bono-publico," said Kirby indulgently, "if you like. (Of course you'll pay me to stand still for it.) So go ahead. Be righteous. How dare I approach your civic virtue with any shady hints! Eh?" Kirby was enjoying this.

The doorbell rang, imperiously.

Shank, in crisis, pulled himself together. He hurried through the house to the door, and when he opened it he was himself again. "Captain Walters," he cried. "Well, sir! You've come at a good time. I have been trying to persuade an uninvited guest to leave. Maybe you can help me.

Captain Walters and another man in plainclothes stepped into the foyer. Kirby was standing in the archway to the living room.

"O.K., Mr. Shank," said Kirby. "Sorry I bothered you. A man can try." He was smiling and at ease.

Captain Walters said, "Hold it, Kirby. You too, Shank. Where is this girl?"

It was the moment of decision for Shank. And he decided. "What girl?" said Shank, cocking his white head, furrowing his pink brow.

CHAPTER VI

KIRBY's car had hit the Freeway long ago and went steadily, fast but not too fast, meeting with no stop lights. The girl had not screamed yet. Or shed any girlish tears, either. Peterson had kept talking, and talking fast. She had seemed to listen. He didn't want to turn his head and be seen talking to her. He wasn't sure how well he was doing. "Understand?" he asked.

She said, "No. If you really are a policeman why are my ankles tied together?"

Peterson sighed and flicked a glance at his rear view mirror.

"If you really are a policeman," she continued stubbornly, "why don't you untie my ankles and take me home?"

He said, for the fifth time, "Keep down on that seat. They might get nervous if you sit up."

She said, "You don't answer my questions."

"I can't untie your ankles and take you home until Kirby's boys drop us," he snapped.

"Oh, fiddlesticks!" the girl said, and she slipped to the floor.

"Oh, what?" he said, startled.

Now she was curled on the floorboards with her forearm on the seat. Now her face was right-side-up at least, to his view. "It seems so *silly*," Susan said.

41

"You beat all," said Peterson grimly. "You know that? Silly, is it? Tell me this—if you believe that I am going to murder you in some desert shack, then why don't you scream and carry on, and try to get away, like anybody else?"

"I won't scream until I think it's going to help me," she said. "I don't want to be 'tapped', you know—whatever that is. But I *will* try to get away from you, just as soon as I see that there's a fair chance."

Peterson ground his teeth upon each other. "I sure don't understand you."

"I don't understand *you*," Susan said. "You hit me."

"Did I deny it?" he said rather flippantly. He could see the boys in the car behind taking the turn-off with him, leaving the Freeway. "You're so calm and reasonable," he said to the girl. "Kindly note that there *is* no fair chance to get away, right now. Don't try it, *please*. The boys in the car behind us would kill you."

"Oh, fiddlesticks!" she said. "How could they?"

"Don't you believe that they are armed?" he asked her. "Eddie showed me a gun."

"Guns!" she scoffed.

"Fiddlesticks, eh?" said Peterson angrily. "Now you listen to me, you little idiot. Silly, eh?" Peterson was really very much annoyed. The trouble was he had a sinking feeling that grown men, running around in cars, carrying guns—when the basic reason for the whole performance was *money*—might, after all, be pretty silly. "I blew my job," he growled, "and probably my career just to keep you from getting killed. And I'm not letting you get killed now. I wish I *had* 'tapped' you. That means hit you, by the way, hard enough to knock you out."

Her chin went up. "Why didn't you say you were a policeman, last night, when I turned around and spoke to you?"

"Holy smokes! I was going to tell *you* inside police business? For all I knew, you could have been a wrongo."

"You just assume," she said in a moment, "that everybody wears two faces? You are certainly trying to tell me that *you* do. You've just lied, all along."

"My job," he told her. He felt as if he swam in a mist.

"In my job, I take orders. I don't say I like having to do what you call 'telling lies'."

"What do you call it?" she asked him.

"Undercover assignment," he snapped. He felt silly. "We prefer more than one syllable per," said Peterson bitterly. "It sounds better."

He was running along a highway near the hills now. The boys were still behind. Susan Miller sat on the floor and rested her arms on the seat, her chin on her clasped hands.

"You took orders from Kirby," she accused.

"Well, of course! Are you stupid or something?"

"You hit me. And you hit me very hard."

He said wearily, "Sure I hit you, and it had to be hard. So that I could get the job of killing you. Now, will you just kindly let me keep you from getting killed by somebody else?"

She opened her mouth. She closed it.

"Fiddlesticks, eh?" he muttered. "The trouble with you is you don't believe in evil." His skin crawled. What a thing to have said out loud!

He heard her say, gravely, "I don't believe in *doing* evil. But I know it exists."

Then the whole thing tickled him. He said, genially, "Mind you keep your head low. Certainly wouldn't seem right. Murderer and victim carrying on a discussion about the existence of evil."

She kept her head low. In a moment she burst out, "Mr. Peterson, you have got me all confused. I just don't know whether you are a good guy or a bad guy. And I thought I knew how to tell."

He chuckled. He couldn't help it. "How did you think you could tell?" he asked.

"I'm *confused*," she cried, resenting it.

"You sure are. You let Shank get you into *his* car."

"Yes," she said, stoutly. "Yes, I was fooled."

"Right you are." He glanced at her. "I suppose, in your book, no good guy ever tells a lie?"

"No," she said. "No, that's not quite—"

"Or ever pretends, for any reason, to be what he is not?"

"No, that isn't exactly—"

43

"Everybody should come out, flat, with whatever is in his head. Like you, eh?" Peterson said, a trifle resentfully.

"No, no. The way I put it, I said a good guy is—merciful."

"My, my," drawled Peterson. But his skin crawled.

"Well?" she said argumentatively. "That seems to me to be just what the difference *is*. Good guys don't want other people hurt. They feel it, themselves. So if anyone is in pain or trouble, then they not only *want* to help, they are obliged. They just about *have* to."

"That so?" he murmured, staring at the road. What a crazy kid!

"And I think," she said, "the habit of it starts with children. If a child doesn't learn that other people have feelings, too, as well as every living thing, and learn to hate cruelty so much that he could never *be* cruel— Don't you see how it makes all the difference?"

"Possibly," he said tightly. (He had a vision of fifteen-year-olds beating old ladies in the streets and feeling what? Pride in their own strength and their own daring?)

"Nice theory," he said. "Kirby, he pulled wings off flies for sport, no doubt. And Shank, he kicked and gouged as soon as he was able, whenever he knew he wouldn't get caught at it. *I*, naturally, hit people like I chop wood. Means nothing to *me*." He hurt all over. "What a simple-minded theory," he groaned. "So you can tell, eh? I wish you'd shut up."

She shut up, for a while. Then she said in a meek sad voice, "I've got a kind of knack, I guess. I don't know what it is. But, outside of my family, people never seem to like to talk to me for very long."

Peterson drove through a mist. He said in a moment, "Does your face still hurt?"

She said, "Yes, it does."

In another minute he said, "*I* can understand why it's hard for people to . . . uh . . . take to you."

The girl put her head on her hands and sighed. "I know they don't."

Captain Walters sat stonily behind his own desk and directed his cold stare at the company he had.

Shank said, "I am simply at a loss, Captain, to imagine what you think you can hold me for. Now, haven't I co-operated? Did I not open my private safe for you? Which I need not have done."

Walters said, "Peterson is my man, Shank. So don't give me that."

"Peterson?" said Shank. "Where *is* your man?"

"He'll be here," said the Captain. "He's got the girl, I presume. He'll be back and bring her with him. This Susan Miller, who overheard too much, who can also testify."

"You go on about this girl," said Shank plaintively.

"Where is the letter?" the Captain countered.

"I fail to recall any such letter as you describe," Shank said piously. "My lawyer should call back soon."

Walters turned his head to look at the thin little man. "Your lawyer, too?"

Kirby said, "Who needs a lawyer? Enjoy yourself. When you've had enough, let me know. I'll wait."

Walters said, grimly, "We'll all wait."

Peterson saw that the car behind him was accelerating. He said to the girl, "Here they come. I'll have to pull over. Watch it."

"Watch what?" she sounded confused.

"Keep your eyes shut. Head down. Or else," said Peterson recklessly, "*don't.* Just pop up and *say* that I am a policeman. That'll do it. True or false, if the boys even think I might be, then I'll be for it. Right here, by the side of the road. You don't have to believe a thing. You can test it out. Suit yourself."

He stopped the car on the margin and the other car pulled alongside.

Eddie leaned out and said, "O.K. You take it from here."

"Right," said Peterson.

"The lady behaving? How is she?"

"Take a look," said Peterson. He pulled in his chest. He shrank against the seat so that Eddie could see. The girl was huddled on the floor of the car. Her head lay on her arms. She did not move. She made no sound.

"Well, so long to the both of you," said Eddie cheerfully.

The other car spurted up. It's tires screeched as it U-turned.

Eddie said tensely to Al, "About seven minutes. So step on it."

Peterson sat still in Kirby's motionless car. "Thanks for that much," he said to her. In his mirror he could see that the boys were in a hurry. The car's image retreated swiftly.

"Are your ankles numb?" asked Peterson. "Let me fix that." He helped her to sit on the seat, at last. He got out his pocketknife and ruined his blue tie.

She rubbed her ankles with her hands. "Now what?" she inquired.

"Phone, I guess," he said moodily. He felt let down. He started the car.

"Why aren't you going back?"

"Because we don't want to catch up to the boys," he answered almost listlessly.

He was reflecting gloomily that he had saved her life but muffed the job probably. He didn't think that Walters would get that letter. So neither Shank nor Kirby were 'gotten'. Unless he and the girl could convince, by talking. If they talked loud and long, perhaps Shank's political career would be nipped in the bud. But that was about all. Peterson, himself, would blow his cover, of course, the moment he turned up with the girl alive. And Kirby and company were experts at revenge. The situation wouldn't be comfortable. Kirby and Shank were also expert liars. The scene in Shank's house would be moonshine. They'd 'prove' they were elsewhere. So what had been accomplished? The girl was alive, but not safe. And evil existed.

The car rolled another mile on the highway through wide flat fields where grapes were growing. Then Peterson said. "Gas station ahead. Hooray! On the left. See it? I'm going to stop there and phone in. But I want you to stay put. I can't let you run around loose until we can get you under protection, or Kirby and company under control. You are too confused. So I'm just telling you. Don't try to run away from me."

"I said I would if I could," she murmured.

"I say you won't do it," he told her curtly. "Try telling this gas-station fellow—whoever he'll be—any story. I'll 'tap' you and take off. Might upset him for days." He relaxed a little and grinned at her. "Think of his *feelings*. Here we go."

He crossed the road and turned in upon the apron of the gas station, which sat on a corner where a dusty narrow side road went among the vineyards. He said to the man whose head popped out of the small tin structure, "Got a phone, buddy?"

"No phone. Sorry, pal. Gas?"

"Yeah," sighed Peterson. "Fill her up. Might as well."

He sat still and the girl sat still. The attendant glanced curiously at her puffed and swollen cheek.

"My wife's got a toothache," Peterson said, in sheer mischief. "How far to the next . . . uh . . . settlement?"

"East?"

"East or West," said Peterson. "North or South. No matter." He felt lightheaded.

"About three miles east, more or less. 'Course if you go north, it's only a little bit."

The car's nose pointed north, along the unpaved side road. Peterson considered it.

The man put the hose in the tank. He moved around and raised the hood.

"Maybe we'll go north," Peterson said. "Less chance of overtaking our friends."

The girl said, in a low angry voice, "That was two more lies. I am not your wife. I do not have a toothache."

"All in fun," said Peterson absently. "All in fun."

"I don't think it is funny."

Peterson grinned. "You're confused, is all. You're trying to part the whole world in the middle, and it doesn't part that way. *You* confuse *me*, plenty, if you want to know the truth."

"Oh, the truth," she exploded. She jerked upright. It was in her mind to shout.

Peterson said, "Don't do it. There's no phone here. Just delay us if we have to explain to him."

She said, "Why should I believe a thing you say?"

"Not a reason in the world," he answered lightly.

47

In Captain Walter's office Shank was restless, now. "I dislike the vernacular," he was saying, "but I can't think of a better way to express myself. Will you either 'put up' or 'shut up', Captain?"

"We'll wait."

"We have waited some time," Shank said. "What are we waiting *for*?"

"To hear from Peterson."

"This Peterson has nothing to do with me."

"We'll see."

Kirby looked up from his pastime, which was to be doing a crossword puzzle in a newspaper. "Five letter word meaning 'evidence to determine judgment'?" he murmured.

Shank shrugged. Walters sat like stone.

"*Proof?*" chirped Kirby insolently. "Right?"

Walters said nothing.

Shank glanced at his watch.

The gas-station man did something strange and sudden. He put down the hood and went dancing away from the car. The movement was startling and peculiar. Peterson sat up.

"Mister!" The man's voice was weak and shrill. He was a good thirty feet away.

Peterson got out and went to him. He thought the man had had a seizure of some kind, or had injured himself. He thought the man was in pain.

"You take a look, there. You just go take a look there." The man's jaw shook. He squeaked like a mouse.

"What's the trouble?"

"No, *don't* look!" the man said, dancing where he stood. "You get that car out of *my* place! Quick! Go ahead, get it away from here!"

"What are you talking—"

"There's some kind of bomb in there."

"There's *what?*"

Peterson started to turn. The attendant shouted. "Waw!"

Too late Peterson saw the car jump. It's tires clawed. The car moved. Susan Miller was at the wheel of it. She was getting away from him.

The attendant was jumping up and down. "Hey! Hey!

48

Waw! She'll blow! She'll blow! There's a time bomb in there. I saw it! I'm telling you!"

Now Peterson saw the whole thing. So Kirby hadn't given him the job. Kirby had had the job done—Peterson included. And the boys had turned back. He knew what that must mean. There couldn't be much time.

"Car?" he snapped. "Quick."

"All I got's my truck."

"Where?"

The two of them ran.

Thought, speech, motion, took only seconds. But Susan Miller, in Kirby's car, was careening along the narrow side road across the flat and empty country. Peterson had the small truck on the road in seconds more. It was not very new, not very speedy. The girl in the doomed car fled them and it was no more than seconds before Peterson knew the score.

The other man was yelping in his ear, "That thing's going to blow! Hang back, mister. She'll blow! We can't do nothing."

Peterson's mind ticked faster than a bomb. Can't catch her in this. Can't signal. Can't warn. And there isn't much time.

"She's going to blow," said the other man with the calm of despair.

CHAPTER VII

Shank was on one of the Captain's telephones. "Yes, Joe. Yes, I understand, thanks. Oh, well, you see I wished to be co-operative, Joe. You know me. Captain Walters insists that he is waiting for a report from one of his men. Now, while *I* know that no such report can concern *me*, still I felt I ought to show good faith, as a law-abiding— Oh, yes, the Captain is surely doing what he believes to be his duty. Thanks a lot, Joe. The inconvenience is not important . . . uh . . . so far."

After a few more pious murmurs, Shank hung up. Walters was boiling where he sat, but he kept the lid on. Shank said graciously, "Thank you for the use of the telephone."

Walters snatched up the phone himself. "Anything?" He listened and he put the phone down.

Shank sat down and circled one thumb with the other. Kirby glanced at his own watch and winked at him. Shank closed his eyes suddenly.

The hair on Walters' neck stirred.

No one spoke.

The sun beat down on the flat land and there was silence on the flesh of the land between the noisy arteries that were highways. A hot silence surrounded the immediate rush and rattle of the vehicles and pushed upon the brief intrusive sounds to make them lonely and insignificant, here on the narrow thread where Kirby's car fled and the truck rattled hopelessly after. The gas-station man jittered with his mouth. "Listen, you *can't—*"

Peterson knew that he couldn't. She was more than half-a-mile ahead and drawing away. Peterson's mind became like a tunnel with one light, at a far end. "One chance," he said. "Wrap your arms around your head. We're going to crash."

"What!"

"*Now.* And God help her."

Peterson wrenched at the truck's wheel and sent it in staggering curves along the road's edge. Then he sent it off the road. The nose of the truck rammed down into the ditch. Impact shook it. Peterson turned the ignition key and listened, fearfully. Would there be fire? The silence swallowed them. He said to the other man, "You O.K.?"

The attendant, crouched, with his arms wound over his head, began to straighten his torso.

"Keep down. Don't move." Peterson unlatched the door beside him. He let his left arm hang in its opening. He let his head rest on the steering wheel. Was he crazy? Was he out of his mind?

"Only chance there is," he muttered. "A child learns . . . is obliged. Makes the difference, *she said*." Sweat poured down his body. "So lie low, friend. Bleed a little."

Now, he could hear a gentle something dripping from the wounded truck. Could still be fire, any moment. Could be an explosion, up ahead, at any moment. Sound that would split silence and let death into this sunny peace where the vines grew so surely and so quietly. She hadn't been far. Was she now farther?

"How long do I have to—" He heard his companion say.

"Don't move. Listen."

Peterson thought, Lord, don't let another car be on this road. Not now. Let the road stay empty. Let it be up to *her*. And God, give her mercy.

He could hear the man breathing. He could hear his own breath. He could hear his heart beat. He could hear himself live. Then he could hear the slow grind of a car's engine.

Then he could hear feet. Slap of soles on the road.

Then he heard her saying, out of breath, "Are you hurt? Can I help you?"

So his hand, that he had ready, shot out and grabbed her and he tumbled out of the truck, shouting at the other man. He had her in both his arms. The three of them ran back the way they had come. Then Peterson pulled the girl down on the ground and the other man fell down, nearby.

"It can't be very long," gasped Peterson. "Can't be."

It was not.

Kirby's car exploded.

They could feel it, the length of their bodies, through the ground. When their shocked ears opened, they could hear the roar of flame, and a thin, tinkling, overtone of destruction.

Peterson turned his face in the dust. There was grit between his teeth. The girl's face turned. He could feel her breath. He could hear her heart beating. He heard her live.

"Baby," said Peterson exuberantly, "you've been fooled! Wreck on purpose. Nobody's hurt. Just a fake! Hey, I am the biggest, fattest, smartest liar you ever met in your life, and Kirby put a time bomb in the car."

She had her cheek to the ground. Her eyes opened wide. Peterson looked into them and almost drowned. He felt

51

dizzy. Reaction, he guessed. In another moment he reared up.

"We'll go back to the highway. Hail a ride. Get to a phone. And look, buddy," he said to the other man, who was sitting up like a rag doll, legs out, face blank, "you stick round and keep folks from messing with that mess. And don't you forget, *you* are going to testify there *was* a bomb. And that wreck is going to be evidence that you were right. Oh, you bet it is! I *thought* Eddie had too much honey in his mouth. Whew!"

He was on his feet, now, and he looked down at the girl. Poor kid. She'd had a bad time. "I didn't hurt you, throwing you down like that, did I?" he asked politely. "May I help you up?"

"Thank you, Mr. Peterson," she murmured, as if she hardly knew what she was saying.

Shank was on his feet. "You must agree, Captain, that I have been patient. Now, while I certainly hope you do hear from your man . . . and of course from this mysterious girl— what's her name?"

Not a muscle had moved in the Captain's face. So Peterson's voice whirled Shank around. "Her name is Susan Miller. Attempted murder, Captain. Kirby's orders. Shank in conspiracy."

Walters was lifted out of his chair with sheer pleasure.

Shank squealed. "Now wait . . . murder! That's nothing to do with *me*."

"We are both ready and able to testify," said Peterson cheerfully. His hand touched the girl's shoulder. "The evidence is in the car."

"It's not *my* car," said Shank, too hastily.

And Peterson laughed. "He sure was chintzy with his car, eh, Kirby?"

The small thin man sat still and his face was sour.

Peterson said, "The bomb's got Eddie's name on it."

"Now, listen," squealed Shank. "Whatever this is, I'm not mixed up in it. Whatever this man Kirby is— Listen, *I* am a respected citizen. You can't—"

Peterson ignored him. "And Eddie is your man, Kirby."

Kirby said, from his dark spirit. "I work for Shank. I am his boy."

There was a lot of talk, and coming and going, while Kirby coiled into himself and Shank wept like a woman and Walters laid on orderly procedures with the calm of authority.

Peterson answered questions, and the girl did, and then she sat with eyes like saucers, listening. When the room had quieted at last she was still sitting there in the straight chair. Walters said to her, "Are you all right, Miss Miller?"

"I'm fine," she said. The swelling on her cheek had almost disappeared. Her skin was almost as taut and fair as ever. There remained the merest rumple on her brow.

"You were pretty lucky," the Captain said reproachfully. "If—"

Peterson broke in. "She's a little confused," he said. "I mean, you can't blame her." Now, he looked at his courtesy-uncle and his superior. Walters looked at Peterson. "May she go now, sir?" Peterson asked. "It's getting late and she's . . . uh . . . pretty tired and hungry, probably." Peterson knew that he was for it.

Captain Walters surveyed the two of them with his experienced eye. "Go ahead, both of you," he said, without expression. "This day is done. I'll talk to *you* in the morning." Walters sat down behind his desk.

Now that he knew the whole story Walters could not, for the life of him, think what else his man Peterson could have done. Except watch his tongue better. Furthermore Captain Walters stood in some awe of what his man Peterson *had* done—after the girl had run away in the booby-trapped car. Walters felt that he needed to think. He became very busy.

"Thank you, sir," said Peterson miserably. "I'll take you home, then, Miss Miller."

The girl got up but she did not go quietly. Oh, no, not she! She had to speak up in her crazy, totally straight-forward way. "Captain Walters?"

"Yes?"

"Don't *you* think he was very quick and understanding?"

"Who?" The captain glared.

"Why . . . Mr. Peterson."

Peterson wanted to die, where he stood. The Captain didn't look very comfortable either.

"I could have been killed," she said earnestly.

"Right. You could have," the Captain said morosely.

"But it wasn't *luck* that I didn't die. It was Mr. Peterson." The Captain growled in his throat.

"And I'm *trying* to understand," the girl said. "I see how you do these things. But it doesn't seem to *me*—"

Her fair brow creased. They watched her, with a horrid fascination. "Captain Walters, does Mr. Peterson *have* to be this undercover kind of policeman? He doesn't seem—"

Walters said grimly, "Peterson is lousy at it. That your point?"

"Oh, no . . . but—"

"Well, he *is*," snapped Walters. "He blows his cover. He practically throws the assignment back in my face, so *he* can rescue a fair damsel." The captain was severe. "You messed things up considerably, young lady, from the minute you got into this."

"But what did *I* do?" said Susan in distress. "Did I do something wrong?"

After a while Walters was able to speak. He said, "Take her away and feed her, *Mister* Peterson. And explain to her what she did wrong."

"Yes, sir." But Peterson took breath and courage rose in him. (Why not? Well, why not find out?) "I'd like to know where I stand, sir," he said boldly. His mien added, I accept judgment. I deserve it! Redfaced, he waited.

The captain, giving judgment, said coldly, "I can't afford to waste your training. But there'll be no undercover jobs for you."

"Yes, sir," said John Peterson stiffly, hiding, for the sake of decorum, his delight and thanksgiving.

Then he took hold of that girl and, firmly, he led her out of there.

She said as they went through the building, "Are we going somewhere to eat?"

Peterson didn't answer.

"I should go home, first," she said, sounding fussed, which, for her, was odd. "This dress isn't clean. And there is Lorna. She might be worrying."

He led her out back, where he had his own jalopy parked.

"Do you *have* to take me to dinner," she asked, "because he told you to?"

"No," he answered.

"Well, then . . . if you don't *want* to—" She certainly sounded confused.

He started his car. "Do *you* want to have dinner with *me?*"

"Are you inviting me?" the girl was puzzled.

"Just answer the question, please, as bluntly and tactlessly as usual."

Her head trembled. Then whatever it was in her came up, like mercury in a thermometer. "Yes, *I* would like it very much," she said. "I have never had a date with a young man, to go out to dinner."

John Peterson licked his lips. He trembled inside. "O.K., it's a date, then. But you'd like to change your clothes?" he asked her mildly.

"If you please," she said, a little timidly.

He didn't say another word. He parked the car in front of the roominghouse. He went in with her. They got to the top of the stairs and there was Lorna Hayes in the upper hall. "Gosh, honey, where have you been? I was about to call the police."

"He turned out to *be* the police," said Susan demurely. "This is Mr. Peterson, Lorna. Mr. Peterson, this is Miss Lorna Hayes. We have a dinner date. I'll have to change my dress."

Peterson and Lorna exchanged glances in the dim hall and knew each other, at once. They were hip people, worldlings. Lorna said, with relief, "Why don't you go ahead and change then, honey? And your date can come wait in my room. O.K.?"

"Oh, thanks," Susan said. Her eyes shone. She used her key on her door. "I won't be long," she promised, rather shyly.

Peterson walked through Lorna's door. He sat down in Lorna's chair.

"It got so late," said Lorna chattily. "I was afraid something had happened."

"Happened?" said the young man with the broken nose. "Yeah. Certainly did."

"*What* happened?"

"What happened, you ask?" He stretched his long legs. "Well, for one thing, we got a big-time wrongo, and we got him good."

"But I meant—"

"And we also got the 'respected citizen' behind him. Shank's cracking up entirely."

"Her boss!"

"Also, come to think of it," said Peterson, "it happens that I'm taken off a job sooner than I—"

"But what happened to Susan?"

"Susan Miller? What happened to her, you ask? Well, she nearly got herself killed." John Peterson looked glum.

"I *told* her not to stick her neck out," said Lorna excitedly. "I *told* her to lie low."

"Yeah? Well, she didn't do that."

"What did she do?"

"It's more what she didn't do," said Peterson thoughtfully. "There I was, luring her into my car so I could kidnap her, you know? But she wouldn't *get* in."

Lorna folded her mouth and her eyes crinkled.

"Let's see. After that, Shank tried to bribe her, but she wouldn't *be* bribed."

Lorna was half appalled, half ready to crow with amusement.

"Sure, she could have lain low in the first place and kept out of it—like everybody else," said Peterson rather angrily. "Also, she could have kept on running away and left me and the other man to bleed and die. She didn't do that, either."

"Honest, I don't know what you're talking about," said Lorna in a friendly way.

"I'm supposed to tell her what she did wrong," said Peterson pathetically. "So I'm trying to figure—"

"She's impossible," burst out Lorna. "Of course, I guess it's not her fault. She was raised on some mountain by a couple of high-minded eggheads, evidently. Only place she ever went was to church. She just doesn't know the score." Something in Peterson's eye egged her on. "This kid is an absolute square. Talks about 'goodness' and 'mercy' and out loud, too."

"Sounds like a prig?" he said. "Makes you squirm? Sure does."

"Yes, she does," said Lorna. "But look, I don't mean . . . I am her friend, I guess. But it . . . just isn't *easy*. I mean, she's *impossible*."

"Too honest," he said. "That's embarrassing. Certainly isn't easy."

"All right," said Lorna. "But she's going to get clobbered in *this* world. She has got to learn."

His eyes turned, but before he could speak Susan Miller came out of her room and across the hall, neat and pretty and remarkably prompt, in a print dress and high heels. Then Peterson saw her face and was surprised when his heart went sinking down.

Out from the black and blue, over cheek bones marred by painted lashes that had blinked too soon, the gray eyes shone. "I'm ready," the girl said.

Peterson stood up, dismayed and depressed.

Lorna was quick and tactful. "Honey, you've smeared your cheek a little. Just let me fix it." She snatched for the cleaning tissue and the cold cream jar.

But Peterson put his shoulder against the wall and said, as if he spoke in a trance, "*Why* did you put that gook on your eyes?"

The eyes were closed. Lorna was already dabbing at them. "Because," said the impossible girl, "I want to be attractive."

Peterson straightened. "Take it all off," he said to Lorna. Lorna made some mighty swipes. The girl took Lorna's hand and pushed it away. Her eyes opened. They looked up into his and he endured them.

He was drowning. He was going down for the third time. He was lost. Oh, well, he'd teach her. There were things he'd have to teach her. But he couldn't bear for anyone else to teach her. Some people wouldn't understand.

"Just bring your one-and-only face," he said to her, gently, "I'm over the shock. I think I can take it."

"GRIPPING IMPACT" —*Chicago Tribune*

"You never know," she reflected, *"when you may meet a black-eyed stranger."* Around the corner, at a party, in a crowd, looming up, breaking the pattern open, warping all the threads.

Katherine Salisbury's comfortable, well-ordered existence had suddenly been ripped apart, and for the first time, she knew fear. Someone was being hunted, and the face of the hunter was hidden. There was some kind of a plot—kidnaping, perhaps even murder. And whether the plot existed in reality or only in the twisted mind of a strange man, the danger was the same for Katherine. For she was the intended victim.

Turn this book over for
second complete novel

About the Author

The list of Charlotte Armstrong's novels of mystery and suspense is impressive. Beginning in 1942 with the creation of the detective Mac-Dougall Duff, as in *The Case of the Weird Sisters*, Miss Armstrong hit the jackpot in 1946 with *The Unsuspected*. Outselling all novels of the type in its first year, it was followed in 1948 by *The Chocolate Cobweb*, and in 1950 by *Mischief*. This book established Charlotte Armstrong's leadership position once and for all. Following this came others including *Catch-as-Catch-Can*, and the present book.

In private life Mrs. Jack Lewi of Glendale, California, Charlotte Armstrong was born in Michigan and spent a number of years in New York. In addition to her books she has written numerous short stories and has won high praise and magazine awards.

THE
BLACK-EYED
STRANGER

by
CHARLOTTE ARMSTRONG

ACE BOOKS, INC.
1120 Avenue of the Americas
New York 36, N.Y.

CHAPTER I

*If, among flamingos, you found a dove . . . Or,
in with the writhing orchids, one small rose. . . .*

He was leaning, as he had a habit of doing, on the wall,
inside the room where the party was roaring, but outside the
party. The black eyes smudged in on his thin tired face
missed very little and so he noticed her in the pale-blue frock.

Women at this party wore reds or blacks or, for shock
value, pure white. Gowns tended to be naked somewhere, or
tight somewhere. Women postured all around the room and
their glances, whether bold or veiled, were calculated. But
this one, in pale blue, sat quietly on a wooden chair against
the wall and looked about her with friendly curiosity. Of all
things! In Emanuel's brother-in-law's apartment! One young
lady!

He heaved himself away from the wall and walked around
until he was beside her. "Hi."

"Oh, hello."

"You need a drink or anything?"

She said, "I have one, thank you."

He leaned on the wall. Now he saw that needlework on the
blue frock had been meticulously and daintily done and he
knew, as he knew many things without analysis, that it was
a very expensive frock, indeed.

"Cinderella, honey," he said, softly, "haven't you got into
the wrong ball?"

"I'm only here for a few minutes," she said, "looking on."
She agreed to her difference and she agreed to his recognition
of it. She was young, all right, not much more than half as
old as he. She had a tooth out of line at the edge of her

5

smile. In her very young upturned face it was a touch of the urchin. It exercised, he noted with surprise, a curious tug on his heart.

He was groping for something, maybe a memory, that might account for that funny little feeling, when she said, accusingly, "You're just looking on, too, aren't you? I noticed."

He didn't show surprise. He didn't, often. He said, "I guess that's right, sis." And repeated, "Sister."

"Do you know who all these people are?" She squirmed on the chair like a child at the circus. "You do, don't you? Please tell me."

He let himself lean on the wall. Looking down on her brown head, he told her. He named the so-called actresses, and the so-called models, and he named some of the men and some of the sources of their power. "Over there, talking to that tow-headed boy, that's our host. A so-called gambler. You know him, sister?"

"I met him," she said gleefully, "just now. I think it's very interesting."

He considered the hooded eyes of their host and all the posturing people. He said, sharply, "Somebody's going to see that you get out of here?"

"Any minute," she confided. "I haven't very long. Please tell me some more."

"You find it interesting," he drawled, "to be among thieves and swindlers and one or two professional killers?"

"Really?" She looked up doubtfully as if now she thought he might be kidding. "Is that really what they do in the world?"

He moved his body out from the wall to put it between her and a pair of eyes and was amused at himself, and disturbed, too. "Why, what do you do in the world, sister?" he teased her.

"I guess I just live in it, so far," she answered, lifting her eyes with so forthright a look that he winced. Such a look, to him, was shocking. "I go to school, of course," the girl said. She put her thumb nail to her teeth, and it was the urchin again. But she took it away. "I just wonder," she said, looking very wise, "what happened to them. In what way did society fail?"

He bit his cheek. "You studying . . . like, say . . . sociology?"

"Not this term. I'm going to take it next term, though." Her level gaze ripped past the amusement on his face. "You think I ought to be home with a nursemaid." She challenged. "Don't you? Why?"

"Only because it's so," he answered, rather sadly.

"So silly," she said loftily. "What can be the harm? In just looking on? What if I sit here for about fifteen minutes and just watch them? How will that make any difference in my life or anybody's?" It was a practiced argument. She had said this to someone before. Now, she looked up and he felt again shock and he shivered. "What's the matter?" she asked at once.

"Hm?" He drank from his glass. "Cat walked over my grave, I guess. Ever have that?" He did not smile. "No difference," he went on, "so long as you don't tangle with any of these characters. Including me."

She smiled. "What do you do in the world? Are you a criminal?"

His dark eyes despaired of her. "That's not etiquette. You do not ask." The girl giggled. "You see?" he said. "You don't believe it for a minute. But for all you know, I might be."

"But you're not?" She made it a solemn question.

"No," he said. "No, it so happens. I guess you'd say I was a writer, if you had to say." He watched her.

"Would I know your work?" She accepted this gravely, quite ready to be respectful.

He laughed and shook his head. "Nothing fancy. I do a kind of reporting."

"Oh." She looked a little pinker, a little flustered. "Oh, but you wouldn't . . . You don't write a column or anything? Because the family would be horrified."

"I'm glad," he said dryly.

"No, no. You see, they'd blame Alan and they shouldn't because I *made* him bring me. I just wouldn't wait in the restaurant."

"Maybe you should have waited in the restaurant," he drawled. Then he stiffened. "Who?"

"Alan Dulain. Oh, do you know Alan? He's over there, talking to our host. It's a thing he had to do for the office . . ."

"What's your influence on this Dulain boy, sister?" The black eyes were curious.

She smiled. "Well, we're engaged to be married," she said demurely, "for one thing. But you wouldn't, would you? Use my name or anything? Please don't tell who I am? I mean . . ."

"I don't know who you are," he reminded her gently.

Then she took stock of him, searching his face with that level gray gaze that somehow touched him with fright, as it had before. "I'm Kay Salisbury," she said. "Kay for Katherine."

The skin around his eyes, as he closed them, was papery thin and stained brown as if with permanent fatigue. "I'm Sam Lynch," he said, "Sam for Samuel. Sister, go home, will you? Just go home."

"I guess I'm going," she said placidly, "because here comes Alan." She stood. She came as high as his chin. She turned gracefully, as if she stood in her own drawing room. (Oh, a young lady!) "Alan, I want you to meet . . ."

The tow-headed young man who came to her side had a crisp kind of face, a sharp nose, a coolly chiseled chin. "Lynch," he said.

"Dulain," said the black-eyed man, mocking the crisp tone exactly.

"Oh, then you've met before?" The girl looked from one to the other but the men had no more to say, and she was the one who broke the stiff moment in which they stood as if the two of them had collided. She said, graciously, "Thank you for talking to me, Mr. Lynch. You were very kind and interesting. Good night."

The black-eyed man didn't touch her hand. He let himself lean on the wall. "So long, sister," he drawled, lifting his own thin hand halfway to a salute. "See you around sometime."

Red came up under Dulain's fair skin as he wheeled the girl toward an exit. "Who is he, Alan?" she whispered.

"He's no good, Kay. Come on, now, please. Time for you to get out of here."

"What do you mean," she gasped, "no good? Alan, he was very nice and he knows all about every . . ."

"He knows too much and he tells too little," Alan said. "Too wise. That kind of fringe character." He wrapped her in her coat. He hugged her arm to his side. They were out of the apartment door. "Well?" he inquired.

The girl's head tilted. She said, judiciously, "It was very interesting."

He laughed. "Go on," he teased. "Lynch is no international jewel thief. He's a tired old phony."

"But I mean interesting . . ."

"Told you there wasn't any glamour . . ."

8

She said, seriously, "Alan, if I'm going to be any kind of wife to you . . ."

He laughed. He kissed her. "Now that you are disillusioned," he said, "and my chore is done, shall we dance or what?"

CHAPTER II

ABOUT two months later, on a day toward the end of April, a big man and a little man entered a restaurant on Third Avenue. The time was nearly noon, but Nick's Bar and Grill was more bar than grill, and the row of battered wooden booths was empty.

The little man was dressed in a well-cut, well-kept dark suit that hung loosely from his shoulders as if from a hanger. He had been in the sun, and with sunglasses on, for, while his face and neck were evenly tanned, the flesh was pale around the soft and rolling red-brown eyes. Blue pale.

His companion was enormous, with thick-palmed, thick-fingered hands hanging out of his shabby brown coat. His face was round and red, as if he had been burned in the sun, somewhere, and when he forgot to hold his straggling brows in a scowl, it was a petulant, pouting, hurt-baby kind of face, with an underlip that seemed about to tremble.

These two sat down.

Fred, the waiter, scurried to the back regions. He pointed behind him with a jerk of the head. "Hey, Nick. Ambielli. Just came in."

Nick let resignation settle on his face. "Take care of him, Fred. If he wants to see me . . ." He shrugged. Fate was fate. "So I'm back here, tell him."

The waiter approached them gingerly. He wished to lay a fresh cloth but the big man's forearms were planted heavily on the table. "Excuse me," the waiter said timidly, "the cloth . . ."

The big man wound his face into a belligerent frown. "And what about it?"

"Nothing. Nothing. I gotta put it on here, please."

Slowly and suspiciously, like a wrestler breaking a hold the big man raised his arms.

"What'll it be, Mr. Ambielli?" Fred said obsequiously. "Drink, first?"

11

"Just bring me a steak, Fred," said the smaller man, in a pleasant cultivated voice.

"Rare or well done, Mr. Ambielli?"

"Well done."

"And that," said the big one ferociously, "means well done, see?"

"Yes, sir. Yes, sure. And yours, Mr. Hohenbaum?" Fred, the waiter, was a name-and-face connector.

"Gimme a chicken salad," the big man pouted, "and some potata chips."

"Yes, sir. Any vegetables? Fresh peas? String beans?"

"Tell Nick to slice a couple of tomatoes, thin." Ambielli moved a thin, tanned hand fastidiously, shifted and leaned back. The blue-white increased in his face as the eyelids fell.

"Nice to see you around, Mr. Ambielli," the waiter babbled, moving pepper and salt. "You're looking good," he lied. "Been back long?"

"Not long," said Ambielli melodiously.

The big man scowled, and the hulk of his torso lifted as if he would rise. "Sit down, Baby," said Ambielli quietly. Fred scurried away.

"Don't like so many questions," Baby growled.

"You got any money with you?"

"A couple of fives."

"Give them to me."

Baby Hohenbaum reached and got the money out, and Ambielli's hand took it with a smooth quick secrecy. The red-brown eyes were a little bitter. "I've changed my mind," he said. "I'm not looking for anyone. We'll manage alone."

"What d'you mean?" said Baby. "Who's going to drive the car?"

"I am."

"Who's going to pick it up?"

"I'll pick it up myself."

"What about your alibi?"

"I'll arrange for that. Nick, here, owes me something."

"I don't like it, boss."

"No?" Ambielli wasn't terribly impressed.

"No. You was always so particular. It don't seem—"

"Forget it."

"But in the old days—"

"New days are coming." Something blazed in the face, the brown unhealthy face.

"Whatever way you want it, boss," Baby said.

Ambielli's thin fingers walked up and down the stem of a fork. "The one thing I need to decide about is the collection."

Baby scowled, indicating that he pondered. "Take old money," he suggested. "Tell him, and wrap it like a package. Check it in one of them parcel places."

"Go on," said Ambielli. "How do we get the key? How do we go there and unlock the lock? And who will be waiting for us when we do?" All this was calm, fluent.

Baby looked hurt. His lips trembled. "They're not going to the cops," he scoffed.

Ambielli smiled. His shoulders moved in a delicate comment. He took from his wallet a piece of paper, a clipping from a newspaper's Sunday rotogravure.

"That's her, boss?"

"Do you know the man?"

The paper was frail in the sausage fingers as Baby began to read the caption. "Miss Katherine Salisbury," he read aloud, clumsily.

Ambielli made a noise through his teeth, like a swift whisper, which seemed to pass like a knife between the paper and the hand. The paper fell. The big man quaked. "Boss, I thought you wanted me to read it?"

"Read in your head. Keep your mouth shut." Ambielli's quick hand adjusted the paper on the table. "That's her fiancé."

"Oh? Oh, her boy friend?" Baby's brows were conciliating and humble.

The fingernail tapping the pictured face was well manicured. "And he is money, too."

"Yeah, boss?"

"A great deal of money."

"Can I read it, boss?"

Ambielli began to laugh. When he did so, the tan, too thin, but not unhandsome face changed its soft quiet character and was wolfish. "Can't you read without moving your lips? Do it while I'm here, then. Keep it down." His laughter was contempt.

Baby rolled his eyes over the forbidden name, and, moving his lips, muttered, " 'In the Easter Parade is wearing a dove-gray soft woolen suit by Mary Kane, tricked out . . .' Tricked?"

"That's right."

" 'In mulberry.' Huh?"

"Go on."

" 'Garnished at the throat by a pure silk scarf in mulberry and white, an exclusive Jonadab print from Jonadab, Madison Ave. Pumps, mulberry swede . . . ' "

"Suede." Ambielli was entertained.

" 'by Martine' " read Baby. " 'Bare-face bonnet by Bellamy.' What!"

"Fashion. That's fashion."

" 'Her escort—' " Baby clamped his mouth over the name.

"Alan Dulain," said Ambielli softly.

" 'is wearing—' Oh, no, boss! It's going to tell what he's got on!" Baby was going to laugh.

Ambielli made the hissing sound through his teeth again. Quick. Commanding. Baby brought his hands down at the sides of his body. Fred brought their food.

"Cup of coffee," the small man said languidly.

"Yes, Mr. Ambielli."

Now, a man came in, came by, skirting the waiter's rump. This customer was in the act of taking his hat off his dark head, and he did not seem to see the pair at the table but passed by and settled himself in the booth next in line.

"How long ago's this chicken cooked?" asked Baby belligerently, his fork poised.

"Since yesterday, only yesterday, Mr. Hohenbaum." Fred, the waiter, backed off.

He flourished his napkin, turned to the newcomer. "Yes, sir, Mr. Lynch?"

"Bring me two lamb chops, French fries, cup of coffee, and," the black-eyed man pinched the rolls in the basket, "a couple of fresh rolls while you're at it."

"Yes, sir. Drink, sir?"

"No."

Ambielli took salt. Baby picked up the ketchup bottle and slopped it on his salad. "Say, boss, I've been thinking . . ."

"Yes?"

Sam Lynch's ears pricked at that one soft syllable. His black eyes moved.

"You know . . ." Baby slurped food, "if you want to live you got to eat."

"True."

"Well, that means groceries, don't it? I mean for the—"

"For the week end?" said Ambielli smoothly. But some

14

move of the hand or eye had set Baby Hohenbaum to trembling again. The silence grew a little odd. "Go on," said the boss. "What's on your mind?"

"Well, it'd be cheaper, you know, if . . . uh . . . it was just you and me had to eat, for one thing."

"You want to be alone?" said Ambielli mockingly.

"I don't mean that." Baby looked hurt. "It's just, you take a dame, you got to go to all kinds of trouble. You can't . . ."

"Wait a minute," Ambielli said. He pushed out of the booth. He took a step or two. "I thought so," he said genially. "Hello, Sam. How's the boy?"

"Live and breathe," said Sam. They shook hands.

"How are things with you? Still on the paper, Sam?"

"Free-lancing these days."

"I saw your piece about Emanuel." The thin lips curved in the tan face.

"That so? Like it?"

Ambielli shrugged. "Did Emanuel like it, Sam?"

"He should have. It was a pack of lies."

Ambielli showed his teeth. "Come, eat with us, boy?"

"Sure. Glad to. Hello, Baby. You back, too, eh?"

The big one was on his feet, his body bent over the table. His head turned on the thick neck, so that the short hair bristled on the fat creases. "Oh, it's you," he growled.

"It's only me." Sam started to shove into the booth, but Baby said, "Wait, get away. *I* got to sit on the outside."

Amiably, Sam let him out, and then slid into the corner. "What's the matter, Baby? Nervous?"

"He's habitually nervous," said Ambielli in his well-spoken way. "That's his quality. Over here, Fred."

The waiter brought Sam's rolls. "Everything all right, Mr. Ambielli?"

"Bring me a bottle of ale."

"Me, too," Sam said. "Company makes me thirsty."

"What d'you mean by that crack?" said Baby angrily.

"Never mind," said his boss with a certain weariness.

"What would this nervous wreck do," asked Sam with an eyebrow up, "if anybody took a notion to make a real crack?"

"You want to try?" snarled Baby.

"Shut up. Eat your potato chips." Ambielli cut meat. "They pay you money for those pieces, Sam?"

"They do. Inside stuff, you know." Sam pulled his mouth awry. "*You* might make me a good piece of copy."

"It's possible," said Ambielli, amused.

"Been West, I understand."

"I've been West."

"You didn't die."

"I didn't die."

Fred brought Sam's food and the coffee.

"I presumed not," Sam said when he had gone, "or we'd have heard."

"Listen," Baby's hackles rose, but Sam patted his sleeve, patted him down.

"You pay this sensitive soul for hanging around?" he kidded.

"Has his quality," Ambielli took cream. "It's well known that he would kill whoever hurt me."

"With or without pay, eh?" Sam blinked understanding.

"Without question," Ambielli said. "It's insurance, Sam."

The big man's expression was ludicrously like a small child hearing praise. He fidgeted. He growled. "You don't need to make cracks about pay. *I'll* get paid. I don't need to—"

Ambielli moved a finger, and the big man's mouth closed.

"Seems to me," said Sam gently, "I did hear that the organization was more or less dispersed, at the time. Or so I heard."

"Boss," pleaded Baby, "you like this earsy, nosey guy?"

"Keep quiet."

"Aw, everybody likes to talk a little shop," said Sam easily. "Relax, Baby. I may be earsy and nosey, but mouthy I am not." Ambielli looked up briefly. "For instance," said Sam airily, "I could say a lot about a certain Emanuel. But I don't say."

"You keep well that way," Ambielli remarked mildly.

"Tell you." Sam grinned. "I've got to have a pretty complete idea of the facts or I can't cover them up neatly in my little pieces I write."

"I can see how it is," said Ambielli sympathetically.

"I'd have thought though," Sam continued daringly, for he had a demon, and it was curiosity, "a man like you would've had a little nest egg someplace."

"Doctor's bills," said Ambielli ruefully. "We're in the wrong professions, Sam. The doctor takes the money. Took mine." He shrugged. "Also, there was always a great deal going out. Maintaining discipline." He smiled faintly. "Overhead."

"You were quite a disciplinarian, yeah," Sam said. He could calculate a risk. He could test, with some extrasensory

16

antenna, a mood. It seemed to him that the man across the table was hungry for an exchange of thought, lonely for speech. He took a chance. "Discipline comes free, sometimes, eh? You see where the old man had an accident?"

"What old man is that, Sam?"

"Watchman. Night watchman on the warehouse. Died Monday in the night. It was in the paper."

"Oh, *that* watchman," Ambielli's mouth smiled. "I saw it in the paper."

"He wasn't important," Sam said deliberately. And he read, in the turn of Ambielli's eyeballs where pride was leaping to deny and in the tension existing in the lump of Baby's body on the bench beside him, a truth he had only suspected. All right. There it was. Now, he knew. The old watchman's death had been no accident, and to Ambielli, anyone who interfered with him was important enough to be disciplined.

There it was. Yet, who could take the jump of an eyeball, the stiffening of a spine, before a jury? Sam knew, but how could he tell? Probably, somewhere in the Police Department, it was known, also, and some cop cursed the same helpless conviction.

Sam leaned back. "Never could understand why they had to have a watchman for a warehouse full of biscuits," he grinned, keeping it light, keeping it easy. "That was a funny angle. Old man got excited, saw mysterious black automobiles in the nighttime. It was none of his business. Nobody was after his biscuits."

"Should have remained a private affair," said Ambielli in soft regret.

Oh, yes, the man was hungry, lonely for speech. Sam's demon pushed from behind. "I always figured it was the watchman, calling in the law that night, last year, that threw the monkey wrench into your . . . uh . . . plans."

"You did?" The words said nothing.

"Well, because," Sam said, lightly, easily, "Emanuel's boys were never all that shrewd. Something must have happened that gave them a golden opportunity."

Baby Hohenbaum twitched convulsively where he sat.

But his boss leaned over, erasing the big man's impulse to speak with a wave of his hand. "You could write a book, Sam," he said, and the words came spitting from the bitter line of his lips. "You know what I was. Emanuel's boys took the golden opportunity to shoot four bullets into me." The

17

red-brown eyes had a yellow flame behind them, and Sam could feel, tangible as heat, the danger in this man. "Emanuel saw to it that, as you say, the organization dispersed. While I went West with holes in my chest, I didn't die. I'm back. I'm broke. I'm sick, I'm out. You going to write a book?"

"Someday," said Sam flatly. "Yeah. But I'll wait for the end of this story because I don't know how it's going to end. It hasn't ended yet."

The eyes warmed. Then the cheeks were sucked in on Ambielli's face. White lids went down, shutters over the windows. When they lifted, you could no longer see in. He began to eat, once more. "You know, Sam," he said, " road-house in the country is a good place to convalesce."

"So nice," Sam nodded. "Money in it, too."

"Darned right," said Baby, and he, too, was happier in the more relaxed atmosphere.

"Takes a little capital," Sam said. "Got a backer, boss?"

"In a way," said Ambielli. Baby snickered and slurped food.

Sam paid no attention to him. "How much do you figure to start with, place like that?"

"Oh, fifty thousand."

"Lot of dough."

"Some people got lots of dough," Baby said, with elephantine glee.

They ate silently a little while. Sam was pleased, as pleased as a hunter with his first duck down. But he was still curious. Also, sifting back into his mind came some words he had heard. Something about groceries. Something about a dame.

"So you're going to write a book, Sam?" Ambielli used his napkin daintily.

"It'll be fiction, you know. The big book. The one I keep telling myself. Someday."

"That's the piece in which you'll use the facts," said Ambielli shrewdly.

"That's the piece," Sam admitted.

There was an amiable silence.

"Started to write a piece of fiction once," Sam said, half laughing, and never knew if he stumbled or if he was led. "Going to do one of those mystery stories. It was good, too. It was so good, I couldn't finish it. I couldn't figure out how anybody could solve the mystery."

"Too good, eh?" Ambielli grinned.

18

"It was good."

"What was the plot, Sam?" Ambielli was amiable.

"Oh, murder, naturally. Fellow kidnapped a banker."

"A snatch, eh?" said Baby Hohenbaum. He turned his big body in the booth and unmistakably he had the air of one who greets with surprise a charming coincidence.

There was a moment of queer, not entirely amiable, silence. Of waiting to see.

Sam said, dreamily, "I wonder where I put that manuscript. You know, I'm smarter now than I used to be. I ought to look it over."

Ambielli said, casually, "Maybe you could finish it?"

"I don't know."

"It's a bad way to be," Ambielli was thoughtful. "Too smart for yourself."

Sam grunted. Baby was glancing under knotted brows from one to the other.

"You ran into the collection problem, I imagine. In your story," Ambielli went on smoothly, "how did you figure out a foolproof collection, Sam?"

"You mean, of course, the ransom money," Sam said, looking as dreamy as he could manage. "As a matter of fact, I think that was easy."

"Have them throw it off a train," said Baby. "I still think—"

"Been done before," Sam interrupted. "Too old-fashioned, Baby. Naw, I had a way. Seems to me I had them send the banker's wife a long complicated rigamarole to follow. You know. She was to go to a place and find a note that told her to go to another place, and so on. Well, so they let her get started. Then, they just simply held her up, early in the trip." His palms turned up. "Took it away from her."

Ambielli made a murmuring sound. "Yeah," said Baby, "but . . ."

"You don't like it?"

"Wasn't she followed?" Ambielli looked skeptical.

"No, because in my story they didn't dare."

"That's plausible."

"What if she was? Anyway?"

"Surprise?" said Ambielli.

"Sure." Sam flicked a finger at the waiter's watching face. He'd had enough of this. He needed a break in the flow of talk. He felt confused and guilty, like a hunter who had shot over the limit without meaning to do so.

"It's not bad," said Ambielli.

"Yeah," said Baby Hohenbaum, "but a stick-up, that's a crime. You could—" His head turned. Crouching, he rose. His big paw closed over the waiter's arm. "You? You want something?"

"Never mind, Baby. Let him go, Baby." Ambielli's voice was thin and disgusted.

"I want coffee," Sam said.

"Yes. Yes, sir."

"Listen, he came pussying up—"

"Let him go."

The waiter went like a mouse to his hole. Baby leaned on a big hand. "But what if he heard something?" he whispered conspiratorily.

Black eyes met the red-brown eyes. Both pair were sorry. Sam twisted his mouth and shook his head.

Ambielli said wearily, "Sit down. Sit down."

"Bad case of nerves." Sam kept shaking his head. "Little dangerous?"

"Stupidity is always dangerous." Lids were white in the tan face. Baby Hohenbaum sat without breath. He was scared. "Nearly as dangerous as being too smart," said Ambielli.

"There's middle ground," said Sam, pleasantly. He was scared, too.

He was glad when Nick, himself, appeared with the coffee. After greetings, after Ambielli had said, "I want a word, Nick, a little later." After Nick had said, "Sure. Sure, boss," and withdrawn, Sam Lynch, who had squirmed silently during all this pulled his hand up from the seat of the booth slowly, and looked at what was in it.

His eyes remained, as they had been, half closed against the smoke of his cigarette. His hand remained steady for he knew how to ride a shock. He didn't often show surprise. He turned the piece of rotogravure, letting it drop off his fingers. "Anybody drop this?" he asked, keeping it light, keeping it easy.

CHAPTER III

HE didn't need to see Baby's hand jump and then retreat. He didn't need to hear Ambielli say, "What is that, Sam?" with such lazy indifference.

How could he prove it? He could never prove it but he knew.

He put the piece of paper on the table, removing his hand, because he knew he could keep shock in the brain only so many seconds before the reaction ran down the nerves to the wrists, to the fingertips. "Picture," he mumbled. "Cut out of the paper. Dulain. Oh, that Alan Dulain."

There was a way to let the shock run through the body and out of him and he had found it. He let himself get angry. "That Dulain," he repeated, angrily.

"You know him, Sam?"

"If you mean is he a friend of mine," Sam snapped, "no. But I met him. I talked to him for an hour once. I cannot look at that face without wanting to—"

"What did he do to you?" Ambielli was amused and curious.

"Not a thing. Not a thing. That's the funny part of it. You ever take a dislike to anybody at first sight?" Sam ran his fingers through his hair. "I just cannot stomach the guy."

"Why not, Sam?"

"You know who he is?" Ambielli did not react at all to the question. "He's a wealthy son . . ." Of what was in Sam's furious voice. "He's blue-blooded, second generation millionaire. Blood blues easy if there's money enough. He's got religion or the current equivalent. He's studying to be a do-gooder, and I hate his insides."

Ambielli was laughing without making much noise.

"Yeah, it's ridiculous," admitted Sam, able to grin. "At my age, to get steamed up about nothing. He's nothing. A kid. But I don't know. He's got himself attached to Miller and Milford."

"Lawyers?"

"This kid's no lawyer. He's getting a degree or something. He's supposed to be getting experience. Or something. I don't know what he does up there. Runs errands. He gets around. Takes himself big. Big. Crime, he's interested in. The criminal type. Crime in society. Ugh, he's so damn silly."

Ambielli laughed louder.

"Had me up in his office once," Sam said. "Wanted to pump a little information out of me. Or so I guess. Honest to Hannah, I'm telling you, we were speaking English, both of us, but . . ." He shook his head.

"You give him any information, Sam?" Ambielli said, lightly, easily.

"If I'd wanted to bare my soul to that Dulain," said Sam earnestly, "if I'd wanted to tell him all I know from A to Z, I couldn't do it. I couldn't communicate with him. It's like we don't live in the same world." Sam held his head. "Listen, don't let me bore you with my troubles." Now, he let his eye fall on the clipping. "So Dulain is going to get married," he sneered. "Well, God pity the girl is all I can say. Where did this come from?"

"Do you know the girl, too, Sam?"

"Hm? No, I don't know her. Salisbury."

It was an error to say the name. Knowledge jumped, in his head, and he was afraid it could be seen through the bone of his skull. It was in a word and the word followed the name. Inevitably. It danced there in his head. He tried to cut it out of his attention, but it stuck with thudding finality, the knowledge he had. How Charles Salisbury, who was wealthy, had made his money.

Salisbury's Biscuits.

For a minute, he was afraid he had said it. He looked across the table.

The little man, who looked like ashes but who burned within, was sitting quietly enough, and there was nothing to be read on his face at all.

Baby said, "Say, Sam, what's this mulberry? A kind of color?"

"A kind of red," Sam said. He leaned back. He began blindly. "You know, boss, I make a living writing up odds and ends." His eyes were out of focus.

"Odds and ends, Sam?" Softly.

"Got to keep my sources. You should realize." Ambielli

22

sat listening, listening for a great deal more than words. Sam could tell. "People do different things in this world," Sam said. "Some are like me. Like to know. Like to watch. Like to understand. But they are lookers-on, members of the audience, not in the show. You know?"

Ambielli kept listening. He didn't say whether he knew. "And it's quite a show," Sam grinned. "Or so I find it. I sure enjoy it."

Then, Ambielli smiled. "You called me a disciplinarian, Sam. Shall I tell you the secret of discipline?"

Sam didn't answer.

"As I've found it?"

Sam didn't answer.

"The secret is this. *Before,* I never worry. But *after,* my punishment never fails."

Sam didn't speak.

"Understand my system, Sam?" the voice pressed softly. "I take care of things *when* they happen."

"Or *if,*" said Sam.

"If and when," said Ambielli. The words were knives. The little man began to inch along his seat. "Now, I want to see Nick, so I'll say good-by. Nice to see you, Sam."

"So long, Mr. Ambielli," Sam's voice was careful. Every note and tone was careful. "Good luck with the roadhouse," he said, most carefully.

The little man's hand on the big man's shoulder suggested that he wait. Then Ambielli walked away.

Sam thought a dog would have smelled the fear on both of them who remained in the booth. The power that little man generated in the dark of his spirit and sent out, tangible as heat, but cold as a knife, drew fear to the pores. Beads of sweat wreathed Baby's face, and he twitched. But he looked sideways with a certain pride, as if to say, "That's my boss."

"Quite a little man," Sam said gustily.

"He's murder. Murder." Baby rubbed his palms on his coat.

And I, Sam thought bitterly, mockingly, know too much. But there wasn't time to sort it out and arrange it, now. Or check the pattern of his coming to know. He must ride the conclusion. He sent antennae to examine this lump beside him. How stupid was Baby Hohenbaum?

He leaned back and made himself limp as if with relief. "Quite a little man," he murmured. "Yeah. You know anything about writing, Baby?"

"Who? Me?"

"It's a bug," Sam said. "Like a germ, see? Bite you. Eats you."

"Yeah?"

"Now I've thought of it, I got to get my mystery story out of the trunk again."

"Yeah?" said Baby. He couldn't have been less fascinated.

"It's easy to work out the first part, you know. The way they picked up this banker. He had habits." Sam drew triangles with a spoon handle.

"What banker?"

"Never mind," Sam said. He spun the spoon. "I'm thinking about my work, Baby. My story."

"Stories," said Baby Hohenbaum, looking as if he were about to spit.

"If I ever write a book about your boss, I'll put you in it."

"Huh?"

"For relief," Sam said.

"Listen, Sam," Baby's brow furrowed. "You wrote this story about this snatch, didn't you?"

"Sure. Sure."

"You're smart."

"Sure."

"What did you do with the . . . who was it, again, that got snatched in this story?"

"The banker." Sam was patient.

"Yeah. Well. Did he stay alive?"

Sam's jaw cracked. His cheek trembled. "If I know what you mean," he said slowly, "you mean, did they hide him out and figure to let him go home once they collected. Or not?"

"Yeah. Or not?" said Baby. "That's what I mean. Or not?"

Sam didn't answer. He devoted himself to breathing easily, to making that effort.

"The thing is," Baby pouted, "what would be the use? Believe me, a lot of trouble would be saved, Sam. You wouldn't need to bother with . . ."

"Groceries." Sam shifted in the seat, his eyes fixed on the sausage finger that was scratching the tablecloth with a dirty nail. "Lots of things. I get what you mean, Baby. I . . . Keep him alive," he said feebly.

"Why?"

"For the happy ending, naturally," said Sam savagely.

"Oh, yeah. In the *story*."

Sam watched the finger smudging ashes in a pattern. "Anyhow," he said feebly, "it's smarter to keep him alive."

"Why?" said Baby Hohenbaum.

Sam said angrily. "Okay, I told you I couldn't finish it!" He clenched his hand and relaxed it again. "There's nothing to worry about, providing you fix it so they got a safe place. Safe, quiet, you know the kind of place."

Let Baby tell him the kind of place!

"But," pouted Baby, "they got to cover their faces and all trouble like that, and what's the difference? They'd still get the money."

Sam felt his heart beating. It was pounding, although slowly, slowly, the blood surged. He thought, I'd better get out, out of here. I can't sit here much longer. He said brittlely, "I gave it a lot of thought, Baby. Believe me. The most danger is the pickup. After dark is best."

"Naw," said Baby, full of scorn. "You're old-fashioned, Sam."

"That so? Okay. *You* write the book." He shrugged. He leaned on the wall.

Baby's fat lips pulled open to laugh. "Great kidder, you, Sam. Listen, you said it already. You're smart. Habits. People do the same thing, same time, like once a week. Like . . ."

Sam looked stupid.

"Like music lessons, say," pressed Baby. "Like . . ."

"Like going to school?"

"I mean, after school."

"Like playing poker," Sam went on with smooth speed. "People play poker once a week."

"Who?"

"My banker. He always—"

"Oh, sure."

"Of course, you have a car."

"Sure."

"Nothing to it," said Sam bitterly. "Nothing at all. But I don't know how to finish the damn story." His ears pricked. "Hell, I'll never finish it." He leaned chin on hands mournfully. "I'm only kidding myself. That's all it is. Most people do, Baby. You know?"

That soft voice said something, down the room, near the kitchen door.

"The boss don't kid," Baby said, looking around rather uneasily. "Well, take it easy, Sam. Don't get discouraged." He brayed.

Sam leaned against the back of the booth. He made himself lazy. "So long," he drawled, lifting his hand halfway to a salute. "See you around sometime."

"So long, Sam," said Ambielli over his shoulder pleasantly. Baby fell in behind him.

Fred, the waiter, came to clear the table, looking ruffled and defensive. "I don't have to take that from anybody, Mr. Lynch," he said righteously. "Not anybody." He gave Sam the check.

Sam, who had been leaning on his hand, lifted his head. "Am I stuck for Ambielli's lunch?" He was ready to bray at that.

Fred leaned down. "They ate on the house. I can quit, you know. If Nick wants to play around, I can quit. It ain't Mr. Ambielli. He's always perfectly polite. Always was. The bigger the man, the better the manners. You've heard that saying." He looked superior. "Too bad, when you think how Mr. Ambielli used to travel. All he's got left is that roughneck, that fat Hohenbaum. Mr. Ambielli used to be a very dangerous man, Mr. Lynch, but he always had manners. I'll say that. Looks terrible, don't he? Sick, I mean. Funny, to see him down . . ."

Sam didn't seem to be listening very carefully. But he heard and his mind made its coments. *Used* to be dangerous. Sam thought. *That's funny.* He could think of nothing any more dangerous than Ambielli, as he was now, down.

He said aloud, "Pretty funny. I could write a book. Not the 'Life and Times of Ambielli.' No, Fred. 'The Life and Times of Samuel Lynch.' Especially the Times. Fifteen minutes here. Fifteen minutes there. Very funny. Really killing. You know that?"

"Anything else, Mr. Lynch?" Fred said, resignedly. He was used to hearing his customers release their feelings in bitter and cryptic speeches which he must hear but never hear explained.

"Shot of rye," the customer said.

Sam closed his eyes. He knew too much. Yeah, all about it. He knew the whole thing. Except, possibly, when. When, he did not know. But he thought, soon. He was like the one member of the audience who had already read the play. It was a kind of freak. He might so easily have followed the plot, like everybody else, with interest. With horror.

This way, he wasn't going to be able to *follow*. He broke into a sweat, sitting there. The pit of his stomach seemed to fall away.

The piece of newspaper was still there on the table. He leaned his cheeks on his fists. It wasn't very good of her. She looked like any nice-looking young girl in pretty clothes. Kind of cute. Nothing special. Teeth didn't show. She wasn't smiling. He shivered.

"Who's that?" Fred said into his neck. "Friends of yours get their pictures in the paper?"

"Who? These people?" Sam hit the paper with his knuckles. "No, no. These people are just people. A couple of members of the human race. Oh, high class people, but just the same, ants in the anthill, pebbles on the beach, flakes in the snow." He gulped the whisky. "You ever see a dog run over by a car?" he inquired bitterly.

Fred looked at this customer. The black eyes were half closed. The black hair was rumpled, the chin was a little blue. This customer was, he judged from his experience, going to get drunk, now. "No, sir," he said, "I never did."

"I never did, either. One time, years ago, when I was young, for I was young once," Sam twisted his mouth, "I was a hero. I pulled a dog out from under a car that was coming right for it."

"That so?" Fred said dutifully. "Did you get a reward or anything?"

"I got something. Know what it was, Fred? I got a broken collar bone. Right quick. Wasn't that a fool kid stunt, though?" He put all his fingers in his hair.

Fred was waiting for the inevitable order. No use to leave. This customer would want more whisky. "Was it your dog?" he asked politely.

"It wasn't even my dog." Sam said slowly. "But I'd . . . seen it around. I'd more or less met the pooch. You know how it is. It wasn't a perfectly strange dog." The black eyes were despairing.

"Another rye, sir?"

"Minute," Sam said. He licked his mouth. "Yes, sir, I was eighteen years of age. I've lived a long time since. Two times eighteen is thirty-six. Am I right? Thirty-six divided by two is eighteen years of age. Which I was. Which I am not any more. Which I . . . know better." He rubbed his face. "Live and learn, Fred. The thing to do in this world, Fred, is enjoy the show. Enjoy the show." He kept on, monotonously. "You only got one ticket to this continuous performance. So stay in your seat. That's the way. Because it is quite a spectacle. It really is. Nobody wants to walk out on the big show, unless and until. Or, you might say, if and when." He was scared and talking from fright. He was terrified for the little girl, the one in the blue dress, the young lady. He was swaying and sweating in that booth.

Fred thought, incredulous, *one drink!*

The customer put his palms to his eyes. "Mother, mother, I can see the car coming." And he shuddered.

"Looks like you got the shakes a little bit," Fred said, more or less sympathetically. "Maybe you don't feel well. I'll bring you another, will I?"

But the customer took out his wallet and put down the amount of his check, plus tip, and the customer reached for his hat. He was not going to get drunk, after all. Fred was just as pleased. "Come in again soon."

The customer, holding his hat against his breast, began to laugh. "I'd like to, Fred. I'd sure like to. I'll see if I can make it." He clapped Fred on the shoulder. "Excuse me. I'm a little high. Just made up my mind. Think I'll quit my racket."

Fred grunted.

"Silliest thing you ever heard of," Sam said hilariously. "At my age. Looks like I'm going on the stage." He left, laughing.

CHAPTER IV

SAM LYNCH was thirty-six years old. He lived alone. He had been married, once, for an unhappy period of three years. He no longer knew where his ex-wife was living or even whether she were alive.

He had come to New York, as young people do, from the middle of the country. And he had gone earnestly to Columbia University for a year. But it was the city that drew him, the city that kept him.

He got a humble job on a newspaper and during those first years he progressed rapidly. He became a reporter. Violence attracted him. He was curious about people and especially about people reacting with violence to violent circumstances. He was always probing and prying to find out how such things had come to pass.

He married, in that good period. He found he did not care, at all, for violent emotions over trivialities around the house. After his divorce he became more and more detached. After the war, in which he was shunted about the world, always landing in lonely places, seeing little or no violence at all, he gave himself over to his demon. He wanted to know.

Inevitably, there came a time when Sam was telling less than he knew. This was because so much he knew he had picked up from a mouth's quiver or the timing of a cough. So that what he knew would come out in the telling as a suspicion only. And so often to try to tell would, quite uselessly, have cut off his chance to learn more. But his bosses began to mistrust him, just the same.

As that side of the balance sank, the other side rose. Professionally violent people about the city began, if not to trust him, at least to put him down as an odd duck, who liked to listen, but who was detached. What he heard he seemed to swallow and keep. And he was alone. He ran with nobody.

What he wrote for the paper was perhaps no more barren and dry than what others wrote for other papers, but his superiors were annoyed. They, too, could sense without proof, and were convinced that Sam *knew* a lot, and they could not forgive his reticence. He kept gleaning. He didn't gossip. So they began to believe that he was loyal to the wrong side.

He lost his job. And he lost two or three more. And he entered into a shady half-world in which no one entirely trusted him. Yet he was able to glean; he listened; he learned, and he knew. No one could prove how much. Those on the wrong side, who let him gather bits and pieces, never heard what other bits he had. Those of the right side suspected him angrily of being an accessory before and after many a fact, but the anger was at this reticence and the suspicion was unjust.

Sam wrote feature stories for one publication or another, in which he skated rapidly over summaries of sensational events, with only here and there a gleaming perception to hint at the hidden wealth of information and understanding from which it sprang. He made a living. He lived alone.

He was close to being what he thought he was—a spectator. Someday, he knew, if no one else did, he would stop gathering and start telling. But he knew that once he did so he would become the historian of one decade. This one, and only this one.

Sam was tall but he did not hold himself well. He stood and walked tired. He slouched out of Nick's that April Wednesday, and went across town, walking no faster, no taller than usual. But he was not laughing any more. He knew that for him an era was ending. At the very least, an era.

And because he knew there was also a good chance he, Sam Lynch, would end, would not see or hear or know much more at all, everything in the world was bright and dear to him. He seemed to see the subtlest variations of gray in the pavements, and each pane of glass, every brick, every stone were vivid and precious. And the old matchbooks in the gutters were pathetic and spoke to him of man.

The trouble was, he was attached. He was attached to this thing that was coming. He could not bear to watch it happen. He could not stay in the audience. He was going to take a part. And he knew, better than most, exactly how dangerous a thing this was to do. Ambielli, up, was bad enough. Ambielli, down, was murder.

30

He would have to be careful.

Still, he thought, he would not do it by telephone. That was too light a medium, weightless and unsatisfying. If he were going to break a rule of his life and tell, he was at least going to do it effectively. And take whatever flavor he could from a deed firmly done. He would convince. He would succeed. Even a futile gesture, he well believed, might be fatal for him. He was bound he would not put himself in danger of his life for nothing.

He would be in danger of his life, all right. He had no doubt of it. Once Ambielli knew who told.

But he would be careful. He would not go to the Police Department. No one knew better than he how quickly and surely the word could travel on the cancerous network within that body. And get out. No, he would tell her people and they, gratefully, could perhaps protect him by their silence. Yes, he would be as crafty and as careful as it was possible to be, and still tell.

Sam had a car, nothing fancy, which he used only occasionally. He thought he would get it out. It wasn't wise to take a cab, or even two cabs, uptown, where he was going. He neither wanted to leave a trail or seem to be trying not to leave one. He didn't think he was being watched at the moment, although he felt vulnerable and conspicuous on the sidewalk. After all, Ambielli no longer had an organization. Only Baby Hohenbaum, that last leaf on a dead vine. But it would be better if he took the car. It couldn't answer questions three days later.

He would have to park it, but even if it were to be seen, parked, in that neighborhood, it might not be connected with him, for it was as anonymous and unnoticeable as a car could be. Yes, among risks, he would choose the car.

For the good reason that he had a plan. His best plan, he saw, was to go on, afterward and get out of town. He'd go up to the shack at the lake. Sam had vestiges of country memories, and he owned a summer place, crude and cheap, and too chilly in April. It was about an hour and a half away. There he would go. And show himself in the village. Be accounted for, elsewhere. Few knew about his place. He took a friend up, once in a while. Once in a great while. Perhaps three people in the city knew he had it, where it was, how to get there. But he thought he knew just how he could fix a kind of alibi.

The thing to do was to pick up, say, a carpenter in the village. It would look as if he had been out to the shack already and found one was needed. Easy to find something for a carpenter to do. Take the winter boards off the windows, for instance.

The worst danger to him would come later, with the consequences of his telling, the abortion of the crime. There would be questions asked. But he would get up to the lake, fast, and be ignorant and innocent, and far away, and pretty well alibied for what he was now about to do.

And after all, he had his reputation. This would be the first time he had ever told. Leaning on the spring wind, he walked toward his garage.

He did not need to look up the number of the Salisbury apartment, for he had looked it up two months ago. It was upper east side, a corner near the river. The main entrance was on one of those queer quiet blocks in which the strong currents of the city did not flow. If traffic were water, then in this place it was stagnant. Sam pulled around to the side of the building and parked. He felt conspicuous at the empty bottom of a stone canyon.

He walked around the drafty corner, and it was like walking a plank, dangerous in itself, and a worse drop coming. The apartment building was staffed like a hotel. He was required to give his name.

Slouched in the lobby, he listened to the words, irrevocably spoken. "Mr. Sam Lynch is downstairs, to see Miss Katherine Salisbury." The sentence, to him, reeked of danger, and of the discipline that "never failed." He was for it, now. His neck was out, all right. Already.

"You are to go up, sir." She was at home. That was lucky. At least it was lucky for somebody.

"Thanks." He turned away, walking tired. He went up in the elevator. A manservant admitted him to a foyer of size from which he was conducted to a living room, vast and dim because of heavy dull green fabric more than half across the daylight. "Miss Katherine asks you to wait a moment, sir. She will be down presently."

Sam saw the stairs curving up out of this big room. It was quite an apartment. He said, "Okay." The manservant picked up a cigarette box and offered it. "Thanks," said Sam. "I'll smoke my own." The man contrived without a change on his face to communicate a certain washing of the hands of this caller. Nevertheless, he held the lighter. Then he went away.

Sam was amused at the service. He did not sit down. He walked on the thick gray carpet, peering at ornaments, as his eyes adjusted to the dimness. Everything here was very simple and very elegant. He was on edge with the knowledge of his own recklessness to be here at all.

The back of his neck told him when someone was on those stairs, and he waited a rigid moment, feeling the sick fall at the stomach again, before he turned. But the woman coming gracefully down was not Katherine Salisbury. She was perfectly white of hair, but her face was so young and rosy that she seemed, for a moment, merely a blonde. Her dress was a dainty print, in green, and it moved softly with the descent of her pretty legs. Her shoes were frivolous. She said, "How do you do?"

"Beg your pardon," Sam said at the same moment.

"Yes?" Meaning, he judged, now who the devil are you?

"My name is Lynch. I'm waiting to see Miss Salisbury."

"To see Katherine?" The woman came toward him, taking tiny steps on her teetering heels. "You are a friend of Katherine's?" she asked, but it was only recognition, or perhaps welcome.

"Yes, ma'am."

"I am Katherine's mother." Her hand was put forth. Sam was too astonished to touch it.

"You are!" he said in flat amazement.

"Of course. I am Martha Salisbury." The woman laughed. "What a beautiful image of surprise. You and I are going to get along nicely."

He touched her hand, then. It was cool and small, with coral nails. She said, "But does Katherine know you're here?"

"Yes, ma'am."

"I do like that. Ma'am." She picked up a bright fabric bag from the corner of a chair. "So many of the young men are using it now. The war, I dare say. Were you in the Service, Mr. Lynch?"

"I was in it," he said, studying her. "Although I'm not so young, ma'am."

"Sit down, please do." He waited for her to seat herself. Something about her made manners imperative. She took out of the blue and yellow bag some bright blue yarn tangled with coral knitting needles. "I haven't heard your name before, but of course that means nothing. Have you known Kay long?"

Her pretty mouth was painted coral. She was a lady, but such a little doll of a lady. The face was not quite so young, close up, but it was pretty. She had an arch to her nostrils, a dainty and well-boned little nose.

"I met her once, ma'am," Sam said. He was wondering what to do.

"And she made an impression," Martha Salisbury nodded. "Katherine does, rather."

"She goes to the Starke School. Every day." Sam neither raised nor dropped his voice.

Mrs. Salisbury tipped her head, not sure whether he questioned or answered. "She's a day student," she murmured. "We like her at home. You met her at the school, Mr. Lynch?"

"It was at a party," Sam said, not meaning to sound evasive, still wondering what to do.

"One meets so many people at parties," she smiled reassuringly. "Isn't this a lovely day?"

He fidgeted. "I'm an old newspaperman, Mrs. Salisbury." He was trying to lead into something. But her brows lifted, her eyes teased him, as if to say, now, I didn't ask. "No, you didn't ask," he said stolidly, "but that's what I am."

"Are you here, as such?" She was puzzled.

"No. No, not that. You see, Mrs. Salisbury . . ." But he wasn't sure. He didn't quite know what he ought to do. She seemed too fragile for his news. And this confused him.

"I don't mean to be a suspicious parent, you know," she smiled. "I didn't even mean to sit down. But you looked interesting." Her hands were skillful with the needles and the yarn.

His face hardened. "Can anybody get in here like this?" He was almost insolent.

But she laughed. "You mean do I often stumble over strange people in my drawing room? Well, yes. I do. Strange to me, that is. Kay has many friends, and, of course, I don't always know who they are." He felt his scalp move. "Have you an ash receiver there, Mr. Lynch?" She bent to see. "Ah, yes, I see you have. What kind of newspaperman are you?"

"I write about crime," he said, throwing the word in bluntly, his black eyes watching her. "Exclusively."

"Oh, dear!" Her hands pressed the yarn in a little gesture of distress. "Do you? Oh, don't you find that depressing?"

His scalp moved; his hair stirred.

"I should think one would grow very weary of the seamy side. Do you *like* it?" she asked. He couldn't find an answer. He had the impulse to hang on to his chair. "My daughter's fiancé," she went on, and a flick of her eye noted that this was not news to Sam, "is very much interested in crime, too."

"Is that so?" said Sam numbly.

"We hear a certain amount about it. Because Alan rather studies it, these days. As a part of his all-round education. Alan has some theories."

Sam sunk his chin. "I'm sure he has," he muttered.

"Alan says that almost any social outcast can be rehabilitated. Do you think so, Mr. Lynch?"

Sam's face darkened, and his eye flashed, and she opened her coral lips in surprise at his reaction. "That's a word I happen to dislike," he muttered awkwardly. "I don't know. Some words you take a dislike to. Or at least I do." He squirmed. "I hate it."

"Why, that's true!" she said, delighted. "Do you know, I never thought of it, but I hate some words, too. 'Poignant,' for instance. It makes me shudder. Does it, you?"

"I'm neutral on that one, ma'am." Sam tried to grin. He rubbed his head. She made him slightly dizzy. It was like watching a petal spin on the skin of a wave, a pretty petal that could never sink.

"You're a writer. Of course you must feel for words." She smiled at her work. "It's nice to see a man absorbed by what he is doing. Alan is quite a brilliant boy. He is so earnest. One day, I suppose it will all bear fruit and he will be quite a great sociologist or social scientist or whatever the term is."

"Do-gooder," offered Sam, rather helplessly.

"And so, of course, crime fascinates him, as a social symptom, you see? But, do you know, Mr. Lynch, I'm afraid it doesn't fascinate me. To me it's unhappy. It's just unfortunate. I rather feel," she cocked her head, "that if the underworld lets me alone, why, I let it alone, you know?" She laughed quite merrily.

Sam put his hands down and curled them on the edge of his chair.

"There, now you think I'm a giddy female." She sighed. "Perhaps I am. Perhaps I'm just not hopeful. Crime we have always with us, like the poor. At least in my lifetime. It's only that I know my place, Mr. Lynch. You men may be in a position to do something about it. Men like you and Alan."

"You've got me wrong, ma'am," said Sam savagely. He would not be yoked with Alan Dulain. "I'm a reporter. Don't twist it. A reporter is someone who sees what goes on and simply reports it."

"Yes?"

"That's all." He was pretty twisted himself, he thought. He gave it up.

"I see," she frowned. "That's your definition of a newspaperman?" She considered it. What she considered was an arrangement of words. He felt she could memorize and repeat them. But she was afloat. She would veer and shift with a turn in the phrase. Petal on the surface.

"I guess so," he said feebly. He gave her up.

"Of course," said Mrs. Salisbury with tender amusement, "my little Katherine is very much interested in crime, too."

Sam had given up. He now could drawl, "Oh, is she? In what way, ma'am?"

"Oh, romantically, of course. You see, a woman in love is a chameleon, really. Twenty years ago, Mr. Lynch, I thought the sun rose and set with Salisbury's Biscuits."

He didn't smile.

"Mr. Salisbury is, or was . . . Salisbury's Biscuits," she said gently. "As perhaps you knew?"

"I know. Kind of cookies, aren't they?" Sam was solemn. "He made a lot of money with them, didn't he? I've seen his warehouse, his great big warehouse full of biscuits, and somebody watching over them, night and day."

She opened her eyes very wide. "But, of course, Charles is retired," she trilled. "He has almost nothing to do with such things as warehouses, any more."

"Or so he thinks," muttered Sam.

"I beg your pardon?"

He didn't repeat.

"The warehouse impressed you, Mr. Lynch?"

"It made a link," Sam said gravely, "in a story."

"Why, isn't that interesting!" cried she. "And you write stories, too?"

Then her daughter, Katherine, came dancing down the stairs.

CHAPTER V

It was like dancing. She was so young and her feet were so quick and sure and the short mane of her shining hair bounced in the rhythm of her flying descent. She wore a chocolate brown skirt and a sweater the color of pale toast, and the quick, slim, sure, young feet were in flat brown pumps with round toes. She came dancing over the carpet.

"Hello. I'm sorry. I was writing a letter, and all over ink. I can't get it off. How nice of you to come to see me."

He winced at the impact of her welcome. She put her hand in his and he looked down at the scrubbed fingers, the ink stain that wasn't quite gone, and something ached in his breast. All of a sudden he was terrified again, and tense, and in a hurry.

"Mother, have you met Mr. Sam Lynch?"

"Of course, dear. He presented himself, and very nicely. We've been chatting away like old cronies, really." Mrs. Salisbury's pretty little hands were stuffing the yarn into the bag.

"What I wanted . . ." Sam began harshly. "I came . . ."

"To see Katherine. Of course," said her mother serenely. She rose, balancing her trim little body tiptoe, because of her ridiculous heels. "And since I came after my knitting, you know, in the first place—"

"No, ma'am. Please don't go. I . . ."

"Now, that's very sweet." She cocked her head. "But you'll find I'm quite well trained. I do know my place." He closed his mouth.

"Silly," said the girl, wrinkling her nose.

Her mother put a forefinger on the girl's own short straight well-boned little nose, so like her own, and she pushed it, playfully. "He's very nice, sweetie. Your Mr. Lynch. He calls me ma'am, and I do enjoy that." She smiled at Sam. "I hope you will come again."

Sam stood there. He should have said, "Thank you," and maybe he did. She prompted a man to his manners. But he held on to the back of the chair beside him, just the same, and silently, he watched her trip away and rise sedately up the stairs.

Kay whirled around and looked at him. "What's the matter?"

He groped for the chairback with his other hand, too, and he bent over it. "She's knocked me for some kind of loop, your mother has. Sister, I'm scared."

"Scared! Mother? Scared you?"

"Uh huh," he said nervously. "Yeah."

"But she's— Nobody in the world is more harmless! What—"

"Who trained her?" he murmured. "Who taught her her place?"

"I don't know what you mean."

"I know you don't," he groaned. "Never mind." He flopped into the chair.

"But she *liked* you. I could tell."

"Because of a word," Sam said. "Because I called her ma'am. Because I remembered my manners."

Her eyes sparked. "Mother's not stupid. She's a very good judge."

He shook his head. "Look, don't people keep track of their kids any more? I'm out of date? The modern world has passed me by?"

The girl laughed at him. She tucked herself into a chair, sitting on her foot, and the tooth was definitely out of line on the right side of her laughing mouth. "Oh, my goodness!" Her eyes were half size with the rise of her cheeks, and bright and brimming, and her mirth was a pretty thing. A laughing girl was a most delightful thing. "But I'm not a *kid*, for heaven's sake! What did you and mother *say*?"

"I told her," he said glumly, "we met at a party." The girl sobered. "She took that for an answer."

"It is an answer."

"No," he said.

"You mean you didn't tell her whose party?" The girl's face pinkened.

"*That* she didn't ask."

"It's just as well," Kay murmured. "Mother's sweet but a perfect sieve. It's Daddy who would be upset, I'm afraid.

38

He's the old-fashioned one. But you're . . . funny. You really don't look old-fashioned, Mr. Lynch."

"Is Daddy around?" he asked sharply.

"I think so," she was vague. She looked a little stubborn. "After all," she declared, "if I hadn't gone to the party, we wouldn't have met. You wouldn't be here."

"I know," he said.

"Didn't you have a good time at the party?"

His black eyes, resting on her face, despaired. He sucked a long breath in and sighed it out again. "After you left," he stated coldly, "one of the guests inquired. Wanted to know what kind of girl you were."

"Now, isn't that flattering!" she beamed.

"No. It wasn't."

The twinkle on her face vanished as if he had slapped her. Sam said, furiously, "You don't know what it's all about, any more than she does. Talk about giddy! How am I going to tell you anything? You're a baby."

"Did you come to scold me?" the girl asked plaintively.

"It looks like I came to talk to your father," he snapped. "Right away. Fix it, will you?"

Her face clouded, and her lashes fell. "Then you didn't come to see me at all?" He made an exasperated sound. "We did have such an interesting talk." The lashes went up. "I thought it was fun. Didn't you? I thought perhaps you wanted to talk some more."

"Sister," he groaned. "No. There's no profit in any more interesting talk between you and me. And you know it. Now, quit with this, will you?"

"But I don't know it," she insisted. "I don't see why—"

"Check back," he said grimly. "You made your boy friend give you a glimpse of what your mamma calls the underworld. You thought it was fun to look in a minute, on the other half. Hm?" Her lips parted. "And we talked. You and I. But your boy must have told you since. Sam Lynch is friends with the wrong people. Maybe he told you I'm one of the crooked ones? That so?" She winced. "Only *you*, in your wisdom, thought it was quite a lot of fun to have me at your side, telling you inside stuff. You said I was so kind. But you really thought I was attracted. And whatever you've been told, you feel pretty powerful, such a queen of a little lamb, don't you, sister? Or you wouldn't mind setting up a friendly little flirtation with a tall dark sinister character like me. And be my little pet lamb, immune, of course, to any hurt, because you appeal to my innate honor which is only dormant." He was furious. *"Isn't that so?"*

She looked him in the eye. "Yes, that's so," she said.

His heart felt as if it curled at the edges. He threw out his hands. He said, "Lord . . ." He said, "Honey . . ." He said, *"No!"*

"Well," she said with a little smile, "you put it in the silliest kind of way, but, just the same, I believe something like that. I don't know why."

He sprang out of the chair and struck his hands together. "Where's your father? I want to see him. And see him quick." He felt frantic.

She folded her underlip under her teeth and didn't budge. Her eye flashed. Her chin went up. "Do you want him to do something for you?"

"Oddly enough," he snarled, "with all his money, he can't do a thing for me."

"Then do you plan to tell him I went to that party?"

"Sister, look, *no.*"

She smiled as if she had tricked him. "You see? None of the bad reasons."

"You don't know all the reasons, maybe." He put his hand on her head, briefly. "You don't understand. I don't expect you to. Listen, I don't want to tell you what I came for, until I've seen your father. I just—I'd rather not."

"All right," she said.

"The fact is," he blurted, "you do attract me. Not the way you think. Go get your father."

"Maybe you don't quite know the way I think," she said primly. "But I'll call Daddy, if you wish."

"I wish you would," he said, stony-eyed. "Please do."

She unwound herself and got out of the chair, keeping her face both serene and severe. He heard a bell, somewhere, but paid no heed, for air was rushing into his chest, and he was afraid, and he was in a hurry, but just the same he did not want her to leave this place where they stood together. Already, a premonition told him that his little vision, the little projected scene in which having given the alarm he would sit beside her and gently try to make her understand, would never happen.

So he was surprised when a man's voice behind him said, "Kay? Oh, I beg your pardon."

"Oh, Alan! Hi!" She walked across the run and Sam turned slowly.

"Hello, darling." The blond boy kissed her upturned face. His arm fell around her shoulder and her hand met his to hold it there.

"You know Mr. Lynch? Oh yes, I remember. Of course you do."

Alan Dulain stood as stiff and cold as his voice. "How are you, Lynch?"

"I'm well," Sam drawled. "And you?"

The girl stood there, in that embrace, and asked with a trace of mischief, "Where did you two meet? Do you mind my asking?"

"Why, no, Kay . . ."

"It was in his office," snapped Sam. "He had me hauled in and he kicked me out again."

"I'm not aware that I ever—"

"Figure of speech. Intents and purposes." Sam bit a finger-nail. Antagonism rippled between them. "Listen, I haven't time—"

"Very sorry," Alan said, stiffly, removing his arm. "I didn't know you were busy, Kay."

"Oh, but I'm not. Not at all." Now she was saucy. "Mr. Lynch came to see Dad."

"Oh, I see."

"You don't. You don't, indeed," muttered Sam. "But never mind. Sister, will you *please*—"

"If it is anything I can be helpful about," began the blond boy smoothly, thrusting himself forward like a shield.

Sam's nerves screamed. "I want to see Charles Salisbury," he snarled. "Do you mind?" He swung on the girl. "Where is he?"

"In the library, I think." She turned as if to lead Sam there.

"Better . . . ask, dear," Alan said warningly.

"Oh. Yes, I'd better." She looked a little flustered and un-certain. "I'll tell him you're here."

"I'd be so happy if you only would," said Sam grimly.

He turned his back on Alan Dulain. Alan sat down and lit a cigarette. He said coldly, "You were not kicked out of any office of mine, Lynch."

"It was kicked out in my language. I don't know what it was in yours."

41

"I am in the habit of practicing the elements of courtesy."

"Sure. 'Thank you.' 'Please.' 'I beg your pardon.' "

"As you wish." The patience in the voice was as insulting as Sam's sarcasm.

Sam turned around and the other crossed his legs. "It ought not to be necessary for me to say this," Alan began.

" 'Tisn't," snapped Sam. "So don't."

The blond man smoldered but he went on quietly. "I told Miss Salisbury that you were no good."

"Katherine," said Sam, "should have listened."

But the other man had control. He said patiently, "She is young, Lynch, as you must see. Too inexperienced, too romantic, to understand what I said, literally. She really doesn't know what it's all about. Therefore, it's up to you."

"Why?" Sam was furious.

"Surely—"

"I'm no good. She's too dumb. But *you* know what's best for everybody. You're sitting on a cloud, seeing the right. *You* fix it, why don't you?"

"I will," snapped Alan. "I'll do that."

They waited in silence. Time stretched, and Sam's nerves with it. He thought of his car down in the street, a badge of his presence here. Where he seemed to have fallen into a bog, to be struggling, weighted by delay and again delay. And delay was stupid. It could only work against him. For his neck was out.

He lit a cigarette, and his eyes fled nervously from the blond boy, who sat quietly, toward the door through which the girl had gone, and then skipped around the walls of the huge dim room, and he put out the cigarette and lit another.

CHAPTER VI

CHARLES SALISBURY had a clean and "talcumed" look. Even his hair looked powdered. His eyes were oyster gray. His suit was gray with a paler gray woven in but lying like a frost on the fabric. He made one think of a seascape on a dull day, all clean grays. Middling tall, erect, he walked in with so measured and deliberate a stride that his daughter beside him seemed to curvet like a pretty pony.

"How do, Alan?"

"Afternoon, sir." Dulain, for his manners, rose.

Kay turned her father with a touch on his arm. "Dad, this is Mr. Lynch who wants to talk to you about something."

The oyster-gray eyes were cool and inquiring.

"Alone," said Sam rudely. He heard Dulain clear his throat. "He's about to warn you to look out for me," said Sam quickly, "so let's take that for said, and let's get this over. Can't we?"

"I was merely going to identify you as an ex-newspaperman." Dulain's voice was buttery. It said, I am a gentleman.

"I'll identify myself whenever it's necessary."

Charles Salisbury said frostily, "What is this all about?"

"I'll tell you what it's about, *alone*."

"Then suppose you wait in there." Salisbury was curt.

"I'm in a hurry," snapped Sam.

"Daddy," the girl spoke gently, "I should have said that Mr. Lynch is a friend of mine." Her reproach was not for her father, Sam knew, but for him.

"Sorry," said her father more genially, "But your manner, sir."

"I've got no manners," said Sam, "not really, and no time for any right now. Let's get to it." None of them knew what drove him. It was a mistake to sound so rude. But his sense of a long time wasted and the presence of Dulain combined to be infuriating.

"If," said Alan, now tolerantly, indulgently, "this is so private, Kay, perhaps you and I . . ."

"No, no," said Salisbury gracefully, "we can as well . . ."

Sam's voice rose. "Listen. Everybody. I want to see Salisbury a minute alone. And quick. *Now, can it be arranged?*"

Salisbury moved his frosted brows. "Is what you have to say at all important?"

"Very important," gasped Sam.

"Very well. I'll give you a minute. If you will come with me."

Sam stumbled toward the indicated door. He felt reduced and compressed into a ruthless order, Salisbury's sense of order, his measured pace, the marching regularity of his arrangements. He also felt like a boor and he felt angry.

And once again Salisbury turned back. "Oh, Alan, about that boat of yours, use my anchorage, of course."

"Ooooh!" cried the girl, young as morning, clapping her hands. "Alan, you bought it?"

"I sure did." The blond boy was happy that she was happy and the father was held, watching, smiling at her pleasure, and Sam groaned.

"Take me out on the Sound?" she cried. "When?"

"Tomorrow? You don't have afternoon classes?"

"No, but, darn it, I've got my music lesson."

"How about after that?"

"Wouldn't it be too late?"

Sam Lynch, leaning on the wall, said heavily, "Yeah."

"What?"

"Too late." He lifted both hands and they were shaking. "Listen. Please. What do I have to *do?*" His anxiety, his irritation cracked in the room. He knew it was wrong to expect them to meet his mood without his information. He tried hard to be fair. He said, without anger, "It's urgent." But it came out flat.

There was a murmuring exchange between the men.

Salisbury said, "Yes . . . er . . . I . . . er . . ." And then to Sam, briskly, "This way."

Sam wheeled but the girl's voice came after him. "I hope you will come to see *me*, some day."

He heard Dulain's voice warn, "Kay."

But she said, defiantly sweet, "Won't you, Sam?"

He said, "I guess not, sister. I don't think so. Thanks all the same." He followed where he was led, leaving the girl and the blond boy without another word or a glance, without turning his head. He followed through a door, down a short passage, into a small room full of books and leather.

44

Charles Salisbury moved toward the desk. He rested his fingertips on its surface. All here was peace, was order. It was due time. "Mr. Lynch?" Now that he gave his attention he gave it totally. Sam stood in this man's aura, a radiation of his decency and order. And Sam, too, leaned on the desk, with no time to waste.

He said, quietly, "Mr. Salisbury, I came here to tell you that I overheard a plan to kidnap your daughter, Katherine."

"What," said Salisbury with a bridling movement of his head, "are you talking about!"

Sam was willing to concede that it took some time. He was willing to wait until this penetrated. He felt sorry for this man. He said, rather dryly, but patiently, "I'm talking about a plan to kidnap your daughter."

"You must be—" Slowly, Charles Salisbury sat down.

"Don't let her go to that music lesson. Don't let her be on the street at any time without a guard." It was too fast.

"But you—" The man did not know how to look bewildered. He simply looked blank. "You must give me some grounds. I can't believe—"

"You don't have to believe it," said Sam, still patient. Still sorry. "You can't afford to take the chance that I might be mistaken." The father said nothing, but sat behind the desk, looking numb and blank. "You can see that, can't you?" Sam pressed more sharply. Then he shrugged and half turned, for he must wait a little.

"Just a minute, young man." Now, the gray eyes showed a glint of anger and Sam suspected it was a way to cover and deny a thrill of fear. "What makes you think you can walk into my house and make so horrifying and sensational a statement without any—" But the father's hands began to flap helplessly. The shell of his placid orderliness was cracking. "You must give me some facts," he said, loud with his dismay. "Do you expect me to take you seriously?"

"I do," said Sam. "And," he continued in a slow drawl, "perhaps you'll notice, I am doing you quite a favor in this matter."

"Then you can do me the further favor," said Salisbury sharply, "of explaining how you happened to—did you say— overhear?" His immaculate fingers tapped on the desk.

"What do you care how it happened?" said Sam roughly. "I overheard it and I'm here to tell you so at considerable risk to myself."

"Nonsense!" said Charles Salisbury.

"What do you mean, nonsense?" But Sam knew what he meant. The ideas before him were so foreign and unfamiliar that the man's mind threw them out.

"What's behind this?" Salisbury's face was hostile and suspicious. "This is absolute melodrama."

"That's right," said Sam gently. He had the image of feeding a strange new food with a small spoon to a reluctant baby. "That's what it is."

Salisbury's face colored. He said, flatly, "I don't believe it."

"And what's the point of my coming up here and lying about it?"

"I don't know. I'm sure I do not know. But you will have to give me something more than a bald statement."

"Will I?" said Sam, ominously. He began to feel he had been patient long enough.

"Who is planning such a thing?"

"I can't tell you that."

"Do you know?"

"Yes, I know."

"Then, why don't you say?"

"Because," Sam shrugged, "if it gets out I'm up here naming names, I'm a gone gander." He said it because he knew it. It was hard for him to remember that this might come fantastic to his listener's ear.

"Oh, nonsense!" said Salisbury again. He rose from the chair and leaned on his hands, fastening his eyes on the dark man's face as if he would bore through to the essence of the mind behind it.

"What do you think I am?" Sam said uneasily. "A loony? Listen."

"This talk about *your* danger. That's too much really." The gray eyes probed while the mouth sneered.

"It's my life," Sam said, "and I'm fond of it. And I've got it in my mouth. And I suppose it's no worry of yours. But *she* is. What's the matter? Didn't you hear what I told you? Don't you read your paper? You think such things can't be?"

The eyes wavered. "I suppose such things can be. But there can be no reason—"

"Reason," Sam laughed. "Money's enough reason. You've got money."

"Some," Salisbury said slowly, suspiciously. "Other men have money."

"You're known to have money."

"Yes, I suppose . . ."

"Have you got fifty thousand dollars in cash?"

The eyes flinched. "No."

"That's too bad," Sam said. "That's what they'll ask for."

The man gasped, and his hands curled on the wooden surface where they had rested. The flat detail, the mention of a sum, had struck through. "Mr. Lynch," he said honestly, "I can hardly take this in. I don't understand. Why should a kidnaper choose me and my family? I am by no means the wealthiest—"

"Ah, don't argue," said Sam, pityingly.

"But I . . . I have never had the slightest connection . . . I'm not . . . We don't get into the papers. How could such people even hear of me? Hear of Kay?"

"Oh, they hear," said Sam airily. "Then, too, the sins of the employee are sometimes visited upon the boss. It's a kind of an accident that they heard of you."

"I don't . . . I don't understand you."

"You had a watchman," Sam bit his lip. "And when I open my mouth too much comes out," he muttered. "Listen, don't try to understand *why*. You don't need to. It doesn't make any difference how come you were picked to be the victim. I'm telling you that you *were*. *She* was. Your daughter, Katherine." Sam began to feel frantic again. "Listen, please don't argue with me. I heard it. I'm telling you. Now you've got to reckon with it."

Salisbury pulled himself together. With a certain courage, with an effort, he was trying to fit this wild thing somewhere in his pattern. He said, "And I insist that you *do* tell me, and exactly, what it was you heard. And wait a minute. Don't go." He brushed around the desk. He left the room.

Wants a witness, said Sam to himself, automatically. He conceded that. He looked gloomily out of the window at the heaped city and its colors, the afternoon glow on the western faces of the heaped buildings, the yellows and the tender reds and the infinite delicate variations of browns and grays. Somewhere in the lovely mass, one pin point, one sick and savage little man with a brown face and a red brain threatened these decent people in their high place. And he, Sam Lynch, knew it.

The witness was going to be Alan Dulain. Of course. Sam whirled around. He was surprised to be surprised. A muscle under his ear tightened, as his jaw cracked. His groan to himself (that he might have known) was inaudible.

Salisbury demanded order. "Mr. Lynch, will you please repeat what you just told me. And will you repeat it in all detail. Let us have, please, exactly what it was that you say you overheard. This is my daughter's fiancé. We will hear you together."

Dulain carried his head high. He had almost a military air of being in place and correct.

Sam said, in a slow monotone, as if by rote, "I heard two men plan to kidnap Miss Katherine Salisbury. They will pick her up from the street, probably in a stolen car, probably tomorrow afternoon as she leaves this house or the Starke School, whichever is her habit, to go ther music lesson. They will either hide her alive, or they will kill her immediately. Probably the latter," Sam said with brutal calm, "because that will be somewhat less trouble to them. They will ask at least fifty thousand dollars in ransom. That's about the whole of it."

Alan Dulain's weight shifted. "*Where* did you hear it?"

"That's irrelevant," Sam said.

"*Who* were the men?"

"I won't say."

"Can't or won't."

"Won't."

The father braced one arm against the desk. "Alan, is this possible?"

"I suppose it's possible," said Alan with faint contempt. "What he outlines is the classical pattern. But you must admit, Lynch, it's a little hard to accept—"

"Admit!" Sam raged. "What's the difference what I *admit?* You want a debate?"

"I'd be more inclined to credit your story if I could understand why you take the trouble to tell it."

"Oh, no trouble," Sam said bitterly. "No trouble, really. Happy to do it. Put my neck out for the ax."

"*Your* neck." Alan's lips curled. "I know a little about you, Lynch, and frankly, what I know doesn't incline me to think you a sentimentalist. Oh, I realize you must be somewhat interested in Katherine. But surely—"

"Sweet Lord!" Sam's shaking hands rose. "Why do I stand here and listen to this? Are you going to do something about protecting her? That's all I want to know."

"You may be sure of that," said Alan Dulain haughtily.

"I may, may I? Well, dandy! Have you got any idea, bright boy, how to protect her? Any slight notion? Or even the glimmer of what it is you've got to keep away from her? *He*," Sam waved at the father, "hasn't. Nobody in this dream castle really believes in the seamy side. I hope *you* at least heard of it."

"Please, please," the father said, "no need to shout. Katherine is in no immediate danger. We must—"

"How do you know?" Sam danced with his frenzy. "Do you even know where she is, this minute?"

"Yes, of course," the father's eye rolled.

Alan said coldly, "If it is any business of yours, she is upstairs, finishing a letter."

"And maybe she isn't," snarled Sam. "Maybe she changed her mind. Maybe they changed their plans. Maybe *anything!* I tell you, she is in as much danger *right now* as if the place were on fire. And what are you going to do about it?"

The father was stiff and still. Alan threw one leg over the desk corner. "I can't help wondering," he frowned, "what is your concern. You barely met Miss Salisbury."

Sam bracketed his temples in a stiff hand. "Look, that doesn't matter!"

"This man," Alan swung to the father who was growing grayer, somehow, "is a pretty devious type, sir. He is a writer of so-called crime—"

"So-called!" screeched Sam. "God damn it, are you guys alive? What's the difference what I do for a living? Or what I'm doing, trying to tip you off. Can't you get it through your fat heads that right now in this town two flesh and blood men are discussing that girl and what they'll do with her when they get her?"

"That is a startling idea," said Alan, unmoved, "but let's not be too startled to think. My point is, you simply are not the public-spirited type, Lynch, as I have reason to know. That's why I don't accept . . . I can't accept this . . . sacrifice." His thin sharp face was cold. "I'm afraid I'd like to examine your motives a little."

"Will you quit with the psychology!" cried Sam almost in despair. "*Listen!*"

"Yes, see here," broke in the father. "We must be very careful that nothing like this does happen."

"Aaaah," said Sam on a deep indrawn groan of satisfaction. "That's right. That's it. Let me ask," he turned hopefully to

Salisbury, "have you any idea how easy it would be for them to get hold of her? Do you realize you got to lock her up? You got to have somebody with her every minute, somebody capable—"

Dulain crossed his legs. "You suggest that we, as you put it, lock up Miss Salisbury for how long?" His ankles swung.

Sam's hair stirred. "What do you want for a nickel? How do I know how long?"

"If we promise to do this, will you reveal the names of the conspirators?"

"What's this? A bargain?"

"So that the law can . . ." Alan hesitated.

"Can do what?"

"Act . . . deter . . ."

"You got a lot to learn about the law, sonny," Sam said. "What kind of case you going to make out of an intuition of an intention? And don't rely on me to testify. What I could testify has holes in it, plenty. Besides I may not be around."

Salisbury straightened. "I don't know what to make of this." He slid into the chair behind the desk.

"Nor do I, sir." Alan frowned.

"It is possible? *Is* he putting himself in danger?"

"I can't see how," said Alan, "since he really isn't telling us anything."

Sam, feeling as if his hair were rising from his head again, nevertheless took hold of himself. He tried to speak calmly. "You can't believe me and disbelieve me at the same time," he said. "It's all one piece. I'm telling you there is a plan. I'm also telling you, if you're warned and take action and she stays safe, and *it gets known who told you*, I am liable to sudden death. Now, make up your minds. Either, I'm plain crazy, all the way through. Or I'm up here doing you one hell of a big favor. Don't forget, I'd like to be safe, too. Nothing to argue. And no bargains. Believe it all or nothing. But let me know."

He turned his back to look blindly out the window. Behimd him, he thought, eye must be crossing eye, hand signaling to hand. For the moment, he didn't care. His vision cleared, and he looked out on the glowing city and to him it was a moving, changing, clashing tangle of men, passionate and violent. And he thought to ask for safety at all was somewhat mad.

Then he heard Dulain's tenor, high and crisp. "Oh, well.

A favor. What do you consider a proper reward for this . . . favor?"

Sam faced around, blazing, and then he closed his eyes. The dark skin around them trembled. "Well," he said in a dead voice, "that's that. Okay. I guess you sold me the idea. To mind my own business." He opened his eyes, not to look at them, just to see his way out of here.

"Wait a minute."

"Get out of my way, you God-damned social worker." Sam raised one hand. He let it fall. "She was a cute kid," he said.

The father whimpered. "No, no, tell us. You can't go."

"Do you believe me?" Sam asked him, almost as if this were light curiosity.

"I don't know." The father's hand moved pleadingly, "As you say, that hardly matters. We must surely take all precautions. But, Mr. Lynch, you must see how indefinite, how impossible . . . And unnerving. After all, what can we do? And for how long?"

"I can see that it's unnerving," Sam said. "I can't help it."

"But what solution?" The gray man craved order. "Is there no way to apprehend these people?"

"No way that I know."

"And no way to prove they exist, either," said Alan Dulain. His face was red.

Sam's whole head was red inside.

"Unless Lynch is willing to be a little more helpful," Dulain went on, "give us names, dates, places. At least something to check. Something besides a word of his, based on his intuition."

Sam said, thickly, "I'll give no names. And it can't be checked. And I was never here. Excuse me for intruding."

"Lynch."

Sam had reached the door, somehow. He turned to the father. "Call the police. Say you've had a tip. And if you've got any charity, don't say where you got it. But first of all, get her a bodyguard. Do something. Because it won't be a kidnaping for long. It'll be murder." Then he flung himself out of the room with an after-image of the gray stunned face on his retina.

CHAPTER VII

CHARLES SALISBURY clenched his hands. "What must we do? What do you think? Who is he, Alan?"

Alan was still flushed. "Told you, sir. Lynch is a cheap writer, a sensationalist. He is supposed to be on friendly terms with some very crooked people. That type. No good. Intelligent, yes, but absolutely no good." His face grew grimmer.

"But, Kay said he was a friend."

"My fault, sir. I took her to a place I should never have taken her and . . . well . . . they met."

"I won't have her in contact . . ." began the father angrily.

"I know it, sir. I know it too well. She begged me. I thought if once she saw how cheap and flashy such a party could be—" He began to pace. "What concerns me, you see, it's possible he would know. He is just the man who might know." Charles Salisbury's hand was on the phone. "What I do not get, is *why . . . why!* He is not the type to tell, sir. Now, whether Kay appeals to him . . . Frankly, I don't see . . . The place was full of flashy women. This could be a nasty kind of hoax. Lynch writes for these hideous junk magazines."

Salisbury took his hand off the phone and clenched it again. He was a decent man and he had thought that, on the whole, his world was a fairly decent one. "I won't forgive you, Alan, if because you took Kay somewhere . . ."

"I can't fit it in," said Alan. "The only thing that happened, in the fifteen minutes she was there, is that she met Lynch. I can't help wondering if Lynch is back of all of it."

"How could that be?"

Alan shook his head. "A twisted, devious type. God knows what he thought he might get out of you. You had no way of knowing his background. Suppose I hadn't been here?" He made this sound a serious speculation, nothing vain.

But the older man said, gravely, "Suppose his story is a bare fact and the man is acting in common decency? You dislike him. I could see that."

"It's true, I have no patience with his type. He's intelligent, and yet, to me, he makes a mockery of the whole effort . . . well . . . of men to combine and . . . well . . . rise. For some reason he violently dislikes me. Oh, I react to that." The blond boy smiled ruefully. "It's difficult to be fair. Meantime . . ."

"Yes. Yes, *what?*"

Alan reached for the phone and the book. "A guard, of course. There's a very competent firm . . . private investigators. I think it's imperative to have a guard. But we had better go about it as quietly as possible, sir."

"I know some people," said Salisbury suddenly, "in the Police Department. If influence—"

"I think this is a better way, sir." Alan dialed. Salisbury sat, watching, with that stunned look still on his face. "I know the man, sir," Alan explained. "I know his reputation. People just do not step entirely out of character without some powerful motive. I'd hate to expose her to some nasty publicity . . . if this isn't true."

Salisbury said, reluctantly, "I suppose you are right."

"Oh, I know the type, sir." Alan shifted phone to ear. "We must explain to Kay. Poor darling. A pity to frighten her."

Salisbury bit his lips. "Or Martha," he said heavily. "What a hideous thing to do to us, if it isn't true!"

Sam Lynch went down the passage, his heels thumping hard on the carpet. He came to the big room where he had been before, crossed it, but when he had passed through into the foyer he stopped and looked behind him.

There was no one in the big room, no one in the foyer, no one to be seen. The vast place was warm and silent, and it smelled faintly and pleasantly of furniture wax. He looked through to the stairway but there was no one on the stairs.

He took hold of the carved back of a chair; there in the foyer and toward the wall, standing against a green drapery, he leaned on his hands. A conviction of failure gathered silently around him. There was more to this business of taking part than he had thought. You could fluff it. You could make a mess of it. He couldn't feel satisfied.

He told himself that Salisbury would act, would surely

do something. The father would go at the problem in some competent orderly fashion. Of course he would.

Nevertheless, he stood still and realized that he was listening. For what? Why, for an effect, a consequence. For something to be done.

But it was warm and still in the empty rooms and he could hear no footsteps and no voices. His hand sweated on the mahogany.

Way down at the side of the building his shabby little car was docile at the curb. It had been there too long. Whatever these people were going to do, they would not tell the clerk downstairs to cover up Sam's name. It wouldn't occur to them. No, he was vulnerable. *He* was not very safe, from here on out. *No matter what happened to her.*

He ought to get down there and drive briskly far away, for his own sake. But he looked down at his hands and he remembered a thick dirty finger. And he thought, if they once lay so much as one finger on her, she won't live. It'll be that late. And he wondered if he ought to try to see the mother, now.

Perhaps he could scare her, really scare her. Put her in the panic she ought to be in, and in which he was. This was a kind of castle, up in the air. He thought Martha Salisbury had probably never, never in all her days, been otherwise than clean and pretty. If she had ever so much as seen things dirty and ugly, they wouldn't have touched her. Not in her place. Even, he thought, had she dealt with dirt or disease or any ugly trouble, it would have been by a magic wand called money. So she would never have really touched or been touched, for money was a long stick.

The perfect cruelty of such a one as Ambielli, the fiery needs of such a one, the dirty hands of Baby Hohenbaum would be shadows to her. Rumors. Folklore. Tales told. She lived in half the world. As did they, those two, for they knew even less, he reflected, about her gentle lighthearted grace. But the twain would meet.

He thought, yes, he could scare her. And if he did, she would turn at once to her brilliant son-in-law-to-be who studied crime and who was full of theory. He tried to be fair and believe that Dulain, no matter what kind of cracks he'd made, would of course do something.

All was so still.

He tried to tell himself that Sam Lynch had done his best.

But he couldn't listen to the argument because it wasn't to the point. He couldn't feel satisfied. Inside his head he was still crying *no, no*. And he could see the car coming and the big hand closing on the girl's throat, and her fearless eyes turning sick at the end to know she was dying in a world she never knew.

No! How could he take his place, go back to his seat on the aisle, and wait for the curtain?

Time was distorted. He didn't know whether he'd stood here a minute or an hour. Then his ear pricked. Something? The dancing rhythm of sure young feet on the stairs.

She came across the long room, past him, into the foyer, and by the corner of her eye she suddenly knew he was there, and her mop of brown hair flew sideways.

He said weakly, "Hi."

She had a coat around her shoulders, a bag under her arm, a letter in her hand. He stiffened his body, rising from that bent position. "Where are you going?"

"Hm? I'm going to put my letter in the corner box. I want it to get off. It *never* does unless you—"

"I'll mail it for you," he said angrily.

"Thanks, but I don't mind." She kept the letter to her breast. She looked up a little slyly. "Is Daddy going to do what you wanted him to do?"

He half closed his black eyes in pain. "I'm not sure. You haven't seen him?"

"Daddy? No."

"Or your friend Alan?"

"No." Then he heard her say, "Can I help you, Sam? Are you in trouble or anything?" And he took his hands from his burning eyes, and at the sweetness of her expression his heart turned over, and he groaned. He said, "You'll be my death. Why is that? What's about you?"

"I don't know," she said gravely. "What's wrong?"

"If I told you would you believe me?"

"Of course," she said.

"Don't say that," he raged. "Don't trust every stray—"

"Don't trust you?"

"You're ignorant. Your uninformed. You're not even half grown—"

"Well, I like that!" she exclaimed indignantly. "If you're trying to tell me not to trust you, all right. Say so. And maybe I won't. But just because *you* don't trust anybody . . ."

"That's so true," he mumbled.

"You don't even trust *me* enough to tell me what in the world you're so upset about."

"I know. Why don't you get that tooth straightened?"

"Because it would hurt," she sparked at him. "And I don't mind it that much. It isn't important." She stopped and folded her lips inward for a moment and then she laughed.

Sam Lynch began to laugh, too. Because he had a vision. It was like looking from a brink across a gulf of horrors, fire and smoke and pain, and seeing before him the thin danger of one taut shining wire, on which, if he had the reckless nerve to place his feet, he might escape. He knew it was a wild idea. He said to himself, I'm crazy! But to trust yourself to sheer, mere balance, that silent and beautiful thing, carries a kind of joy, and so he smiled, and his black eyes were glowing.

"Fuss about nothing," he muttered. "We'll skip that." Then he began, softly, "Sister, I did something foolish."

"Oh?" She was ready to be serious.

But he stepped around the chair and he took her arm. "Yeah. Of all the dumb things to do, I brought you a present."

"Present? For me?" She let him turn her. She didn't notice they'd begun to walk.

"And then I came all over shy. I was hanging around wondering if I had the nerve to . . . It's downstairs."

"What in the world?"

"Well, I couldn't very well bring it up without . . . uh . . . It's not the kind of thing you can keep in your pocket. It's in my car."

They went out through the door of the apartment. Her hands were careless and sure on the knobs and locks. "Well, I'm certainly not going to let you get away with it," she said.

Sam punched for the elevator. He fidgeted. "You'll think it's pretty silly. I fell for this, myself. How do I know, though, if you like—"

"Like *what?*"

"Would you let me go first?"

"Why?"

"I . . . got something to fix . . ."

"About the present?" He nodded. "But you're going to give it to me? Aren't you?"

"If you'll come and get it. And, of course, if you fall for it, too."

"You mean come to your car?"

"Well, yes, because— Would you?"

"All right. Where is it?"

"Down at the side. It's getting toward dusk," he said, stammering a little.

"What's that got to do with it?" She really had no least tinge of suspicion, no shield and no armor, *no fear,* and it fascinated him. It fascinated and terrified and challenged him.

"Didn't you ever hear," he rattled along, "don't go with a man who says he'll give you candy?" His heart was excited. "Didn't your mamma tell you?"

"It can't be candy," she said emphatically.

"Well, no. It's sweeter than candy. That's if you like them. I'd guess you do."

"Sam, you've got me so curious. Why all this mystery?"

The elevator was there. "Oh, I'm a mysterious fellow," he said, as if he were clowning. "Hsst. We are strangers. Say nothing. But follow me."

The girl giggled.

They stepped into the car. He didn't look at her. Halfway down she said in a very aloof and remotely gracious manner, "Hasn't it been a lovely day?"

"Sure has," he said, casually, not looking at her. He wished his heart would quit its racket before it shook his chest apart. At the street level, he saw the side way out. He went that way.

He walked fast out of the building. He was too near the car. He thought, I don't have to do it. But he knew he was going to do it.

If she came. If she was such a little fool as to follow.

He ducked into his car and in the glove compartment found the old scarf. He ripped it lengthwise once, then twice. He pushed the front seat over. The open door hid him, all but his feet, from the sidewalk before. Back of him, this was a dead end. He bent down. He listened. Then, on the sidewalk he could hear the gay rhythm of her feet.

CHAPTER VIII

ALAN put down the phone. "How soon?" demanded Salisbury.

"Be up right away. These are good people."

"Even so, we'll keep her close at home, right here, for a day or two. Also, I think that in spite of what you say, I am going to call the police and put this whole situation before them. True or untrue, innocent people ought not to be—"

"I don't—"

There came a tap on the door. And Martha, saying, "Are you there, Charles?" The two men looked at each other. Martha's husband braced himself. He dreaded telling her. He wasn't sure of her reaction. He couldn't imagine it.

As Salisbury called, "Come in, dear," the phone rang.

Alan picked it up and put it down. "For Kay. Phinney's got it."

Martha Salisbury said, "Will you boys take tea or strong liquor?"

"We'll take strong liquor." As Salisbury linked his arm with hers, she looked up at him oddly.

Alan followed them into the big room. Phinney, the manservant, said to him, "Beg pardon. Telephone for Miss Katherine. Do you know where she can be, sir?"

But her father turned and answered, "She's upstairs."

"No, I think she came down," said her mother. "I thought she was with you."

The father said, stiffly, "Perhaps, the music room." The manservant went that way.

Martha Salisbury unlinked her arm, tripped to the foyer phone, and trilled, "Hello? Oh, Phyllis? Just a minute, dear. Kay's here somewhere." She held the phone. Her eyes watched the stiff silhouettes of the two men, watched and widened.

Alan said, "Why, I imagine she's upstairs."

"She must be," Salisbury said.

59

Then Martha leaned and called, "I wonder if she could have gone down to mail her letter. Don't you imagine . . . ?"

No one replied. The silhouettes were rigid. The manservant returned and stood still, rather at a loss.

Alan said, "I'll look upstairs." He turned and went up very fast.

Martha said rapidly into the phone, "She'll call you back, Phyl, dear. I'm sorry." She hung up.

"Kay?" Alan's voice came faintly from above. Then, higher, "Katherine?"

"What the matter?" her mother said.

Salisbury had begun to breathe in gasps. "Katherine?" he called. He started rather blindly toward the back regions of the apartment. He passed his wife without seeming to see her. "Katherine?"

The manservant moved all the way down the room to the windows.

"What's the matter!" Martha teetered on her tiny feet. She ran on her silly heels toward the windows, veered toward the stairs.

Phinney turned from the window. "I thought perhaps I could see her in the street, madam. But there's no one near the mailbox now."

Mrs. Salisbury swayed. Alan, on the stairs, looking down, white of face, said, "Katherine?"

Salisbury was in the foyer again. "Katherine?" he pleaded.

Looking at her husband's face, Martha Salisbury raised her hands. She called, "Katherine!" and in her high clear voice cracked the alarm. "*Katherine!*"

It was dark. All around the board shack were night noises, lip-lap of lake water near the rotting porch, sigh of a tree, twinkling patter of a small creature across the thin roof.

The place had plumbing and nothing else in the way of civilized convenience. Interior light came from a kerosene lamp with a dirty glass chimney. Windows that had been boarded over for the winter still wore their crude board barricade outside the glass. The room was higgledy-piggledy—bunks, chairs, a rack of books, a table, a small round iron stove. No curtains, no rug, no "gay" decorations. The two Indian blankets on the two bunks were bright enough but they did not match each other.

Katherine Salisbury pulled a piece of one of the blankets over her freezing ankles.

The foundations of the world had cracked, down on the street, near home, and for a long time she had felt as one who whirled in a void, where there were no solids at all.

She had been shocked and frightened, of course, but at the same time, angered. And now it was that sense of outrage that predominated. She was no longer afraid that she would be hurt in the sense that she would suffer pain. But the outrage was that her parents and her lover did not know what had become of her, and she, by force, was prevented from telling them. She was anguished, thinking of their anguish.

For herself, she felt young and healthy and confident of her youth, and she lay with her wet hair against the boards at the head of the bunk, with her coat huddled around her, and the blanket on her ankles, and she tried to think. To be quiet and think.

He was as silent as she. They had talked too much. Her throat hurt from so many futile words, such useless arguments. He sat on the hard chair, elbows on the table, hands in his black hair, and what she could see of his face was bleak and exhausted. They had struggled, she against the crazy thing he had done to her hair, and they had argued.

He was exhausted, this Samuel Lynch. This strange man. Yet, she mused, how shrewdly he had guessed that smug proprietory feeling, that I-am-the-exception-to-the-rule idea, that childish vanity in which she had felt so pleased with herself. How easily he had fooled her. How easily she had been led to think he had a puppy in his car, for her. Something small and living, down on the floor. She had been so sure. And had climbed in, because he wanted to shut the door (to keep the little living thing in, or so she'd thought).

Then his rough hands descending over the back of the front seat, and the violence. The scarf around her throat, cutting off her power to make sound. The up-side-down tumbled impossible tangle of her limbs as she was shoved down upside down on the floor, the narrow place. To be helpless in that outrageous way, bound and without balance, upside down with her mouth full. To struggle and kick only in inches and in the dark, under the old coat. It was *all* outrage.

She shivered, now.

"Cold?" he said, not looking up.

She said, "Yes."

He got up wearily and took the top off the stove with the iron gadget and thrust a few more sticks inside. The rosy light played over his face, coming from below, marking the hollows of his cheeks and of his eye sockets. He looked exhausted, gaunt, tragic, and immovable.

She pulled her coat collar to her chin.

"Hungry?"

"No."

"I guess there's beans," he said indifferently. He sat down.

At first she'd thought he meant to injure her, perhaps even to kill her. She'd been for a few bad moments in terror of her life. But now she knew what she thought and it explained everything.

At first, his whole story about this Ambielli and his brutal companion had seemed to her pure fiction. When he began to tell her, she had thought he was making it all up.

But now she believed that some of it might be so. But, she thought, Sam must be on the wrong side. She judged he was on the wrong side somewhat reluctantly. Harassed by some little feeling for her, yes. Nevertheless, he was compelled to obey this Ambielli. It seemed obvious. It explained everything. Ambielli has something on him, she told herself sagely. She had no idea what. She took it no further. Such things were possible. People "had things" on other people. She didn't doubt that. Not any more.

All his queer angry words, his warnings not to be so trusting were because he hadn't wanted to obey. She should have taken warning. She hadn't. She'd kept on feeling, in them, through them, that he cared about her, somehow.

She still couldn't help feeling that he did. Even this silly self-defensive story that he'd kidnaped her only to keep her safe, it was because he didn't want *her* to realize he was on the wrong side. He cared what she thought of him, even now. Just the same, there was no leverage for her in this feeling he had . . . if he had it. She couldn't budge him.

There was no use in any more arguing. It was so clear, so logical to her that *if* all he wanted to do was keep her safe, *then* all he had to do was take her home again. It was nonsense to her that her people had been warned but that he mistrusted them. Alan would have known exactly what to do. And Alan would do exactly right. There wasn't any question about it.

No, there was something wrong with the premise. Must be.

Her safety could be so easily accomplished. It must be something else Sam worried about. Well, he admitted he was afraid for himself. Yes, she concluded, he is afraid for himself and that's what really worries him. He's been made to do this, for Ambielli. He was afraid not to obey. He'd met me. He could get up to see me because I knew his name. So he was the one to do it, of course. Maybe he never wanted to do it. But he had to obey, and now he is afraid to let me go.

She supposed the others were handling the other part of it. She believed, now, it would be (for her and for Sam) a matter of waiting in this hidden place until he got the word, the order to let her go. The anguish stabbed her. Oh, her poor people! And she thought angrily, I won't wait. What if I can get away?

She believed that Sam would try to hold her. But she couldn't believe he would hurt her, and then the monstrous thing that had happened to her rolled like a film in her brain and shook the intuition through with doubt. She told herself not be a vain silly little fool all over again. Probably he would hurt her if he had to.

"Hair dry?" He got up and came toward her. She tried not to flinch as he put his hand on her head, not too gently, and stirred her locks with his fingers. "Good enough," he said. "You look like the devil."

She sat up and got our her comb and began to tidy her hair. It was difficult without a mirror. She said, "May I?"

He turned his hand to the lamp, giving permission, and he nodded. She climbed off the bunk, picked up the lamp, and walked, stiff legged, into the bathroom. Shadows shook on the board walls.

The shack backed up against an earthen bank, squeezed between it and the water. Across the back, a strip of space was cut into a narrow kitchen and this narrow bath. But there were no doors to the outside and the windows were nothing but flat slits at the top of the back wall, level with the land above the bank. There wasn't any way, even for the young and strong and slim, to get out of either of those two shallow interior cubby holes.

Kay combed her hair. As she did, she realized that this bleaching of her hair was a wild thing, a stray. She couldn't fit it in. It was a fact not explained, not understood at all, in her theory.

He'd been frantically anxious to do it. So anxious he'd even left her, tied, tumbled, and wedged as she'd been in his car, long enough to buy the chemical. And he had been ready to tie her down to a chair and bleach her hair by force, had she not given up the struggle. She couldn't see how it mattered much. Her hair was a mess, blotched and stiffened, streaked with paler shades, and that was all. But she certainly didn't look like herself with it so streaked and drab and her face so colorless.

He'd said, "Never mind why, sister. I can't tell you why. I can say, but you can't take it in. Not yet. Put it this way. I'm trying to figure out how not to die for you. Or put it this way. I'm studying how to keep *you* alive, if I do. Thing is, I have a hunch we could have a caller. So I'm looking ahead. That is really funny. Sam Lynch looks ahead. Funniest thing I've said today. Never mind. You can't take it in. You will, when the time comes. But I got to do this *now* because you can't do it in five minutes. Never mind, sister. Put it that I'm crazy and you can't go wrong."

Then, after that, he'd made her go over her clothing and take off cleaners' tabs and name tapes, and he'd made her empty her purse. He'd burned all the papers, even her driver's license, and he'd banged at her compact with a hammer, destroying the monogram on the outer case before he threw it in the lake.

"But *why?*" she'd cried.

But he had thrust her down on the bunk and said, "Be quiet." And he'd sat down, holding his head. After a while he'd said, carefully, "If anyone comes, you are to get away. You are *not* Katherine Salisbury and you mustn't admit it, until you get yourself home."

"But, Sam, why?"

"You'll understand, when it happens."

"When what happens?"

"Something, to me."

"Oh . . ." She was exasperated.

"All right. Let me breathe. Quit arguing. I've done the most damn foolish thing I ever did in my life, so far. It's so foolish, I'm dizzy. Dizzy looking at it. I'm going in circles. I think I'm thinking but I'm not any more sure of it than you are. Maybe a wheel's busted in my head. So I mind my own business for a million years!"

And then he looked at her, furious, hair mussed, eyes

blazing, and he shouted, "Who are you?" And she had trembled down under her coat and kept quiet.

And, in the quiet, she built up her fine theories so that she thought she understood almost everything. But now, looking at herself, she thought, he meant to disguise me, to hide who I am. What can the reason be? And she thought, with a creeping warmth, there can't be any reason but the one he said. To hide me from harm.

She came out of the bathroom. His head lay on his arm. He didn't move. She was well aware that he knew where she stood. She put the lamp down softly, and in the descending glow she could see, plainly, that there were a few pure white hairs at his temples and before his ears.

She said, "Sam, you're getting gray."

He said, "I'll be white by morning. Go to sleep."

"But . . ." Her throat hurt with all the arguments.

"I don't *know* what I'm going to do with you. I don't know what's going to happen next. I can't say because I don't know."

"Sam, take me home."

"I know what I'm *not* going to do with you. I'm *not* going to throw you back to the wolves. Be quiet." His head rolled on his arm.

She went over to the bunk, curled under her coat, and pulled the blanket over her feet. She was rigid. How far were they from a telephone? Would he sleep, she wondered. Where was the key? Could she be silent at the door? Could she hide out there in the dark?

The lake licked at the shore. Little feet tapped two arcs around the shingles. The trees whooshed and hooshed in the night wind and the lamp flickered.

CHAPTER IX

LIGHTS burned all Wednesday night in the Salisbury apartment. Then it was Thursday. It was incredible that Thursday could come, and go. It was a day so full of tension, and so empty.

At the Starke School, Katherine Salisbury was not in attendance. She missed her music lesson.

Sam Lynch was not seen in his town haunts.

Alan Dulain did not appear at his office.

Charles Salisbury stayed away from his club. His wife, Martha, begged off from her luncheon.

Excuses were made, but the reason was not told. Charles Salisbury made the decision. He announced coldly that he would not call the police. Not now. Alan was sure that there would soon be some communication. It was the classical pattern. Salisbury made the decision to wait for it. He said, and said it only once, "I want my girl."

At dawn, he called the three servants together and asked them to say nothing to anyone. He told them that he feared Miss Katherine might be in the hands of kidnapers. He warned them that newspaper publicity might be unfortunate. He used the word gingerly, because Martha was there. He emphasized the *might be's*. He begged them to obey him.

Meantime, he pretended to believe there was a real hope in checking the hospitals, but he did not believe it. He hoped Martha believed it. They kept up. It was good manners and it was, of course, fear. On top of all other fears, they feared for each other.

They waited.

Alan and his hired men spent the night checking the hospitals. And looking for Sam Lynch.

This was the one thing they could do. They could find Sam Lynch, who knew all about it. The police could have found Sam Lynch, of course. But so could Alan's men, and quietly. Sam Lynch could tell them more. When they knew more, they would know better what to do. How best to find Katherine.

To himself, alone, her father added, *if she is alive*. To Martha, he pretended that of course she was. He would fall into the classical pattern of this crime; he would keep faith; he would pay; everything would come out all right.

It was a pattern. But he was afraid. The pattern was false. Murder. Sam Lynch had said it, and Salisbury had the word burned into his brain. Less trouble. Well, *he* would make no trouble, no trouble at all. Just in hope. Time enough for the police, later. Police for revenge.

Alan deplored the decision. Alan was for bringing in the organization, now. But he deferred to the father, and he was busy hunting for Lynch. If it had not been that they had this one line of action, Salisbury might not have been able to hold to his decision, or Alan to defer to it. Or Martha to bear up.

The Salisburys built Sam Lynch into a great hope. He had warned them. He had known. Surely, now, he would tell them where to look for her. He must have been on their side. Alan said grimly that Lynch was on some side, all right, and he must be found.

Thursday went by.

Katherine Salisbury missed her music lesson. No one said why. Her name was not in the newspapers. Not on the police calls. The servants said nothing.

Yet, in the tangled city, her name was spoken.

But not by Reilly, Alan's man, who that morning went up and down the block in which the Salisbury apartment was located. He rang bells, he stopped a few people on the sidewalk, he showed photographs of Katherine Salisbury. "She's eloped," Reilly would say. "Her family's having a fit." He would wink. "You see her around here last evening? Get into a car? Anything like that?"

No one seemed to know. Some were indifferent. Some were unsympathetic. Some were suspicious.

That afternoon, in a room far downtown, where a little man sat at a table and a big man, on the bed, cringed against the wall, her name was spoken.

"Katherine Salisbury either skipped out or was taken out," Ambiellie said, red-eyed.

"They're looking for her all right, boss," Baby said in a monotone designed to soothe.

"Don't tell me what I know. I know that." The little man got up and hit the big man viciously with the edge of his palm on the big forehead. "Be quiet when I'm trying to think," he said, and all his soft-spoken shell was cracked away.

"Yeah, boss."

The little man stood, flaming, and he was murder. "If she skipped out it's coincidence," he said, "but if she was taken, somebody's in my way."

"Listen, boss," Baby cringed lest there be a blow. "We don't need to worry. We can set it up for somebody else."

Ambielli's red eyes steadied. "This one's set up," he said contemptuously. "I never worry."

While the Salisburys waited, high in their apartment, people moved in the city.

Late on Thursday, in with their evening paper, folded inside, a message came. The Salisburys took it, read it, and looked at each other with a fearful hope.

When Alan came in, about nine o'clock on Thursday evening, he thought them so weary as to seem distraught and inattentive. When he told them there was nothing yet, no girl in any hospital under any false name, they seemed scarcely to admit to their minds this news.

He took his drink and sat, tense, young, frowning with the responsibility, endeavoring to give of his special knowledge his best advice, to bear the weight of the problem on his competent shoulders. "There's not much doubt she's been hidden somewhere. We still can't find Sam Lynch." He looked grim. "That must be significant."

"You're being careful?" Salisbury asked. He held a hand between his weary eyes and the lamp. He felt the awful responsibility of acting for the sole objective, moving flawlessly in the pattern, making no error in an utterly strange and perfectly horrible world.

"It's all undercover, sir. Don't worry. Nobody even guesses she's gone. But Lynch just is not around. However, there's a rumor that he keeps a car. They're trying to discover where. If it has gone, too, I must advise using the police organization. They can find a car, sir."

"Not yet, Alan."

"But how long? I can't understand," Alan beat his knee, "why they don't communicate. If it is what we think, they're bound to communicate quickly, *before* the police get into it.

Don't you see? They should have done so already." He was puzzled by a break in the pattern. He did not notice the motionless silence of his host, the movement of Martha's elbow as it pressed her knitting bag to her side. "When they do, we may get hold of something more to work on. At least, we will be sure what this is. We will have something to turn over . . ."

Salisbury said quietly, "You're not, in any way, going against our wishes, Alan. Are you?"

Alan's face tightened. "I only wish I could convince you. This isn't for you to handle, sir. You are too close, too emotionally involved. Amateurs cannot deal with this thing. My men aren't amateurs, of course, and they are doing their best but it needs the organization."

"I want my girl," said Salisbury for the second time. Although his voice was quiet it was as if he had screamed. He was sorry to have said it. He looked anxiously at Martha.

She was knitting. Her hair was oddly tousled. It was a strange effect. She sat so quietly, knitting under the lamp, and her hands were swift and her voice was calm. As if she had everything under control except her white hair, which rebelled and rose from her scalp to betray her.

Martha said, "If we could find Sam Lynch. Where can he be? He knows."

"He certainly must know," Salisbury murmured. The sum Lynch mentioned was the sum they asked. Lynch had known.

"He *more* than knows," Alan was grim.

"And yet," Salisbury spoke with an admonishing doubt, "he did come here to warn us. And although they left the building at about the same time, they did not leave together. I believe he is on our side. I think he would help us. If it was his plan to take her away, why did he warn us?"

"The man's mind is so twisted," Alan said, "so devious, so split, I don't suppose, sir, that you and I could follow his reasoning. I'm *sure* he is involved."

Salisbury, watching from behind his hand, felt an impulse to cry out at the tense young face, don't be so cocksure! The boy was behaving well. He'd done no breast-beating, no brow-clutching, and he had been industrious. Nevertheless, something about him plucked at the nerves. Some glib use of words, as when he said "emotionally involved." And some arrogance, as of an expert in these things, and even his very assumption of so much responsibility was irritating.

"Lynch will be found," Alan said as if this was doom, "and Lynch will talk."

Salisbury didn't feel so sure. He could imagine Lynch never talking at all, since dead men don't. But he kept this image to himself. "I suppose your people can do little more tonight," he murmured. "Alan, Martha is too tired. I rather think she must take something and sleep."

"You, too," Martha said. "Both of us, Charles."

They seemed to lean on each other, and by leaning, hold each other up. Yet they dared not admit to each other anything but hope. The father thought, ah, my brave love! and felt a fullness behind his tired tearless eyes. "Must rest," he murmured.

Alan sensed no dismissal. "If only I," the pronoun bore some emphasis, "had heard all Lynch had to say. Maybe he let drop more than you realize. There may have been something."

"I've told you everything," the father said.

The blond boy turned to the mother. "Tell me everything he said to you."

Martha's hands became still. Her pretty face, framed in the wild white hair, lacked the airs and graces of her prettiness, but all its lines seemed to have been carved deeper, cleaner, to a most somber beauty. She told how Sam Lynch had identified himself. How they had spoken, and she so frivolously, about crime. "And we spoke about you and your interests, Alan. I said how Kay was interested, too. As I had been in Charles' business. In the biscuit business. He said something about a warehouse. I gathered that he wrote fiction. I don't remember why."

"Warehouse?" Alan frowned.

"Yes. He said . . . I remember the words . . . 'somebody watching over them night and day.' It was a strange thing to say."

"Watchman," cried Salisbury. "Wait. I remember that word."

Alan's held breath demanded more.

Salisbury dredged it up. "Something about visiting the sins of the employees upon the boss—"

"An employee? A watchman?" Alan jumped up. "Must mean something. Who is your night watchman at the warehouse?"

"I don't know. Have no idea."

"Can you find out."

"Yes, of course I can. Wait." Salisbury turned from the phone. "The name is Perrigrine. He is on duty now. Had the job only a week, since the old man died."

"The old man died?"

"Yes, in an accident."

"Wait," said Alan. "How long was the old man there, sir?"

"I can ask."

"No, wait. There was some kind of shooting affair, last year. And your watchman testified. Remember? He saw something suspicious. Wait, I'm recalling it. He called the police before the thing happened. That was it. It was the time Ambielli was nearly killed. A gang thing. Classical underworld feud. Everyone knew that Emanuel was behind it. Ambielli was pretty well ruined. He left town."

"But this . . . what has this to do—?"

"Ambielli," Alan said thoughtfully.

"What about Ambielli?" snapped Salisbury.

"Is back in town."

To Salisbury the thought came, in sequence, quietly. *And the old man died.* It came so quietly that he began to say it. "And the old man . . ." Before he came to the end of the phrase his mind ran ahead of his tongue and he stopped.

He heard Alan asking, "What kind of an accident did the old man die in?"

Salisbury shook his head. He didn't know. He was wondering. He wanted to ask when Ambielli had come back to town, but he didn't dare. He sat, looking at it. The hideous idea. An old man, on duty, saw something. Dutifully, called the police. Now, died. *Now.* Months later! "Oh, no, ridiculous!" he said loudly.

"If Lynch was hinting," Alan mused, "he couldn't have meant Emanuel. No reason for *him* to carry a grudge against you." Alan chewed his fingernail. "Can't be. It *is* ridiculous."

Charles Salisbury lifted his hands. "What grudge against me?" Such a grudge, he thought, as killed an old man, months later. "How could *I* be held responsible? I had nothing to do with it." Reason protested. But, all the same, his mind reached outside a strict and reasonable order and he thought, no, it wasn't a grudge exactly. But it was a way, almost a whimsical, an accidental way for me to have been heard of, known about, and chosen for this. Since I have a daughter. Salisbury's eyes winced.

"Ambielli is back in town," Alan said, "I've heard as much." His pupils slid sideways. "I don't believe it, 'visiting the sins . . .' That's sensationalism. Must have been Lynch's idea of a red herring." His mouth curled.

"But if Mr. Lynch were honest," Martha said gravely, "and if it were this man he overheard, then where is Lynch?"

Salisbury thought to himself, if Lynch were honest, he may be dead. As the old watchman is dead. He didn't speak. He moistened his lips.

"Oh, lying low," said Alan contemptuously. "Keeping out of the way. So much is plausible. People like Lynch have an exaggerated dread of the Ambiellis. Part admiration, of course. But I don't think he was honest. If so, why not name the name?"

Salisbury said, "Because of the dread."

Alan raised his brows.

"Lynch was afraid," Salisbury said slowly, "and the name wasn't essential, yesterday."

"Or," said Alan skeptically, "those cryptic hints were dropped to confuse and mislead us."

"I d-don't . . ." Salisbury stuttered. "You say it's plausible that he is afraid. But you won't grant he thought he was putting himself in danger."

Alan smiled. "Why would he put himself in danger?"

"Because he had a decent impulse."

"*That* is out of character. I assure you."

So sure? thought Salisbury. Are we never out of character? Is there never anything wild, not named in the catalogue?

"My mind is open, of course," said Alan, and Salisbury blinked. "I had better phone the agency. Better see what they can turn up on Ambielli. This may be helpful. May be important." Alan had a bustling air.

"I wish," Salisbury shielded his eyes to hide alarm. "Alan, let it alone a day. I beg of you."

"But—"

"If they communicate with me . . . Don't you understand?" Let it alone, he was thinking, because perhaps they haven't hurt her yet. Don't start up trouble and suspicion. Not now. Not yet.

The young man was earnest. "Believe me, I no more want to risk . . . anything than you do, sir. I don't feel it is a risk. Or that you realize how perfectly discreet these men can be. There won't be any fanfare, or the ponderous movement of the department. Which, I agree, may have its spies. But I am sure—"

"I am not so sure as you are," Salisbury said sharply. "I want no risk. No added risk."

Alan pursed his lips together.

Then Martha threw back her rumpled head. "Indulge us, Alan," she said tartly.

Alan said, gently, "I know how you feel. I do understand. How paralyzing it all is." He squared his shoulders. "That's always the hideous difficulty in these things."

"Good night," she said abruptly. Both her hands held to her knitting bag.

Charles Salisbury showed Alan out. When he came back, his wife was sitting with her eyes shut, holding in both her hands the piece of silk that had been hidden in her knitting bag. She said, "I'm glad we didn't tell him." Her eyes opened, and they were cloudy. "He makes me nervous."

"Yes."

She said, "As if it were a case. A type of thing. Not Katherine."

Not, thought Salisbury in agony, the only Katherine in all time, all space, forever. He said, aloud, "I know." He came and touched the purple-red scarf in her hands. It was the sign that had come with the message. It was their hope. "Another day," he sighed.

"I wish it were tonight. I wish the note had said tonight."

"No, no. Don't you see? They give me time, the daylight hours tomorrow, to get the cash. They want the money. That's their only objective."

"Yes, of course. Of course, Charles."

"So they give me time to get the money. It's reasonable." He pretended.

"Yes. Yes, I do see." She bowed her head to his reasoning. As they both must.

He thought, ah, my brave love. And Thursday was gone, but it would be a long day, Friday.

CHAPTER X

IT was incredible that Thursday had gone by. Kay, wakening to day, thought, but this is Friday! How could it be? "Is it *Friday?*" she said.

"Far as I know, and Friday afternoon at that. Why don't you sleep nights?" He was hoarse. As far as she knew, he hadn't slept at all.

She sat up angrily. "Because I'm looking for a chance to get away."

For a moment, his black eyes laughed at her. Then he told her soberly that there was no chance.

"Why not? Sam, let me."

"You're too young and foolish, that's why not." She wondered if he were evading. "God knows what would happen to you," he grumbled.

"God knows what'll happen to me anyway. *You* don't."

"That's right. There's coffee. And salmon."

"Salmon!"

"On crackers, it makes a meal. This isn't the Waldorf, sister."

She went into the bathroom and locked the door. Across the dirty narrow window pane she could see the wild green and yellow grasses. She washed her face and combed her hair, flung open the door and said, "It's a pigsty." She straightened the bunks, quickly, energetically, with righteous anger. She neatened the shelves. She went into the narrow rustic inconvenient camp kitchen and she fell upon the disorder there.

For the fist time, with shock, she saw that there was a door in the left wall, which was the outside wall. She stepped softly and put her hand on the knob. It wasn't locked. It was only a cupboard. She sighed. Then she knew he was leaning on the wall, watching her, and she began vigorously to arrange the things in the cupboard.

"Well, busy as a bee."

But she skipped the chance to squabble and, turning, said seriously what she had been thinking. "You don't trust anyone. But I *do*. Sam, this is stupid. We can't wait here forever, just because you don't know what to do next. I trust my father and mother."

"Naturally," he said. "And Alan?"

"Naturally, for heaven's sake. Sam, will you listen to me?"

"Yes, I will," he said quietly.

"All right. I will believe all you say. And I will do my best to protect you. I promise," she told him earnestly, "I won't tell anyone what you've done. I don't have to tell."

"You will protect me, sister?" He wasn't exactly amused. She couldn't read his eyes.

"Then, Ambielli will never know."

"Too late."

"Why, do you say—?"

"I don't know. I have a hunch." He looked so tired as to be almost ill.

"You must see that I will be guarded, *now*," she cried. "After *this*. You must see that."

"Yes, I see that," he answered numbly.

"Are you . . . so afraid of Ambielli?"

"Yes. I'm afraid."

"But he couldn't blame *you*," she said softly, "if I ran away."

"No." His face didn't change but she knew he was sad and disappointed.

"Then, take me home, and you stay there, too. They can guard both of us."

"Alan would love that, sister."

"But—"

"Maybe Alan could rehabilitate me. He's got his theories. He's a moral snob, all the same."

"What!"

"Once soiled, never quite white again. A guy who forgives with his head. Nothing moves in the heart." He lay his head against the wood of the wall. "Look at my mouth hanging open."

"You're so stupid about Alan," she raged.

"And you trust him, sister."

"Of course. Of course."

"Well, you'd trust anybody."

"I would *not*." She stamped her foot like a child. "Oh, Sam, I can believe—*maybe* I can—that you were trying to do something for my sake. But I think, if you didn't senselessly hate Alan Dulain, you'd never have gotten into this mess."

"Maybe not. That's very shrewd. That's a right shrewd notion."

"Isn't that true?"

"Don't nag me."

She said, "You're tired."

"To the bone," he admitted. "Yeah, I'm pretty tired, sister. Dare say."

"Coffee?"

They sat down at the table together. For a moment, it was companionable. It was almost cozy.

"Listen, sister," he said hoarsely, "when you see your mamma, tell her, will you? I never made a pass."

She thought, startled, we're shut in so close we're reading minds. She said, aloud, turning the subject, "Why do you keep listening, Sam? You're always listening."

"For wolves. I've told you and told you, there are wolves," he muttered. "There really are. I told you about Baby Hohenbaum."

"Baby Hohenbaum," she nodded.

"He only knows one thing. Without pay, even. The boss is God. And I told you about Ambielli. Ambielli kills. He thinks nothing of it. He's got nothing much to lose, either. He's raw. He's death walking. Sister, you can't kid around with death. It's so permanent."

"I know." She sucked in breath.

"So don't say it again." His eyes shut, wincingly. "Please, I beg of you. If I could figure out *how* to take you safe home, believe me, I would do it. Glad to get rid of you. No offense." He looked so tired! "Well, seems as though nobody's coming out here. Maybe, after today, if nobody comes, I can reconnoiter."

"Another day?" she exclaimed in dismay.

"Another night," he said. "Sister, I'm confused. I freely admit it." He reeled in the chair. "I had no business thrusting an oar in. Not my style. Nor my habit. A reporter, I said to your mamma, is one who sees what's going on. Watches, you know? Looks on. Well, I'll tell you, that's more my style."

He rubbed his face. "No man of action, I. No hero. You don't believe in the wolves, though. Not yet. That's the trouble."

She thought, he's getting so tired and confused, before he knows it, he'll let me go.

And by that close magic he answered her thought. "No, I won't let you go. I can't trust you yet."

"Ah, why?"

"You're too inexperienced, too romantic."

"Sam . . ."

"Alan said so. And the difference between Alan and me is this, sister. I tell *you*. Alan tells *me*. That's the difference."

"Alan," she said severely, "is a fine person. He is very intelligent and well informed, and he is heading for all kinds of important good works, and his ideal is service to mankind. I don't like the way you talk against him."

"Good works, eh?" Sam looked wild. "Oh, yes. A do-gooder. He's going to do this sorry world a lot of good. But not in my dictionary, he doesn't. Listen, shall I tell you the way for a man to do good? I don't claim I *do* it, you understand, but I *know*. You're born and you grow. You live and learn, and you take out of yourself what it is you've got and you lay it on the line and you offer it. Out of yourself, what you can do, for other people to use if they can. *This* is service. See? See it?"

She felt as if he were shaking her, as if her head bobbed.

"That's the good you can do, sister. And I was a darned bright audience, I was really that, and maybe I never should have left my seat." His voice rose from the mumble. "All right. But I know it's doing no good, sitting up, telling all the other little people how *they* should behave. No, no. Rehabilitating the poor dumb clods. And how do you know when they are rehabilitated? It's when they think just like Alan thinks. Otherwise, they're out of line. See it?

"Yes, yes, sure," he snatched it out of her mind, "he wants to be a teacher. And we got to have them, and some men are teachers and that's what they've got to give. But let me tell you this, sister. A decent teacher *listens*. If he can't listen, he goes out of date so fast it knocks him silly. He has respect.

"But Alan, he doesn't listen. He can't hear. He's got no respect." Sam pounded the table. "I tell you, you've got to have respect," he shouted. "How can a man set himself up, he knows all the answers. How *can* he? He can say to me, 'this I've found,' or, 'this seems to me.' And maybe he can sell something. But not to me, unless he's got respect. Respect, I say. That he might hear something out of the *other* people."

"But, Alan—"

"Doesn't even respect you, sister." Sam sagged. "Oh no, he doesn't. He tells me, *me*, you understand, behind your back, confidentially, how young and foolish you are."

"I suppose *you* respect me," she cried, startled and angry.

"I do. Yes, I do. I tell you you're a fool kid. That's my opinion. But I listen. Sister, you can tell. Some things, you've got. I'm tuned. I hear."

His hand moved toward hers but didn't touch. She thought, he hasn't touched me, and marveled, not counting the violence long ago.

"Things I . . . say?" she faltered.

"Not with the voice." He rose, stumbling. "So I should weep over you." He rubbed his eyes. "Because you're cute or something. I think I'm delirious. Going to sleep. Don't try to get the key. Don't run away. I'll sleep. Then, think. You know? Think better. Think of something."

"It's a good idea," she said mechanically.

He slept, at once, with no transition. He lay on the bunk, heavy and gone. She felt a little lost, a little light-headed, as if some steady drag were cut away.

She moved softly back into the kitchen and worked a little more at the task of putting it in order. Her mind was absent. Her mind was trying out the idea that all Sam told her was true. If he had heard Ambielli in the restaurant, if he had told her father and Alan and been uncertain of their belief, if he had been so frightened for her, and she so patently a fool, and if Ambielli was so dangerous, then, of course, he was confused and frightened now.

She wondered, as he wondered, how could he take her home? She thought, those cruel and revengeful men will be like hornets, watching my house, all ready to swoop and sting us both to death. Especially Sam. Or, she thought, they are looking for Sam. They know he knew. Maybe he is the only one who could have stepped between.

She, too, began to think they might have callers, here. She looked up at the narrow kitchen window, and a shudder shook her all up and down and her heart swelled lest she see a face, eyes peering through the grasses from the high ground.

She thought, but I needn't be Katherine Salisbury. I don't

look very much like her. If I'm some other girl, then Sam didn't do it. She thought, that's crazy. That's impossible. And she knew what Sam had meant. If they were to come after him, then she must run away and hide herself.

In a little while it occurred to her that since she looked so different, it would be simple and safe for her to go home by herself. She thought she would tell Sam when he woke. Perhaps he hadn't thought of it.

Then she knew he had thought of it, but not until she tried out belief in him, tried *listening*, could he trust her.

But now he would. And, rubbing an old rag over the worn sink, dreamily, she fell to thinking. They always teach us patterns. But they should tell us. There are odd things, and inconsistent things, and things that do not fit. They can lead to unpredictable deeds, done for unguessable reasons, by unexpected people. *You never know,* she reflected, *when you may meet a black-eyed stranger.* Around the corner, at a party, in a crowd, looming up, breaking the pattern open, warping all the threads.

Why, Ambielli, who had his plans, thought he knew his fortune. But there was a black-eyed stranger in his cup.

And even Sam. Even, she thought, a wild, stray turn of your own heart, that you can't explain, can be like a black-eyed stranger, the upsetting chance.

CHAPTER XI

Friday wore away. Alan was told that Martha Salisbury had collapsed. Actually, she walked in her room, up and down and around, and she was only wearing Friday through.

No one was told what Charles Salisbury's errands were, that day. Quietly he went about them, doing what he had to do. His losses would cut deep.

Martha did not receive Alan Dulain, and Salisbury took care to cross the boy's path only briefly. The father was irritable with strain, and he knew, vaguely, that he contributed to a picture of a disintegrating despair. But he could not help that. When Alan left him for the last time, in early evening and marched away, face pinched, head high, shoulders squared, Salisbury thought, poor kid. But he did not think it long.

At nine o'clock, having sent for the car but driving himself, he set out on the journey. He did not think that the men Alan called his private people would be watching the apartment. Nevertheless, he did his amateur best to note whether or not he were followed and concluded not.

The words penciled on the piece of brown paper, mysteriously found wrapped around the soft mass of Katherine's scarf, were now engraved upon his brain. They were his hope. He knew exactly what he was to do and he intended to do it, exactly. He would act in good faith. Nothing would fail by fault of his, now.

He was alone. He had told no one but Martha. He had the money exactly as he was supposed to have it, old bills, in a manila envelope, addressed to Smith, lying at his side on the seat, unsealed. He left on time and on the dot of the instructed hour he swung uptown. He drove slowly, careful to obey every least regulation, lest there be an unforeseen delay.

It had been a long time, he reflected, since he had gone

forth with his teeth biting his heart back, with the need to call out such reserve of strength merely to keep himself steady. It had to be done and done just so. This journey was his effort and his alone. If she were still alive, hope lay in obeying. If she were not, it made little difference that the police would come into it a little late. No, he would lock mind and imagination and emotion. He would meticulously obey.

But if, as the note promised, all went well and she returned in eighteen hours, as it said, *when he got his girl back,* then how he would strike! With thunder and with lightning, with the Law, with all other grim power he could muster, he would rip them from whatever hole they thought to hide in, were it to take a hundred years!

But not now. Lock down the lid of now against all that.

He took the turn, up the hill, in Van Cortlandt Park. He came out on a broad avenue, rather bare of traffic. On this he kept northward, proceeding sedately but steadily down the inside lane, for he had a left turn coming, although he was still at least two miles below the designated side road. He pulled up for a red light and sat reading the note again, not from paper, but as it lay printed in his head.

Somewhere a shadow shifted. Something loomed. The right door handle turned. The door opened. A huge shoulder, a head bent so that what lay black over the face might have been a shadow . . .

A voice said, in a startling falsetto, "You Salisbury?"

He could not nod. His neck was too stiff. But he said, "Yes," and he thought, Alan's man, oh no, no. He said, sharply, "Don't keep me, please."

"This the money?" the voice chirped. A hand in a brown glove picked up the money.

"Don't!"

The face had no features. There was cloth tied tightly over it, and the profile was all a black curve, hideously without the jut of a nose. The hand, the money, the head, the shoulder withdrew, dodging lightly away, and the door clicked.

Utterly shocked, Salisbury found himself squirming across the front seat and half falling out the door. A car at the extreme right of the avenue took a skittering start and turned right. Its taillight bounded merrily away.

A woman leaned out of a car behind his, that had only

just, he realized, rolled slowly up. "Anything the matter?" She called boldly. The driver beside her was a man.

Salisbury said, piteously, "I don't know. I don't know."

She turned her head. Then, like a go-between, she called, ".Need a push?"

"No. Thank you. No."

The car went into reverse and backed with an air of impatient disgust. It roared in a sharp twist around to the left of his car and its taillight went bounding away.

He got back behind the wheel. He had to wait, having missed all the green. Then he drove slowly on.

He did not know what to believe. It was out of order. Little use following all the instructions now. Nevertheless, he made the proper turn. He found the designated iron fence. He walked along the concrete base in which it was embedded to the tenth tall spike from the gate. There was no message in that designated spot. He hunted for a long time.

He did not know whether this was good or bad. He did not, he realized in anguish, know whether or not he had accomplished his mission. He thought, if he had, if *this* had all along been their plan, then not to drop the one more word it would have taken to tell him so was as brutal, as cruel a thing, as he could conceive.

He would tell Martha that he was hopeful. But he was terribly afraid. He was afraid he had made the wrong decision, from the beginning. With what, he wondered, had he been so meticulously keeping good faith?

It said, in that square penciled printing, eighteen hours. As the night wore through, the Salisburys were hopeful. They asked each other, who could have known the money was there except he who had sent the instruction? And they said hopefully to each other, "Of course. It must be so." As it grew light, their spirits lifted and when ten o'clock came, Saturday morning, they even toasted the passing of half a day, the dark half, in a little wine. She would come. She would call.

When they began to brake time, to will it not to go so fast, neither knew. Or when each realized noon was too near. Saturday was racing across the calendar. Salisbury thought bitterly, he had kept faith, but with what? He didn't say it aloud. The flying clock raced round.

83

CHAPTER XII

SATURDAY noon. Baby Hohenbaum was eating green grapes. He ate them steadily, one at a time, in rhythm. The boss sat, knees together, hands in his pockets, in a fat blue chair. His chin touched his collar-bone. He was coiled there, wickedly, Baby knew, and from time to time, Baby rolled his eyes to look at him.

Baby said, between grapes, "Nothing to worry about."

Ambielli, with his neck still twisted, turned his eyes balefully. "If somebody talked I'll take his tongue out."

"Aw, boss," Baby looked at the bunch of grapes lovingly as if it were money. "Why do you want to worry?"

"I never worry. I never fail." The head raised on the neck. "Look down, see if he's there."

Saturday afternoon. They were in the big living room, and Salisbury, who had not been able to touch his lunch, was trying to eat a sandwich. Martha said he must.

She was knitting. But something horrible was happening to the thing that came slipping from the needles. It was changing shape. The neat tight rows had loosened, each more than the last, and the garment that ought to have grown according to count, evenly, was spreading, and it was becoming crooked, too, sagging, and hanging off the coral needles lopsided and a little mad. As her hands worked, it kept mushrooming and distorting, silent and hideous; it was the outward and visible diagram-in-wool of panic.

When she said, "More coffee, Charles?" her voice was all right.

"No. No. This sandwich is very good. What's in it?"

"We must ask Phinney," she said brightly. "I'm glad you like it, dear." Neither of them would ever know what was in the sandwich.

"Yes," he said, choking, "it's very good. Won't you try a part of one?"

"No, dear. I had lunch, really. I'm not hungry at all. Not yet."

"It's early for tea," he said.

"Of course it is." It was not.

The room was very quiet when they were not speaking. "Isn't it a little cool in here?"

"Would you like a fire, Martha?"

"Oh, no. No, thanks, dear."

"Going to be a late spring."

"It does seem so."

Their eyes met, and he thought, oh God, the bravest heart can break! He went and sat beside her and leaned close. "Show me how you do that, darling."

Her hands steadied. "Simple. You put the needle in, so."

"Yes."

"And loop the yarn, so."

"I see."

"And pull it through."

"Is that all?"

"Not quite," she said. "Sometimes, you see, there are variations."

The doorbell rang, and the same thrilled shock ran through their bodies as they leaned together and breath pulled into them both, in the same gasp. Before they could move, Phinney's feet had hurried. Alan Dulain burst in.

He seemed to run full tilt into their expectancy and, as if it were a barrier, he stopped and looked. It was as if all three of them cried out, What? What?

Then Alan said, "Anything?"

"Nothing." Martha echoed, "Nothing," and Salisbury saw the yarn slide off the needles, as it should not do, and the coral point dipped ahead, just the same, and he knew enough to understand there would be a great hole in the emerging fabric. And he thought, we are going to fall apart pretty soon. Just like that.

"How are you, Mrs. Salisbury?" Alan pitied her.

She said, "Alan, have you heard anything?" and her voice was all right.

Alan was being cautious. He must be able to see, thought Salisbury, that we are falling to pieces. "Well, we've checked all hospitals again with no result. There is no chance it's an accident or anything of the sort. I hoped you had heard something. By now." His air accused them.

"We hoped," she said wanly.

"Darling, won't you lie down? Take something?" Salisbury thought, if she goes to pieces, so will I. Right here. I'll fall on the carpet.

But she said, letting her knitting fall at last, "It's four o'clock, Charles. I think we must tell Alan."

"Yes," he said.

"All day. Too long. Something is wrong."

"Yes," he said.

"Tell me what?" said Alan a little coldly.

"There was a demand for ransom, Alan."

"When?"

"Thursday."

"*Thursday!* And you didn't tell." The boy's face was hurt and angry, and at the same time it hinted, I thought as much. "Where is it?"

"Here."

Alan snatched the brown paper. "What was the thing with it?"

"Her scarf." Martha took it out of the knitting bag. "This."

Suddenly Salisbury was glad they were telling. It felt like action. It felt like movement.

"It's her scarf," Alan frowned.

"Of course it is."

"None of her handwriting?"

"No." (Salisbury cried out; inside, don't point that up!)

"Do you think," Martha sat straighter and her voice was clear. "Is that a stain on the scarf?"

Salisbury felt his skin crawl. All this time. And she had not once said this to him, and he felt shaken. He had not thought he was being spared.

Alan took the pretty thing in his hands and crushed it, not looking down. "For God's sake, tell me what you did, sir."

"I did as it says."

"You went out . . . last night?" (You fool! You old fool! No one said it. Salisbury heard it.) "You found this place? You delivered the money?"

"I didn't get far with the money. A masked man took it off the seat."

"What!"

"We think it was planned. I did drive on. I found the place. But there was nothing there."

"Nothing at all?"

"Nothing there."

"Do you mean you were stopped? Robbed of it?"

"At a red light, Alan. He took it easily. He knew what it was. He even called my name."

(Ah, you foolish old man! Salisbury heard it.) "What did he look like?"

"Seemed a big fellow. I was startled. I couldn't see. He was masked. No face."

"Where did he go?"

"Car. Turned the corner."

"You didn't follow!"

"I reacted too late. Then I went on ahead. You see, I wasn't sure. I couldn't think straight."

"If there only had been a trained observer hidden in your car. Or someone behind. Anything. If you'd only told me."

"I hoped . . ."

Martha, looking at her work, said, "I dropped some stitches. Look, I dropped . . ." Salisbury held her closely in his arms.

Alan snapped, "What time was this? Has it been the eighteen hours?"

"It's that, Alan."

"She's not here."

"Not here."

"No call."

"No. Nothing."

The father watched the other's eyes, and he thought, oh, God, what statistic is he remembering? What is the rule in these cases?

"You marked the money," Alan said, and his tone added, of course.

"No, I . . . did as it says."

Martha said, sharply, "Charles!"

And he answered, quietly, "All right. All right."

Alan walked up and down, very much upset. But he controlled himself to speak moderately, even gently. "I'm sorry you didn't let me in on it. I wish you'd seen fit to tell me. There might have been a chance. Professional people would have known what to do."

"Done now," said Salisbury, bitterly.

"Even this printing might tell an expert . . ." Alan stopped walking. "And fingerprints. Frankly, sir, I believe we must turn to the police. I can't see there's anything else to do. She isn't here. It's late. All this time lost. My men found Ambielli but—"

"Your men found!" As it penetrated, Salisbury was lifted to his feet. "But I begged of you."

"It was obvious to me that you were both nearly out of your minds, not, as you say, thinking straight."

"You had no business . . ." Salisbury cried. "Didn't you hear me beg of you?"

"I ought to have been told about this note, sir."

"I told you that *if* they communicated . . ."

"You didn't tell me anything."

"You didn't listen," Salisbury cried.

Alan looked hurt. "There is nothing to be so upset about," he soothed. "My people simply located the man. No harm. They found the room where he stays. They're quietly checking."

"No harm!" cried Salisbury. "*I* kept faith. But *you*, in my name, did not. It may be . . . It may be . . ."

"Not at all. Ambeilli doesn't know he is being watched."

"How can you be so sure? What if he does? What if he thinks I was not alone last night. Somebody followed me. What if he thinks I did *not* obey?" Salisbury heard himself bellow. "Don't you understand? *She isn't here.*"

Alan said, scornfully, "I can't believe—"

"Call your people off!"

"If you insist, sir." Alan was stiff. "But I think it's unnecessary . . . as a precaution. And I think we need to know more about Ambielli. Especially now. As you say, she isn't here."

CHAPTER XIII

SALISBURY dug his knuckles into the bones above his eyes. He looked at his wife's white head, which showed a faint shimmer of motion, a continuing tremor. He thought, she can't bear much more.

"This hint about Ambielli," said Alan, "is a fairly promising clue. The best we have until we find Lynch himself. I was bound to do what I thought was wise. For Katherine's sake. Yesterday you seemed completely paralyzed and helpless. If you had trusted me."

"I had," Salisbury mumbled. "Don't you see that I had?"

"These men are discreet. They've done this sort of thing. You just don't know, sir. I'll take the responsibilitiy."

Salisbury said, sharply, "You can't 'take the responsibility.' That's meaningless. That's a word. Done, now," he snapped. "Let's hope they are as discreet as you think. Can you reach them?"

"I can, shortly. That is, they know where I am. One of them will call. But I don't agree. We must go to the police, sir, and I think you must admit it. It's beyond you, sir. I'm sorry. That's the truth."

Salisbury thought with swift sick self-doubt, the boy is right. I suppose he is right.

"Not yet," Martha said softly. "It's barely time. It may be we aren't counting from the same beginning. Not yet. You see, if they—"

"Don't Martha."

"It doesn't make much difference," she murmured. "So just wait a little bit, a little longer." Martha got to her feet. She said in breaking tones, "Don't give up hoping. But I think I must go upstairs."

"Of course, darling," Salisbury felt relief. "Yes, do. It's best. Let me call Helen to be with you."

"Yes, call Helen. My nice maid, Alan. After a while, she can brush my hair."

Salisbury thought she was falling to pieces but then, looking into her face, he saw it was not so. It was only that she knew they would be stronger apart, just now. He could lean on her statement of hope. She on his. That was why she said, now, "When Katherine comes, Charles?"

And he answered, gravely, "I will call you."

When she had gone, Salisbury threw out of his mind the cluttering self-reproaches. He felt free to betray his panic, and therefore, in the moment, free of it. He said crisply, "As long as your men have been checking, what did they find?"

"I can tell you that soon, sir. They know where I am."

"And what about Lynch?"

"Nothing, yet. He is simply not around. And his car is gone. However—"

However, thought Salisbury. Katherine may be in the most terrible danger or all danger for her over forever. *However.* "Go on," he snapped.

Then the phone rang. Phinney's feet pattered in the foyer. Salisbury drew again that gasping breath.

"For Mr. Dulain."

"Yes, thank you." Alan strode. "This will be Warner."

Salisbury thought, I am wrong to go by the heart and the blood, which paralyzes. I was wrong to try to obey. You fight treachery with treachery, secrets with secrets, guile with guile. Maybe it's strength in the boy to worry at a crack in the mystery, to dare to try. I am old. I am ignorant. Too stiff. Too cautious.

Alan cried *"What!"* And his eyes turned in his startled face. Salisbury ran nearer, and to be running, in his own apartment, within these walls, on his own carpet, was in itself catastrophe. *"Ambielli's downstairs!"*

"What!"

"This is Warner. Says this Hohenbaum forced him to go to Ambielli and he—And now Ambielli wants to see *me!*"

"Tell him to come up . . . to come up . . ." Salisbury staggered.

"I don't underst . . ." Alan shook his head sharply. "Warner. Bring him up. Yes, both of them, then." Alan put the phone down. "This I can't . . . This I don't fit in."

"What does it mean? What does it mean?" Salisbury thought, things don't always fit. The world goes out of order.

"I don't know, sir."

Salisbury cried, "So Ambielli caught on to your man. Your discreet person."

Alan looked troubled. "But I don't understand."

"You . . . you . . ." Salisbury threw his hands up. "You expect a hired man to be a tool, infallible like a chisel that won't slip unless your hand slips. Your man, Warner, slipped, Alan. And what it's done to Kay!"

"It's done nothing," Alan said. "Ambielli hasn't got her. If he has, why would he come here? It's too bold. What could he gain?"

"If he has," Salisbury whimpered, "I must explain. Surely if I tell him, I kept faith. If I tell him to his face." His words were going as wild as his thoughts. God's mercy, he thought, Martha is lying down. "Mercy," he said aloud.

Alan said, pityingly, "Ambielli is not the type for mercy, sir. Don't tell him much of anything. I think I can cover up what you are afraid of. Let me talk to him alone."

"No. No. No."

"It will be easy enough to show that we didn't get onto him through the note, or anything that *you* did, sir. Let it be as it was. I never knew about the note. I've got suspicious of Ambielli in another way."

Salisbury took the brown paper and put it in his pocket. He felt dizzy. "Yes, all right," he said. He was old.

"You had nothing to do with my ideas."

"Yes. All right."

"Let me handle it. Watch him. See what you think. I don't believe he's got her. Because I cannot understand why he comes here. Yet, if he hasn't got her, it makes no sense, either."

Salisbury said, "I don't know. I don't know. It's not necessarily sensible." He reeled across the room and sat down and shielded his eyes. A wheel turned sluggishly in his head. "You can't tell him Lynch came here."

Alan moistened his lips. "Why not?"

"Don't you see? If this is the man . . . If Lynch was honest . . . If Lynch isn't dead already . . . You can't tell because then we would never find him." Salisbury felt frantic.

"Take it easy. Just—"

"I don't know," Salisbury said. "How can I know?" He thought, or you either. Blind ignorant, both of us.

But Alan had put on a foxy look, a narrowing and brightening of the eyes. "I think you're right. No use giving it away, that we know about Lynch. When we find Lynch and make him talk, that may give us some pressure on Ambielli. Only way to deal with his type, sir, is by some threat."

Salisbury thought, Katherine is ill, somewhere. That's all it is. We should check the hospitals once more.

"Also, these people are perfect cowards, as a rule," Alan said, "and one will rat on another."

Salisbury began to watch through his fingers for this Ambielli.

Downstairs, Warner was turning from the phone.

"Boss, I don't think it's so smart." Baby looked as if someone had taken his candy.

"No danger. Be quiet."

"Boss, they can't tell you something they don't know, can they? How can they?"

"Oh, I think they'll tell me," Ambielli said. "Just be quiet."

Upstairs, as Phinney let the three of them in, Salisbury saw that the first was a rather small man in a decent dark suit. The second was a huge man who planted himself within the room and continued to shift his weight from one leg to the other as if to sink those great thick limbs into the floor. Last, came a thin man with sparse hair and a shrewd face and this one spoke. "Dulain. Ambielli."

"Mr. Dulain?" The small man had a pleasant voice.

"Mr. Ambielli?" Alan held himself stiff and high and Salisbury thought, the little man's amused. "You wanted to see me?"

The little man ignored this. He looked down the distance to where Salisbury sat. "Our host?" he inquired softly.

"Mr. Salisbury knows nothing about this," said Alan haughtily. "I wish you had arranged to meet me in my office."

The huge man's weight seesawed. "The boss wants to see you," he growled. "You get seen."

"I came where you were," purred Ambielli.

Alan ignored the big man altogether. "Do you wish to speak to me privately?" he asked the little one.

"That isn't necessary." Ambielli sat down. The big man came and stood, uneasily, near and to the rear of his chair. The thin man, who must be Warner, seemed uneasy, too. No one was easy, except the small man with the tan face and the white eyelids, who sat in the chair.

"You wanted to see me?" Alan repeated.

"If there is anything you wish to know about me or my affairs, Mr. Dulain," said Ambielli in his soft voice, "I would suggest that you come to me directly. Baby, here, is very sensitive to indirection." Baby growled. "And I, myself, don't care for it. What was it you wanted to know?"

What he was saying, even the manner of saying it, seemed to Salisbury quite businesslike and clear. Quite orderly. The only odd thing about the little man was the big man.

"I wanted to know," said Alan, "where you were and what you were doing on Wednesday."

"Oh, yes," said Ambielli pleasantly. "So much I concluded. Now, if you ask me, I'll tell you. If you tell me this first. *Why do you ask?*"

It was clear to Salisbury that Alan wasn't handling anything. There was a dimension to this little man that Alan did not sense. Alan asked what he had to gain, but there were shadings, here, of pride, even of curiosity, that Alan left out. Alan was now hesitating, clearing his throat.

"Oh, come," said Ambielli. "Obviously, something happened on Wednesday in which you think I may have been concerned. Let's not waste time over the obvious. What happened, Dulain? And *why me?*"

"Yeah," the big man uttered his loyal growl, "what's the idea?" But Ambielli's hand stirred where it rested on the chair. The merest straightening of a bent knuckle, it was. But the growl died in the big man's throat.

This was, so far, the only odd thing.

Alan put his ankle on the other knee and both hands on the ankle and he tried to smile boyishly. "It seems, some months ago, there was a shooting," he began.

Salisbury thought, no, he can't do it. Not the casual relaxed stuff. Nor the silken threat. No, his picture of people, of other people, isn't thick enough.

"A man employed as a watchman by the Salisbury Biscuit Company was on duty near the scene," Alan went on.

"Oh, yes," said Ambeilli. "I see. You are speaking of the night *I* was shot. Go on."

"You remember?" Alan's eyes thought they were gimlets, and Salisbury felt embarrassed for him.

Ambeilli laughed. "Naturally, I remember." Salisbury still watching from beneath his hand, still at a loss to know what kind of creature this was, saw for the first time a wolfish

95

flash. "And by the way," said the little man in a pleasant gossipy manner, "I see where the same watchman was killed, only a few days ago."

Then he and Alan spoke exactly together. He said, "In an accident." Alan said, "In an accident?"

Ambielli smiled. "Why, I suppose it was an accident. Or so I read. Too bad. Of course, he was old."

The big man was stock still.

Salisbury thought. It must mean something. Why so still? It isn't evidence. It isn't anything. But why so still?

"I am wondering," said Alan loftily, "if someone who . . . resented the watchman, now carries a grudge against Mr. Salisbury."

"*This* Mr. Salisbury?"

It was too flip, too patronizing, too much of a sneer. Salisbury took his hand down. Didn't this man know so well which Mr. Salisbury that he made a mistake, here? Salisbury was tense, where he sat, and his eyes felt as if they were bulging as he sought an intuition of the truth. He croaked, "Obviously."

"I beg your pardon." The eyes flashed his way.

Salisbury said, "Lots of men have money. Did you choose me for such a fantastic reason?"

"I?" said Ambielli. His finger moved and the big man, growling as an animal might, obeyed, as a trained animal might have obeyed, and stopped growling.

"Well?" said Dulain.

Ambielli said, "What are you asking? Whether I have a grudge? It seems rather a thin notion." Alan looked stiff. "Not yours, Mr. Dulain? No, I see. Grudges." Ambielli shrugged. "Frankly, there was a time I may have felt angry with that watchman because he interfered. But such things don't last." Alan shook his own shoulders as the little man shrugged. "We recoup our losses and we move along. Stupid to dwell on such things too long. Don't you find it so?"

His eye shifted to Salisbury. It was cool and communicated nothing. Yet all this was too smooth, too obliging, even. There was a sneer in it somewhere. And something restless, some hunting thing, moved in this man. Salisbury cracked his fingers.

Alan looked stiff and was silent. Then, Warner, the thin one, said, "I can tell you what they were doing on Wednesday."

Ambielli said, "Perhaps it would save time for us all if you would. Do that."

"They went out on Long Island, around one thirty, with an agent in the agent's car. They spent the whole afternoon and up to eight P.M. looking at a piece of property. Roadhouse. The agent says so. The present owner, who was out there, too, he says so. Lawyer who met them there, three men working on the road, a cop who thought the place was closed and wanted to see did they have any right to be in there, all say so. I got dozens. They were there."

"It's solid?" frowned Alan.

"It's absolutely solid. They were there."

"This," said Ambielli thoughtfully, "was on Wednesday. What happened to Mr. Salisbury on Wednesday?" He really wanted to know. Salisbury was sure of it. This was a hungry curiosity, as if he *needed* to know.

"Then they couldn't . . . ? These men didn't . . . ? It isn't possible?" Salisbury blurted, his doubts churning.

"There is such a thing as hired help," said Alan Dulain. "Men of this type often arrange an alibi."

Ambielli looked much amused. "You've made a study," he mocked, "of my type?"

But Salisbury said brokenly, "Then you don't know where she is? If you do, please . . . I kept faith. If you do, then you must have the money. Why isn't she home? Why hasn't she come home? I don't care for anything but that. Let everything go. Just let her come home." (He thought to himself, what a pitiful old fool I sound!)

"Oh?" said Ambielli. "Someone is missing?"

"My daughter. My daughter. My daughter."

"You had a daughter?"

The verb, the tense of the verb, pierced Salisbury's breast and tore his heart.

"She was snatched, huh?" said Hohenbaum in what sounded like perfect amazement. Ambielli turned a trifle in the chair and looked at him. "What d'ya know?" said Baby. Ambielli smiled.

Alan got up. "All right. That's what happened. Wednesday. You're alibied. Solid." He tried to make it a threat. "Where were you *last night*, Ambielli?"

"I, Mr. Dulain?" said Ambielli. The threat went the wrong way. It was the little man who was dangerous.

"Warner, get hold of Reilly or somebody. Tell them to check on where these two were last night."

"It's very interesting," mocked Ambielli, "to see how your type works, Mr. Dulain. Now, what could have happened last night?"

He knows, thought Salisbury. Of course, he knows. But then, I told him. Is it this man? If it were, he knew all at once, there was no hope.

Alan was saying, "Was it *this* man? Was it Hohenbaum? Mr. Salisbury!" Salisbury came to attention. "Is this the man who took the money?"

Salisbury could not focus. "You had the impression that he was large," nagged Alan. Now he could see the pouting mouth, the red hurt baby face. He shook his head. "How about his voice?"

"It was falsetto," Salisbury said.

"Say something falsetto."

Baby Hohenbaum growled. "Huh?"

Ambielli began to shake with silent laughter.

"Like this." Alan squeaked.

Baby stared. "You go to hell," he said sullenly.

Ambielli wiped an eye with a finger. "Excuse me," he said, almost strangled by mirth.

Charles Salisbury turned his head. "You can sit in my house and laugh?" he said lightly.

"Excuse me." Ambielli repeated the words, but what he threw at Salisbury was not remorse and not apology. There was a thin edge on the words, a dangerous anger, like the cutting edge on a piece of steel, like a knife. And it cut. Salisbury suddenly saw the screaming core of this little man. The thing inside that cried, I do what I want. I laugh if I please. I . . . I . . . I . . . He thought, the man's a threat walking. He's like a bomb. *This is the man.*

"You haven't answered, sir. This is a large man," Alan fussed. "Even if you can't identify, could it have been Hohenbaum who robbed you?"

"I don't know," Salisbury said quietly, in quite a different voice, "whether it was. Yes, it could have been."

"Robbed you?" murmured Ambielli. "Interesting. Rather a clever method, eh?" He cocked his head. "Wasn't that in a book, Baby?"

"What book?" said Alan in flat surprise. Alan was lost.

"Yeah," said Baby. "I think it was, boss." The big shoulders were beginning to heave. But the finger quieted him.

"Why do you think she isn't here, since I paid?" Salisbury was able to speak quietly. His despair was quieter than his hope had been. (If it was this man, explosive, a thin shell of soft words around that brutal "I," then he had no hope.)

"I really couldn't say," Ambielli was pleasant. And aloof. "I know nothing about your daughter, Mr. Salisbury."

"We don't know nothing about it," chimed Baby Hohenbaum almost indignantly.

Warner came back from the phone. "Somebody will check. Office says Reilly is on his way up here." There was more he could say. His eyes rolled with secrets. Alan's eyes left his face uncertainly.

"Have you taken this to the police?" It was Ambielli, purring.

"No."

Ambielli's finger was up. "The money was, of course, marked?" Salisbury heard himself groan. Ambielli said, "Or recorded by number at least?" Nobody answered him. Ambielli clicked his tongue. "You should go to the police, you know." He sounded almost reproachful. But it was mockery.

Alan said, "We know."

"Then I shall expect them," Ambielli sighed. "All this will have to be repeated. All this nonsense . . ." the words began to bite suddenly, "about a grudge."

"I think you may expect the police," said Alan.

"To inquire? About a grudge?"

"To inquire. Whether you have Katherine Salisbury."

Ambielli smiled. "You ask me questions. But you pay no attention to the answers, Mr. Dulain."

"You haven't told me where you were last night."

Ambielli shrugged. "I was at home. Baby was with me." The growl began to come out of the big man. But Ambielli rose. "So you thought I might have had a grudge?" he said thoughtfully. "So you inquire. You must be desperate." The mahogany-colored eyes rested on Salisbury curiously. "She hasn't perhaps eloped? I see you don't think so." He kept a faint frown.

The phone rang.

It was for Alan, and he went to answer. Salisbury let his breath go. How long would he gasp and feel his heart stop at a bell? How long before the heart would agree with the brain that she'd never call?

Ambielli was standing, looking, listening. Hunting?

Alan put the phone down and Warner, who had been beside him, faded out of the foyer, somehow. He was, and then with no fuss he suddenly was not there. Alan came back into the long room and said briskly, "I think that is all, for now, Ambielli." He sounded like a man who had another appointment.

Hohenbaum was ready to be insulted at this dismissal, but Ambielli only smiled. "Any time. Anything I can do, any time, gentlemen." He seemed agreeable but in no hurry. "If you will only approach me directly. And perhaps, next time, at my office. I, by the way, am buying the property I so luckily and with so many witnesses went to see on Wednesday."

There was mockery in it, somehow. "If you . . ."

Salisbury choked on the threat. What could he threaten? They had learned nothing, for sure. There was no proof.

"Yes, Mr. Salisbury?" The threat reversed. The little man stood with his head turned over his shoulder.

"If you are behind . . ."

"Behind whom?" The vowel in the pronoun vibrated and sang.

Salisbury shook his head helplessly.

Alan licked his lip and said, "Just a minute . . ."

"Yes?"

"Let him go," croaked Salisbury. "Let him leave here." He thought in a moment he would attack that insolence bodily.

Alan said, "We'll go to the police, you know." He sounded feeble. "You don't mind?" It wasn't even a threat. It was nothing at all. Unless it was delay.

But Ambielli did not delay. He began to walk toward the foyer, not looking back, and Baby followed. Phinney was ready to let him out the door. Alan licked his lip again. "Wait!"

And Ambielli flashed around to face him and said, sharply and shockingly, "Do you know Sam Lynch?"

But the shock came a little late. There was only the shortest interval for him to examine the flavor of their surprise. On top of his words, from the inside door to the foyer, Sam Lynch walked in.

He stopped in his tracks. "Well," he said, "Boss? Fancy meeting you here?"

Ambielli's head was lowered and his eyes, directed upward, were turned high in their sockets. His hand moved freezing the big animal beside him who had begun to swell. Ambielli drawled, "Fancy?"

The cold went down Sam's spine. His head swiveled as Ambielli walked by. Baby walked by. They went out the door. Reilly, who had come in the back way behind Sam, said, astonished, "Hey, was that *Ambielli?* Up *here?* What for?"

"To ask," muttered Sam.

"To answer," Alan snapped.

"Bet my life," Sam said.

CHAPTER XIV

SAM sat down.

He had the impression that Alan Dulain was barking at him, and then barking at this man Reilly, and at somebody else who was there. There was a general sense of barking and confusion, but all he could think about was the fact that he was marked to die.

He thought, it couldn't have worked out more disastrously if it had been planned this way. He thought, this Warner who had let them in the kitchen should have mentioned who was there. Probably it was planned this way.

As he had said to the girl, "Ambielli's got principles. They are a little off, slightly out of whack, you know. But he's got them. He'd kill me just for telling. There's a kind of cockeyed point of honor mixed up in that. For this, for you and me out here, he'd kill me. And no question. But not until he is sure. It's a little cockeyed, but he's got his reputation. He'll take care to discipline the proper party. It's beneath his dignity to make a mistake, and a man like Ambielli has got his dignity. A little out of whack, maybe, but it counts. It operates."

He said to himself, "That's torn it." Ambielli would be sure, after this.

When he had wakened, around midnight, Friday, he had felt like blushing for the stuff he'd let fall out of his mouth. Talked like a drunk, he'd thought. The girl had fallen asleep, a warm little heap on the other bunk. He'd felt meltingly tender toward her and that was embarrassing. He'd blown the lamp out.

All was so still. He'd done a reckless thing, to go to sleep. But no one had come. She was safe. He'd drowsed in the dark, smiling over her safety, which was his secret. He'd slept again.

Not until the light of Saturday were they awake at the same time. When she told him what she'd been thinking Sam listened. He narrowed his eyes and hardened his face, because she was so pinkly and warmly rumpled with sleeping and he got the melting feeling again.

He'd agreed. Sure. It was reasonable. More or less disguised as she was, she did have a better chance of getting home without Sam. "That's if you believe there's a big bad wolf. I've got a feeling you do, now."

She said, "Unless I believe it, I can't understand you."

"Can you understand me?" he'd teased. She nodded, and he'd felt his heart curl. "That's more than *I* can say." He'd grinned at her. "I guess you're right, sister. I'm poison to you."

Of all things, she'd said, "I'm sorry."

He went out and put the coffee on. He shaved. They ate. After a while, she'd said, "When may I go, Sam? Now?"

So he told her. She was right, all right. But he said, "Don't you see I feel like I'm deaf and blind? A man like me, locked up out here, Thursday, Friday, and no news. It's driving me crazy. I didn't dare leave you. Now, though, if Ambielli knew about this place, he'd have been here by now. Or so I judge. I'll have to go by myself, first."

Oh, she'd wept and she'd howled. He'd said, "No. I've got to look around. I can't send you by yourself when I'm deaf and I'm blind. And I don't know what's happening or what you're walking into. Now quit that. I can't do it. Listen, I stuck my neck out so Ambielli wouldn't get you. That much I'm not going to undo. I should die for nothing?"

"Oh, Sam."

"All right. You're right. The way it is, either one of us is safer alone." Then, he'd said all that about Ambielli's principles.

But she'd wept and she'd howled. Finally, he'd put her aside and got out the door and locked it against her. And listened to her howl.

He was sorry. But it was the only thing he could do. She couldn't get out, he knew. So, in case he never got back to let her out, he'd put the second key to the door and a note saying what it was down in the coffee can. Where she'd get to it in time. Down under the coffee. It was the best he could do. He was no man of action, no hero. He was a man, though, who had to know. Couldn't stand this blind stuff any longer.

Couldn't send her walking out into Ambielli's arms. Come back with the cops if he had to, he thought. But maybe he wouldn't have to. It was an awful slippery world. All kinds of things kept happening. And he'd had no news. Ambielli could be lying in the morgue, for all he knew. Sooner or later, Ambielli was going to go to work on disciplining Emanuel, and one of them would end up in the morgue. Who could tell? Who could tell, from here? He had to know.

So, he took his car out of the shelter, a roof with legs was all it was and took the run up the rutted place dug in the slope. It was a leafy green morning with spots like golden dollars dancing on the ground.

No one would hear her howling. It was April. The lake cabins were empty. The weather was chancy. It was a gamble. He was trying to get away from doom. Any gamble was a good gamble. Any gamble at all. He jumped into the soup and he was a fallen fly in the soup but he was bound to struggle.

Sitting in Salisbury's chair, Sam thought, now, it had not been very heroic. Heroes didn't act like flies. Were supposed to walk up to doom and look it in the eye. He thought, well, I got a good view, now.

He'd made it to his place, all right, all the way down through the city that was so beautiful in the morning. His rooms were flat and stale and strange. He didn't know why he'd come there. But he went to the trouble of borrowing a gun from a friend of his on the top floor. George didn't know, yet, he'd loaned it. The gun was in Sam's pocket. Much good it would be. Sam was no marksman.

Then he'd mooched around. Listening. This Reilly approached him in Nick's. What a waster of histrionics, all that scene. Sam playing so innocent, playing so baffled. Why should he talk to Alan Dulain? Why should he go to this uptown place? Then, Sam playing his curiosity was getting the better of him. That was in character. Such a good touch. Sam had been pretty proud of his act. And he wanted to see Dulain, at the Salisburys', where he'd be at the heart of it, and deaf and blind no longer. So, he played letting curiosity get the better of him. He figured it was a gamble. Nick might not tell. Any gamble was a good one.

Flies in the soup probably kid themselves they'll make it.

He'd thought, better to be dragged there than be seen going under his own steam. He'd thought to judge on the spot whether he'd have to tell them where she was.

Well, now he knew. He'd have to tell. So much was settled. And he was going to die. Oh, they'd fetch her home, all right, and that part was a relief.

But Sam didn't want to die. He wanted to stick around. He didn't want to leave the show. It was so damned marvelous, he didn't want to be deaf and blind and know no news forever. He sat in the chair, looking at the floor. Even the threads in the carpet were marvelous, marvelous.

But he knew he'd have to tell where she was and they'd go fuming out there, making noises, and *she'd* be okay. But Sam would die. They couldn't get Ambielli for anything. Ambielli hadn't done anything. How could they?

Maybe Sam Lynch would walk in terror a little while. That would be all. Ambielli had his reputation and he was raw and touchy and Ambielli wouldn't skip it or laugh it off. He couldn't. Sam couldn't expect it.

If these people would keep Sam Lynch covered but they wouldn't. Couldn't. He didn't expect that of Alan Dulain. Or of that poor father. He knew *they* weren't going to figure him for any hero. No, he couldn't expect it. For a minute, he thought, wait. They *could* lock him up. And they'd probably be glad to. Put Sam Lynch in a nice safe cell. They'd be justified. They'd have a right.

He didn't think he'd make it, that far, probably.

He stared at his shoes. How marvelous were shoes! What a thing! How cunningly the human race knew how to clothe the human foot. What a device!

He realized that Alan Dulain was shaking him by the shoulder and yelling in his ear, "Where is Katherine Salisbury?"

"Isn't she here?" Sam said stupidly. He had to have a little time, a few more minutes. Everything was so marvelous. *She* was safe. Ambielli wasn't going out there to get her. Ambielli was busy, downstairs waiting for Sam.

"You know damn well she isn't here. You knew it before it happened."

Sam did not care for this Dulain. His brow lifted. "You mean to say she's been kidnaped?" he drawled.

"What do you know about it? You'll talk, Lynch."

"Last time I talked, you took very little stock in what I had to say."

"You'll talk this time. The whole truth this time." The blond boy's face was pinched with rage.

Salisbury, her old man, said, "Don't do that, Alan. Lynch, you will tell us? I believe you meant to tell us before. Tell us now."

Sam opened his mouth to tell. He said, instead, "What were you folks telling Ambielli?" He was looking for a loophole. He didn't want to die.

"None of your concern," said Dulain.

"Oh, brother." Sam sank in the chair, "No? You think so?"

He heard Salisbury groan. "So it was Ambielli you heard that day?" cried Dulain. "So that's going to be your story? Well, it won't wash. You slipped. I thought something would slip if I let the two of you meet. You're in this, Lynch. I always knew it."

"Take your hand off my shoulder," Sam said. "Take your hand off. That's better. Now, what is this?" He pulled himself together to pay attention.

Dulain was burning up. "You're working for Ambielli. You did the dirty work. While he fixed his alibi."

"Ambielli's got an alibi, eh? Good one?"

"A dandy," Warner said.

"You checked it, Warner?"

"Yeah, Sam."

Alan swung around to Reilly. "Where did you pick Lynch up?"

"Saw him go into his place." Reilly shrugged. "He came back, that's all."

"Where were you?"

"Out of town," said Sam. His black eyes took in this Dulain. Really in a tizzy. Katherine Salisbury was going to marry this Dulain. He asked himself with surprise, why should he die for Katherine Salisbury?

"What's *your* alibi?" Dulain was shouting.

"For when, bub?"

"For Wednesday. She went out of here when you did."

"Is that so?" Sam looked stupid.

"Where did you go?"

"I went out of town," said Sam irritably. "Wait a minute, will you? I'm trying to think." In the back of his mind a new fear was boiling up. Once he was dead . . . He felt sick. Ambielli wasn't just going to quit, was he? It was like a guy dying before the war was won, and nobody else in the army. He didn't trust *them* to know what to do.

"Think," said her old man. "Can you help us?"

Sam thought, I can help you, Pop, but who can help me? And if you don't, who will help her and keep her from Ambielli? "What did Ambielli say? What was *said?*" he demanded.

Dulain made a gesture of impatient disgust but the father began to tell him. "Alan said he had remembered about that watchman and that Ambielli might have had a grudge . . ."

His eyes, thought Sam, were a little like the girl's eyes, the same earnest honesty. "You thought Ambielli would take that?" he said aloud. "Naw, it was a silly idea. Why did you tell him that?" Sam looked at Dulain with curiosity. "What got into you, to cover me?"

"I wasn't covering you. I was trying to cover Mr. Salisbury."

"I didn't think you'd be interested in covering me."

"I'm not," said Dulain. "I don't give a damn what happens to you. I want Katherine."

"I hope you do," muttered Sam. "I hope to God you do."

"I'll get you for this, Lynch, if it's the last thing—"

The father said, "Wait. Listen, Lynch. It was because . . ." He took a piece of brown paper out of his pocket.

"Out of town!" said Dulain furiously. "Are we to take that from you?" He snatched the paper. "Give him a pencil," he commanded. "Now, Lynch. Print what I dictate."

"You going to dictate, boy?"

"I am and you'll print."

"Why?"

"Never mind. Print."

Sam said, "What is this?"

"Print it. 'Take the first left after the third traffic light. Go west three quarters of a mile to iron fence.'"

Sam's damp fingers slipped on the pencil. He felt a grin begin to form on his face, a battered thing. Then he put his tongue out of the corner of his mouth and began to print laboriously.

Reilly was looking over Dulain's shoulder at the brown paper. "Oh, oh," he said.

"Am I perchance printing part of a ransom note? Perchance?" Sam saw Salisbury's hand over his eyes. "Continue," said Sam, cutting the comedy. "Sorry, Pop."

"The way that's done," Reilly said in a low voice, sounding troubled, "you can't tell. It's a trick. You take cardboard. You cut a square hole. Every letter is drawn square with a guide, see. How about fingerprints?"

"Have it tested," Alan snapped.

"Better have it tested," drawled Sam, "in case this fellow never read a book or went to the movies. Maybe he can write but he can't read. Say, tell me, when did this show up?" Sam's fingers were spread. The yellow pencil jiggled in the press of his thumb against his palm. Marvelous, he thought. A pencil! What a thing! What a device!

"Thursday," Salisbury said tensely. "Eighteen hours are long gone. Why isn't she home? Can you explain it?"

"You mean!" Sam exploded. "Don't tell me you've paid!"

"I . . . thought I did."

"Don't keep telling *him*—" began Alan.

"I want to listen to this, sunshine," snarled Sam. "Shut up a minute. Get out of the way."

Salisbury told him and Sam leaned back. He let the chair take him. He closed his eyes. He thought, oh, this is marvelous!

He said, "Was there anything from her? Surely you didn't pay off without some sign?"

"They sent her scarf."

Sam looked at it. He said, "Mulberry, eh?" in an odd tone. "Pretty exclusive, I guess. That pattern."

"What?"

"You shouldn't have paid off. You should have gone to the cops. You know that."

"*I* knew that," Alan said.

Salisbury's haunted eyes met Sam's. Sam saw the hurt and looked away. "You should have figured it for murder, sir," he said somberly. "From the very beginning. From the first word. Well, down the drain." He jiggled the pencil. "When did they say she'd be back?"

"By now. An hour ago." The old man was steady. "Why isn't she back, Mr. Lynch?"

Sam answered mechanically, "Don't be too sure. There could be a hitch somewhere. Things don't always go in order. It's a slippery world."

He was thinking. That fox! That Ambielli! Must have been hanging around, ready to pick her up, maybe on Thursday. She doesn't show. So, he snoops. They let it out. Maybe the servants. Let it out she was missing. Or, calling hospitals, they let it out. Or asking questions. Lots of ways Ambielli could catch on she was gone.

Ambielli must have been burning. Somebody hijacks his prey. So, he steps in. *He* hijacks the money. Oh, oh, it was

109

marvelous! A world such things could happen in, you wouldn't want to leave.

And now, Ambielli had the money, and what did he care where the girl was? She'd been no trouble to him, no groceries for Baby to buy, never a face of theirs to see. She was no danger to them at all, and Ambielli didn't want her any more. Wouldn't want anything to do with her. All he cared, now, was to discipline Sam Lynch. *If* Sam was the one. *If* he got sure.

But, Sam thought with growing excitement, anyhow *she* was safe and she could get home by herself easily, now. And she might even . . . the girl, herself . . . oh, she would if she could . . . little sister with the gray eyes . . . she'd even said so . . . *she'd* protect Sam Lunch!

Then he wouldn't have to die!

If he could make it back out there, let her go, tell her what to say. Tell her she never saw any faces. The ransom was paid, and she was released. Simple as that. Or she could even give a partial description, not possibly Sam Lynch. Some way to cover. Some way. Maybe it would work.

In fact, Sam *had* done the dirty work and Ambielli had his profits, safely, and he had an alibi, a dandy, they said. Sam thought, I could even get Ambielli to buy that. But he thought, No. There's his reputation. What else was he up here for, if not to see what he could find out about who did this to him? He got the money. Used *my* method. Of course, he's got it. So he wasn't up here for profit, but for his dignity. He came to find out. And he did find out. Or, did he?

Maybe there was still a chance, if he could get out there to the shack alive and stay alive until she came home and told the story. Dulain would never do it, never cover him. (Don't tell. Don't tell. Death to tell.) See if he could get to her alive. Little sis Salisbury with the crooked tooth, she had heart enough and little enough sense to do it for him. At least, he thought, she'd listen.

He said aloud, "Did you speak my name?" Nobody answered. He looked at Warner. "You were here, Joe?"

"Yeah, Sam."

"*Did* they?"

"Ambielli did, Sam."

"But *they* didn't? *You* didn't?"

"Just then, you came in."

"Oh. Did Ambielli have a car?"

"Him and Baby rode up with me."

"Oh." Sam thought, but they'll get a car. Have one by now.

Alan was listening, his ears almost pointed. Not really listening, Sam thought bitterly, but waiting to hear what he expects to hear.

He heard Salisbury say, quietly, "Is there any way you can help us?"

"Maybe so," Sam said.

"Help *us!*" burst Dulain. "He knows all about it. He's in it. Don't you get that? He's trying to figure how to shake you down a little more. He . . ."

"Alan, this time I'm going to assume Lynch is a decent—"

"Then you're a fool, sir. He is not decent. He is on the wrong side of this somehow. Why do you spill everything you know to *him?* Everyone's telling *him?* But he hasn't told us one thing. Not one thing. I can't understand."

"Boy," said Sam, "that's the truth." He looked at his shoes. He thought, and why should I die for Katherine Dulain?

"If he can help . . ." the old man argued.

"Don't listen to him, sir. We'll get help. He'll try to talk you out of going to the police. His type never wants authority in on it. He'll be mysterious. A phony like this! It'll be agony, sir. And more money, no doubt. And all the while, you know quite well, she may not even be alive."

The father knew it quite well, Sam saw. Sam said, angrily, "That's right, Dulain. For all *you* ever listened or did about it, she could be dead."

"You—"

"There are wolves in the woods," raved Sam, "that ain't been rehabilitated yet. But when I come crying wolf, you say, '*I* can't understand this kid's motive, so he must be a liar.' And if Alan Dulain can't understand it, it can't be human. Aw, you're so damn silly. Why didn't you call your police on Wednesday?"

"Why didn't *you?*" spat Dulain.

"Because I was scared. But you got nothing to be scared of, a hero like you. Go ahead. Call them now. Sic them on Ambielli, why don't you? Go ahead. Do that. Do something useful." Sam ground his teeth. "Call them *now.*"

"Will you swear," said Dulain craftily, "that it was Ambielli you overheard plotting—"

"I can't quote him," Sam said through his teeth, "for God's sake, he didn't *say.*"

"Then how can I sic the police on him?"

"You won't do it? Just do it, right now? Just for the hell of it? You're going to debate, boy?"

"If you don't tell . . ." Alan shrugged. "What have I got? You said yourself the grudge idea was silly."

Sam said, "Yeah, it was silly. Never mind."

The question churned in his mind. How get Ambielli? For extortion, or whatever it would be called? For the taking of the money, which was a crime, and Ambielli had done it. This Sam *knew*. But how could he tell? "Because I told him a little plot," he would say, "and the little plot was used." It was a long way from proof. A long, long way. He could hear the sarcasm. "Now, Mr. Lynch, you contend that you and only you in all life and time could think up such a little plot? Do you mean to say, Mr. Lynch, that in—how many?—years you never mentioned it to another soul but Mr. Ambielli?" Sam groaned. Laughter in the courtroom.

Then, get Ambielli for the murder of the watchman? That was a crime, and Ambielli had done it. And Sam *knew*. And knew by nothing but the intuition, without evidence or witness or clue.

All right, get him for kidnaping? Which was a crime. Oh yes. *But Ambielli hadn't done it.* Sam's eyes felt hot and the lids dry.

"Do you think," he heard the father say, "that Katherine is alive?"

Sam pulled himself together. "I'll find out for you," he said carefully. "If you'll let me go. I've got contacts. Dulain knows my reputation. Think it over. Meantime, where is there a bathroom?"

"Phinney," called Alan, "will you show Mr. Lynch?"

"Thanks," snarled Sam, "for understanding." He thought, wants to confer. Glad to get me out of the room. Going to debate a while.

He closed the door of this bathroom. The window was not transparent. No way he could be seen, as he wrote on a page out of his notebook, wrote it down boldly. Exactly where she was and how to get there. Housekeeping in this air castle was perfect. Everything was spotless. It couldn't be long before one servant or another would be cleaning around in here. He put the piece of paper under a box of medicine in the cabinet. He thought if he made it to her, he could warn her to destroy this note. He thought, if I don't make it, and I'm dead, they'll find this pretty soon. Or she'll be into the coffee can.

He thought, I'm a great one to leave little notes around. Got a lot of faith in the written word. Naturally.

He began to think again of the fly in the soup. All the little fly could do was beat his wings. Some flies got out, though. Some of them made it. If they hadn't got their wings too sticky. He thought, I never saw a fly who wouldn't try.

CHAPTER XV

HE unlocked the door and came out. There had been some kind of flurry. He could sense the trailing eddies in the air out here, the settling of the dust. The stalky little operative, Reilly, was gone.

He said, irritably, "Well? Do I leave? Or you want to burn the soles of my feet or something?"

"You may go," Dulain said.

"You been on the phone, boy?" Sam wanted a few more minutes. He didn't feel ready. Besides, his demon was on him. He wanted to know why they let him go. "What's on your mind?" he asked.

"Charles?" All their faces tilted to look up and Martha Salisbury looked down. Then she saw Sam Lynch, and she came down the rest of the way and walked across the room to him. He had forgotten about her. If he'd thought to wonder where she was, he'd have guessed they kept her drugged someplace, some dim luxurious quiet place where Martha Salisbury could lie safe in a dream.

But here she was, and her small feet came marching. She said, "Oh, Mr. Lynch, I am so glad you are here at last." Her voice was all right. And he saw that her pretty doll face had fallen tight to the bone but she was not doped. Her eyes were all right.

He hadn't reckoned with her.

She said, "Do you know where Katherine can be?" She asked him, respectfully.

He mumbled, "Ma'am, I'm going to try . . ." He left it hanging. He was ashamed. He thought, I didn't give her enough respect. I should have respected her.

Salisbury was swiftly at her side. "Lynch thinks he can help, darling. He thinks there could have been a little hitch. Things don't always go by the strict hour, so he says . . ."

But the little doll lady wasn't having any. She said to Sam

115

Lynch, "I've been thinking about it." She spoke to him as if only he and she were grown up. She said, "People who would do such a thing as this, wouldn't honor a promise. Or I shouldn't think so."

"It . . . it depends, ma'am. Some kinds of promises . . ." He was evading. He hadn't reckoned with her and he didn't want to. "There are different circumstances. It's hard to say. Can't be sure."

"But isn't it true that the safest thing for them would be to kill her?"

"Ah, Martha." Salisbury was dismayed.

"When I think about it, Charles," she said, "that seems so plain. Maybe Mr. Lynch, who knows more than I, can show me I'm mistaken."

Sam said, respectfully, "Yes, it's dangerous to them for her to stay alive. She may see too much. You've thought that out, ma'am. But it is also a pretty terrible danger the other way. Once you were sure she was never coming back, you'd move heaven and earth." Salisbury's eyes glittered. But Sam had to go on. He couldn't leave it hanging. "Still, you'll do that either way."

She said, "So I was thinking." She threw her white head back. "Ought we to be sure she is never coming back? Is it time?" And she stood there, and he was to answer.

"Oh, no, no, no," Sam couldn't help it. He touched her shoulder. He said, "Don't be sure, yet, ma'am. Don't hurt yourself with that. Try not—"

She wrenched away and picked up the mulberry scarf. "But this silk. It's not alive, Mr. Lynch. I wish I could tell you how I know. It just isn't Kay. She's flesh and life. This silk is dead."

"Martha. Martha."

"Yes, Charles. Yes, all right."

If you took the words, they didn't mean anything. They sounded mad. But Sam knew what it was about the scarf, and his heart hurt for this little lady who had turned out to be as tough and marvelous as this. He said, almost stammering, "I think she's all right, ma'am."

"You know more than we?" Oh, she put it right up to him.

"I don't suppose she's so happy," Sam said as lightly as he could, "but I don't think she's hurt at all. I think she'll be home."

She said, "Thank you." Her eyes didn't leave his face.

"Ah, darling, sit down."

"Yes, Charles. *Will it be long?*" She was asking *Sam*. He was supposed to *answer. He must have told her.*

"I don't know," Sam said in a panic. "I couldn't say. I really don't know."

He knew without looking what Dulain wore on his face, the smirk, the just-as-I-thought-all-along expression, the big ha-ha. Dulain said, "You're a liar."

Sam said, "Uh-huh." He was very tired. He thought, well, this tore it. "You haven't got a lot of tact, Dulain. But you're right, as usual. I am a liar." He put his hands in his hair.

CHAPTER XVI

The Salisburys were silent.

"You are Ambielli's man," Alan said.

"No."

"You're a liar. 'Boss,' you called him."

"Slip of the tongue. Courtesy," said Sam bitterly. "That's a word, boy. Arrest me. Call a flock of cops. Call for the wagon. Oblige me. Please."

But now Alan drew back. "Why?"

"Why not, for God's sake? I'm a phony. I'm a crook. I'm a kidnaper."

"Then Ambielli's got her and you—"

"No. That's not what I said."

"You're a liar."

Sam said, "Go up to Shawpen Lake. I've got a shack up there. That's where she is."

Salisbury jumped up but his hand was in his wife's hand holding tight.

"Who's got her there?" Dulain demanded.

"I have."

Martha sat still but the men made a hostile phalanx. Alan said, "Who's on guard?"

"Nobody."

"You're a liar." Alan snarled. "That's impossible. Wait a minute."

Sam looked down at his shoes. He knew their voices were crossing and clashing over his head but he stopped hearing the words. He thought, so I get to be a hero. I trip myself to glory. He had to grin.

Martha was still sitting there holding that scarf. But Salisbury was shaking him and shouting, "Take me there. Take me there. Right now."

Sam roused. "You can find it," he said almost indifferently.

"No, no, take me there. Now. Quick."

"You want to live, don't you?"

"What?"

"Better not ride with me."

"He'll take us there," Alan cried.

Sam lifted a brow. "What makes you think so? I told you. You're a big boy. You go."

"It's a trick!" Alan was furious.

Sam hoisted himself up. "It's a *what?*"

"You're a liar."

"For Christ's sake!"

"You're working for Ambielli. This is only a trick."

"Yeah? You think so?" Sam felt his eyes glazing.

"Why do you want us up in the country? What's that going to do for you?"

"Not a damn thing. Unless it gets me killed."

"Who's going to kill you?"

"The boss," Sam said.

"Then this is a double cross."

"Not exactly."

"Who got the money?"

"Ambielli."

Alan said, "You make no sense."

"How true," said Sam. "How right you are. You're often right, Dulain. Better get going, somebody." He leaned back.

"And where will you be?"

"In jail, I hope. Please?"

"Salisbury money. False arrest."

"Drop it, Alan," Salisbury said. "Hurry."

"But wait a minute, sir. Don't fall for this. He must have something rigged."

"That would be my type?" said Sam.

"Katherine," the father cried. "I'm going after Katherine."

"Wait."

Sam said, "Yeah. Wait. Don't forget to put me away. Call the cops, one of you."

"Time enough," said Dulain, looking sly, "when there is more evidence than your word."

"The time is now," Sam said in alarm. "I confessed, didn't I? You got witnesses."

Dulain frowned. "You admit you took her?"

"I *admit.*" Sam said. "I *told* you." He looked up. He felt like laughing. He said, "Wolf. Wolf." It sounded like woof, woof, like an imitation of barking.

Alan lifted his chin and a new expression formed on his sharp face. Pity? Sam watched, warily. Alan came nearer, looking down. *Looking down.* He put his hand on Sam's arm, in pity. He said, "Tell me about it, Sam. I'd like to understand. What was in your heart?"

Sam sat still and watched the hand, the clean square cut fingernails. His lips twisted. "Guess."

"You were married once, weren't you, Sam? Did you ever have a child? Does Kay remind you . . . ? Is there some frustrated . . . ?"

Sam pulled his sleeve out from under the hand. His black eyes were blazing. He said, "Guess again. Just keep guessing. If you never listen, you'll never know. You'll always have to guess."

Alan said slyly, "Why should you be angry? Because you couldn't fool me?"

Sam said, "You're not a hard man to fool, Dulain, with your system. Whatever isn't clear to you, why, that's crazy." He got up. "Hey, you, Warner? You going to turn me in?"

Warner looked at Dulain who shook his head. "Later", Warner said.

"Might as well be going," Sam mumbled. "Might as well mosey along. Don't know what I'm waiting for."

"This place. This lake." Salisbury understood nothing, nor did he necessarily believe in her presence at this place. There was no order to his thinking. He was going to ride on the mere hint, the mere chance. "How do you get to Shawpen Lake?"

"Highway 6," Sam said. "Look at the map."

Dulain said, haughtily, "We'll get there."

"I'm sure. Well, so long." Sam moved his head as if to bid them all good-by but he was blind. "And if I don't see you all again," he murmured, "it's been marvelous."

"You'll see us," Alan said. He heard the lady say, "Good-by."

The door shut. Salisbury cried, "Alan, where's your car?" He was locked in the present tense. He was going only one way, after Katherine.

Alan snapped, "Warner, get going. Catch Reilly if you can. Follow Lynch."

"I can try," said Warner, "if Reilly ain't gone already."

"Call back here."

"Okay."

"Where Lynch goes, *I* think that's where she'll be."

Salisbury was caught for a moment by this idea. He hesitated. He swung back to the urgency of his simple present purpose. He began to grope in the closet. "I'm going to that lake."

"I, too," said Alan. "Naturally. We'll call back, too. But if it's a trick. It's almost got to be a trick."

Martha cried, "Charles!" and she was pointing. "What's that?" Salisbury looked down to see what it was that had fallen to the floor.

It was a scarf.

Martha came quickly and snatched it up. All their eyes traveled back to where the other scarf still lay on the sofa.

"Another scarf?" Alan looked blank. "Whose scarf is this one?"

Martha had her face in this one, the one from the closet. "*This* one is hers." Salisbury knew. (This one would carry her scent. It would smell of her living flesh.) "What . . . what does it mean?"

Alan's face was white with anger. "Lynch knew that other scarf was a phony. He let that slip! There's been some monkey business, and he knows what. He knows too damn much he doesn't tell. I don't believe a word out of him. He couldn't say a straightforward—"

Martha said to her husband, "Hurry."

He spoke to her as if she were grown up. "You'll take any message?"

"Yes. I'll be here."

"Call the Police Department."

"Yes, Charles."

"Tell them everything."

"Yes, Charles."

"Don't tie up this line," Alan said.

"No, Alan."

"We'll call you."

"Yes, call me."

Salisbury touched her arm. "You believe Lynch?"

"I do believe she is living," Martha said.

In the tangled city the traffic moved—trucks, taxis, busses, some private cars.

Sam stepped out of the stone doorway of the apartment house. It was half a block to his car. Well, he would get there or he wouldn't. He didn't even look, right or left. One foot fell after another and each fall surprised and even shocked him. He got into his car. It jumped under his shocked hands and feet.

Warner raced down the back way, stepped out into the side street, hurried to Reilly in the car, caught the door as the car jumped from the curb.

Still a third car, which was double parked to observe both exits, now jumped, too.

Traffic swarmed.

Sam thought, now? No. Now? No. Now? He knew there was a car after him. He went west and north and west again.

Warner said, "Take it easy."

Reilly said, "Don't kid yourself. It ain't easy." They were absorbed, and did not look behind.

Behind, Baby said, "When do we close in, boss?"

Ambielli, skillful at the wheel of the stolen car, said, "When we are alone." He was frowning.

Baby growled. The boss said, soothingly, "We can arrange to be alone."

Martha telephoned. She said crisply, "I must not tie up this telephone. Will you send someone here to talk to me?"

Sam thought, not yet? He dared to try a trick or two. But he thought it was a silly idea. He'd never shake them.

Baby said, "He's trying to shake them, boss."

Ambielli gnawed his lip.

"He ain't heading for that lake, boss."

"If he could shake them, he might."

"Has he got her up there, boss?"

"Possibly," said Ambielli. But he kept frowning.

CHAPTER XVII

THERE is only so much weeping and wailing you can do, Katherine discovered, all alone. When there is no one to listen to it, you can cry only so long before it gets silly.

She turned the energy of her anger at Sam against the shack. She would get out. She was young and strong and this place couldn't hold her. Not if she used all her strength and all her anger. Such a thing as imprisonment, the physical fact, had never happened to her. She couldn't believe in it.

The door, she found, was heavy and strong and the lock was one she didn't understand. Some kind of double bolt. She broke a kitchen knife trying to slide the bolts back, and the flying steel, she realized, was dangerous. She thought of the pins in the hinges but they were on the outside. She soon concluded that she could not get out through that door.

The windows were boarded over, and the boards nailed from outside. She got a sash up but there was nothing to use against the wooden barrier. She tried battering with the chair. Nothing happened. She could get no leverage to pry. She had nothing to use that was both thin and strong. She hacked with a kitchen knife but the wood was tough. She might whittle at a seam enough to make a peephole, no more.

Glass in the high slits across the back of the shack could be easily broken out. But she could not pass through an opening eight inches high.

She attacked the walls themselves. It was the same thing. No weapon. No tool. She knew there must have been an ax, or at least a hatchet somewhere here. If so, it was gone. The hammer was gone. He'd taken them away. He'd put the tools outside the walls where she couldn't get them.

He was a monster!

There was no chimney. She couldn't crawl through the hole where the stove pipe pierced the roof.

The roof?

She couldn't get out through the roof. Her hands were full of splinters and pain. Sam Lynch was a monster!

It was all a monstrous madness. There was no Ambielli. There was no wolf. There was only a madman called Sam Lynch who didn't know what he was doing, and far from keeping her safe, everything bad that had happened was his doing. She thought, what a fool! What a romantic little fool I am! If I ever get out . . . !

But she couldn't get out.

It was terrifying. She thought, first, of fire. She'd burn! She crept to look into the iron stove. But the iron gadget for lifting the lid was gone.

He's a monster! she raged. I'll freeze!

Or she'd starve! Her teeth chattered and she had to talk herself out of a real panic.

Katherine, listen. There's food in the kitchen, water in the tap. She wouldn't starve or die of thirst. She wouldn't freeze, not in April. Blankets on the bunks. She wouldn't burn, because she couldn't feed the stove, and the fire in it was dying. She wouldn't touch the kerosene cook stove in the kitchen.

Maybe someone would come by. She could watch. She curled up near a window and peered through the cracks between the boards. She could see leaves and more leaves and a little of the incline that fell dizzily down the bank. The road, such as it might be, must run high above where she was. She couldn't even see it.

Maybe she could hear. The woodsy place was at first too quiet. It became an uproar of scary, unrecognizable little skittering noises, scrapings, creaks, rustles. Snakes? Even a snake couldn't get in to this prison, she hoped.

She couldn't get out.

Sam would come back. He would. He must. He wasn't that much of a monster. But she had better do something besides huddle here for if there were wolves in the woods, there were snakes in the grass, madmen in the cities. . . . She got up and washed the dishes. She said to herself, severely, Okay, you're locked up all alone in this shack in this wild place. But you better not make such a big thing of it.

When she came to the coffee pot she drank a little of what was left. She was leery of lighting that dirty, rickety-looking, dangerously unfamiliar kerosene stove. So she drank the coffee cold.

All day she alternately lay watching, listening, thinking,

or she bustled, trying to do something. Nobody came by. Sam Lynch couldn't care for her. She must have been right in the first place. He worked for Ambielli. If there was such a one, such a creature.

But Sam Lynch couldn't really care for her. A man like that? Alan said he was half crooked. *His* principles must be a little off, a little whacky. And how could he be attracted by such a one as Katherine Salisbury?

Always called her sister. Strange man. She mustn't think like a vain little fool. What could there be about her to interest him? What could there be? She looked at it, trying to look honestly. He must be working for Ambielli (and had a conscience). But she thought, no. Either he is a madman, all mixed up, fighting things just shadows in his brain, or he has blundered into a terrible mess because he cares for me.

Sam was old. He didn't touch her and she certainly didn't want him to. She thought, it doesn't go by any pattern. That's the trouble. And then thought, fleetingly, Alan won't know what to make of it.

Oh, she wished Alan would come. Alan knew how to be a hero. If he knew where she was he would just come.

But she thought, uneasily, It's a simple world if you know how to be a hero. That makes it easy. For one thing, you'd know when to die.

Sam kept saying he didn't want to die.

Well, she didn't, either.

She was lying on the bunk, her eyes wide open. Dark was piling up in the corners. This boarded up room was always dim. Dark would be early. If night came down and its black dark, what would she do?

Nothing to do. Go to sleep. She sat up, looking and feeling stubborn. She knew it was worthless to be afraid. It was too confusing. She took a match and lit the lamp. The shack seemed, at once, warmer and cozier. She took light into the bathroom and washed, and tidied her hair, and brushed at her rumpled brown skirt. Her face looked strange to her, thinner and tighter. I'm aging, she thought. Aged in the woods. She laughed at that, but, all alone, you can't laugh long.

She thought, darned if I am going to be so scared of that old kerosene stove. I'll make supper. I'll have something hot. I'll make some coffee.

But as she marched out to the main room, then, at last, she heard a car.

Salisbury stood in the dingy booth and said into the phone, "Martha? Did they call?"

Martha said, at once, "Yes, Charles. Mr. Reilly called back. They lost Sam Lynch. A reckless driver forced a truck to ram into them. He thinks the reckless driver was Ambielli. Where are you?"

"We're on the wrong side of the lake. Lynch didn't warn us of the turnoff. Now we have to work around it. Are the police—?"

"The man is here now."

"You're telling him everything?"

"Yes, Charles."

"I'll call you."

It occurred to Salisbury as he hung up what a bare and bald exchange of unhappy facts the call had been, between him and his love. Neither of them had spared the other anything. Or mentioned hope. But they were strong and hopeful, just the same.

Sam saw the swerving of the cars behind him and saw the traffic knot, and he skittered around a corner and was running free. He corkscrewed west. Finally he found a curb and drew up and sat still, trying to close his staring eyes. The eyelids kept fluttering, wanting to fly open. They would not rest. But he needed to rest a moment, having escaped with his life.

What now? The girl's old man would get up there to the shack. Sam wouldn't go there. She'd be home, soon. But Sam would stay away. What must he do, where go, to lie low and yet observe?

The northbound traffic on the avenue was sliding by, not fifty feet away. A blue car went, in the pack, past the street where Sam sat. It took a spurt as if it had an impulse and it switched to a left lane. It went west on the next westbound street, looped south making left turns all around, until it was on the avenue again. Northbound. Same as before.

Quick sharp horn blasts touched off a motorist's reflexes and opened Sam's eyes. He could see no trouble. The light changed on the avenue. A blue car got off to a slow start in the near northbound lane. Out of the window of the blue car Baby Hohenbaum was hanging, as if he were looking at his front fender. There was no doubt it was he. And it was the blue car's horn that still emitted yelps like coughs.

Sam rode the shock. Either it was a fantastic coincidence, good luck or bad luck, or it was not. Or it was: Hey, Sam, lookit! Or it was tag. Or it was: hey, Sam, tag, you're *it!* Sam's black eyes were despairing.

Ambielli said, "He make the turn?"

"Yeah, boss. Coming out slow."

Ambielli showed teeth. "Ask the cop," he nodded slowing up. "Ask him how to get to Shawpen Lake from here."

"I know how."

"Ask him."

The car's noise smashed the busy silences. Kay ran to look through the crack and made ready to scream a fine great scream, to tell a stranger she was here. And get out. Get home. Be saved.

But it was Sam's car rattling down the incline, lurching under the shelter. "Ah, so," said she aloud, "he deigns to come back." She was furious.

His key worked the lock behind her. She didn't even turn around. "Good evening," she said coldly.

He came and turned her with his hands. "Sister, do this for me. Listen. Listen good. There isn't much time."

"What is it now?" she scoffed. "Wolves, I suppose."

"All right. You're mad. I get that. Listen, I've got in ahead of a procession. My God, I hoped you'd gone. I hoped you'd gone. Listen, I got up the back way. They asked for the lake. Maybe they wanted me to know it. Maybe they *permitted* me to get here ahead and alive, just to make double sure. Makes no difference. You got to get out. Go home."

"Well!" It was the first bit she understood at all. "Gladly."

"Don't take any time," he warned. "Do this for me, sister. Death I don't care for."

"So you've said before." She was scornful.

He looked worn. His black eyes were desperate. "Put your coat on." He began to push her arms into the sleeves. "Got money? Here's money. Climb up the bank farther down the shore. You'll be on the road. It's a dead end, that way. But you go that way. Come to a field. Just cross it. There'll be a paved road the other side of the field. Go to your right on that road. You'll come to a corner, about a mile. That's the highway. You can do that?"

"I can do anything to get away from here," she blazed.

"You're mad at me." He stated it sadly. "Listen, there is a

bus, on the highway. You could take it. You could get a couple of towns along before you tell a cop who you are."

"I'll tell the first cop I see."

"All right," he said.

"I could have done that days ago."

"I know. I know."

"You didn't care about my safety."

"I cared some," he said. "Listen, sister. Ah, I wish you weren't mad. Maybe you would lie for me." They were going toward the door. "I told your people. They think I'm a liar. You could make me a liar."

Her heart swelled. "You told . . . ? You saw them? How are they?" she cried, looking up at him.

"Your mother is quite a little lady. Looked it square in the face."

"*What* in the face?"

"Your danger."

"*You* are my danger," she cried, furious, wanting to wound him. "Every single thing. I could have burned!"

"You're alive," he said sadly. "The key was in the coffee."

"It's worthless," she cried out at him. He couldn't follow. He couldn't know she meant his fear.

"Yeah, yeah, I am your danger," he agreed. "Hurry. Get away from me."

"Sam . . ."

"Go on. Get—Wait. Do you hear anything? I don't hear anything."

"Sam, you . . . You think I am *your* danger. Is that it?"

His eyes flickered uneasily. "Yeah, that's my heroic position. I didn't intend to die for you. I kept trying not to, sister. I could write a book."

"Oh," she cried. "You're always . . . What are you talking about? I think you're crazy."

"Oh, I am. I am. Never mind. Go on, get out of this place before anybody shows up. At last you'll be safe."

She pricked her ears up. "Who is going to come?"

He looked at her and his face was frantic. "I don't know," he yelled.

"What are you so afraid of, Sam? Please."

"I told you." He talked rapidly. "It's a procession. Or I fear so. Why would they ask if they weren't on their way? Only I told your people. And Alan's on the way, too."

"Alan!"

"And who is going to get here first I do not know. Maybe by now Alan's found the turnoff. Or maybe it's Ambielli."

But she was joyful. "Why, if it's Alan!"

"Yeah, then you're all right," he looked desperately sad, "if you'll be careful. And make them be careful. Ah, sister, will you remember? I won't be here. Either way, I'll die. Ah, hurry."

She didn't budge. Looking at him, she said, "I was scared this morning. It's a bad feeling."

"Telling me." He stood looking at her intently.

"But it's worthless," she cried. "Why can't you throw it away, Sam. It's got you mixed up. Don't be so."

He groaned. "It isn't the hero who does it the hard way. I've died my thousand deaths, believe me, already. Please, now . . ."

"Oh, I'm not going, if Alan is on the way."

He sat back against the table and covered his eyes. In a moment he said, pathetically, "What am I going to do? What am I going to do? Cried wolf too often. What am I going to do if I can't scare you? You're not scared. You won't hide."

"Sam, you come with me. We can both hide, in the trees, and see who is coming."

"I am your danger," he shook his head. "Get away from me. You want to be hunted down in the dark? Don't hide with me."

She shook her head, thinking of shadows in his mind. She felt sorry.

"I wish you weren't mad," he complained, with his eyes still hidden. Then, softly, "I had a hunch you'd listen. I thought you'd lie for me."

"Sam, I am." She pitied him. "I am listening."

"Ambielli, once he's sure I've got you, is going to . . ."

"Kill you. Yes, I know." She'd heard this too often.

"But he doesn't want you any more. Your papa paid ransom to Ambielli. Never mind that. You'll never get the straight of it. Means you can freely go home. Leave, please leave me. If you leave me, I can try to cover."

She bit her thumb. Her hand fell. "You're afraid of Ambielli," she said slowly, "because you did save me."

"Yeah, I saved you, sister." He said harshly, "I am your hero. But don't you lie for me. A more pitiful hero you never met than me, sister. I had you saved, that is. Right now I'm kicking your life around again." He grabbed her. "Want to be a witness?" he raged at her. "Ambielli wouldn't let a witness live. For God's sake believe that. *Get out of here,*" he bellowed. "You can't wait for Alan now!"

She pitied him. "Sam, what must I do? How . . . lie for you?"

"Aaah," he murmured, holding her elbows, thrusting against her stubborn push to stand still. "You could have said you saw no faces. You didn't know who took you away. Told this to the cops, the papers . . ."

"Lied to . . . Ambielli, Sam?"

"In effect. And so to everybody."

"Everybody?"

"Especially Alan, that's what I meant. You could do it, if you'd go."

She took a step in the direction he wanted her to go. "How could I lie to Alan?" she asked uncertainly.

"Not forever. Ambielli isn't going to live forever. I never meant forever." Now he had her moving. He was pushing her to the door. "Ambielli's got to be sure. You could still lie for me. Sister, if you'll go."

She pitied him and all she really believed in was his terror. "Sam, I'm going to stay. I'm not afraid."

He let go of her suddenly. "I don't hear anything. Do you?"

"No." She stood there quietly. She shook her head.

"Should have got here by now," he said anxiously. Suddenly he reeled back toward the table and sat down in the chair. "Mother, Mother, I'm mixed up. Maybe it wasn't Baby's face. Maybe I couldn't see. Maybe the cop said another lake. I'm hearing things. Ah, how right you are. It makes me worthless."

She said, quietly, "Sam, don't you see? I can explain it all to Alan and Daddy. Without lying. Ambielli won't find out for sure, through *us.*"

"Of course not. Of course not. Only fancy." He drew a long breath. "All right. It is possible that I am too devious. I would run, I would twist, I would hide. But, sister, I can listen. All right, there's a fifty-fifty chance, at least. You're not afraid. All right, it's worthless."

She sat down quietly. "I am too devious," Sam said feverishly. "So Alan says. How right he is. You notice? Types he calls us. All right. He's right. And I hate him because I don't want him to be right. And that's a fact. I want to think we're mixed-up mixtures, every one. I want to think we've got our deviations, and we've got a chance, because we can listen, and the whole world's a slippery place because of that. I don't want to know myself a type, and doomed to do what a smart one like Alan reads in the tabulations. I don't want to think you are a romantic young thing, period. It's too God-damn simple! And I don't believe it and I can't do it and I don't want to!"

"*And I'm not,*" she said indignantly. She was drawn to him, to comfort him. She stood.

"Well, you'd have to be, to lie for me. And how that's devious!" He put his head down on the table. "I can't hear anything. God knows, I make mistakes."

She said gently, "I don't know much about you, Sam. I just know you got into this mess, you're scared the way you are, on account of me."

He said, "I don't know what it was, either. I just didn't want *you* to die. Took a freak notion."

"For a stranger," she said.

"For a . . . one," he said oddly.

She said, "You aren't a type, either. We just— It's funny."

"Go home. Go home. Run away. Don't stay. *I'm afraid!*" He looked frantic.

Something turned her head.

There was a face against the glass, high in the kitchen wall. She could see it through the doorway, just as she had once imagined. It was a real face. Eyes, nose . . .

"Sam," she said, by some instinct, very quietly, "there's a face . . ."

CHAPTER XVIII

He didn't move.

"Sam, is it Alan?" She stood beside him, her hand lightly on his shoulder.

"No," he said, "because I didn't hear anything."

"What shall we do?"

"Sit in my lap," he said. And he turned and drew her down and cradled her in his arms. Yet, he didn't touch her. He sat like the Lincoln in the monument his tall body brooding around her. He sat still as stone.

She put her left arm up around him.

"I never wanted to play it this way, sister," he murmured. "Know what to do?"

"I'm not me?" she whispered.

"Small hope. But every fly tries."

"To wiggle out," she said. "Is it Ambielli?"

"Must be."

"But Alan is coming."

"Try to . . . waste Ambielli's time. They might get here. Like the marines."

He kissed her. But it was play acting. He didn't really touch her.

She slid her fingers into his hair. "Sam, you have a gun," she whispered, "haven't you? I can feel it in your pocket."

"Your name is Bonnie Mae. Miss Mae."

"All right, Sam. Why don't they come in?"

"Time is wasting. Don't complain."

She sat up straighter and took his face in two hands. His eyes were sick and terrible. "You fool, Sam," she said in a loud flat voice. And she kissed him and let her lips slide on his cheek and said, below his ear, with curiosity, "Why don't you kill Ambielli?"

He pulled his head back to look at her. The flat dusty look was gone from his eyes. "So simple?" he inquired. "To get

135

Ambielli? You and all your ignorance and all your money, and I never thought of it!"

"Don't have to sit and be killed . . ."

"Take the risk?" he inquired. "Walk right up to the risk, and then it's self-defense? Who trained you up? Your mama? Sister, there is no such thing as a type. There is not."

"Of course not."

"It's a lie. It's a big lie."

"It's a big fat lie."

He kept laughing and he rocked her. "My blood-thirsty lamb, will you let me?" He no longer needed to explain. They were finished with plodding through screens of language. She used her body to conceal his hand that put the gun in the table drawer. It was necessary to conceal the weapon they would use, if and when . . .

Now their hearts beat with exactly the same rhythm as they listened. It was odd. It was an enlargement of the heart, a doubling.

Suddenly he let go his embrace and she nearly fell. He said, in perfect suspicious surprise, "Somebody's out there!"

And she was easily surprised, too, and easily she turned as if she were shocked to look at the door.

He put her aside, and she allowed him to do so reluctantly as if she hadn't heard what he had heard and didn't believe he had heard anything. Sam got cautiously up. He said in rather an angry tone, "Somebody sure as hell is out there."

Somebody tapped on the door.

"Who's that? Who's there?" Sam's cry was prompt.

The voice, outside, was matter-of-fact and calm. "Sam?"

"*Huh!* Wait a minute, Bonnie. Company, for the Lord's—"

"What kind of company?" Kay said shrewishly. "I thought you said nobody's going to be up here. Listen."

"Wait a minute," Sam, close to the door, said, "For the Lord's sake, is that *you*, boss?" in a squeak of astonishment.

"It is I, Sam," Ambielli's voice replied.

Katherine Salisbury flounced over to a bunk. "Why don'tcha let the Professor in, Sam?" she snapped. "Don't mind me."

Sam's eyes rolled to look at her and they were full of laughter and her heart caught in her throat and settled back and she puffed out her bosom and crossed her legs high and the sense of danger sang in her head, her arm, her breast, and it was marvelous. And she heard him say so, heard him murmur, "Oh, this is marvelous!" and he swung open the door.

"Hi, Ambielli. And Baby, too. We-ell, come in. Come in."

The small thin unhealthy man standing in the door was dangerous. The big man behind him was only his weapon, controlled by the fingers of his hand, obedient to his anger. "Stand still, Sam," he said softly.

Sam's mouth opened and closed. The big man pushed through, slapped and felt of Sam's pockets.

Kay looked on with round eyes. He really did do that. He felt of Sam's pockets. It was such a familiar thing. It was almost like being home again, in a world one knew. This was a way to behave, a convention.

She said, trying to keep a flat twang in her voice, "Who's your friends, Sam?"

"Listen, Bonnie . . ."

"Stand still." Sam stood still.

The big one turned to look at her and his lips were pushed forward to a pout and his brows knitted in pain at the in-justice of everything. But Sam slouched there, as if he weren't worried, but just resigned to waiting out this time-wasting misunderstanding.

Kay said, "Whoever they are, they got nice ways. I'll say that."

"Wait a minute, Bonnie. Please." Sam didn't look at her. It was right that he didn't. It was a good act. But she could feel the red-brown eyes of that small man scorching her now. She leaned on the wall at the head of the bunk and she dragged her own eyelids up insolently and she stared back at him. She said to herself, inside her head, who do you think you are?

"This is Ambielli," Sam said. Kay thought to herself, made her mind repeat it, Ambielli who? Which one? The big one or the little one? She knew these thoughts went out across the room just as if she had spoken.

"What's the girl doing here?" Ambielli said and his voice was thinned, sharper, like a nervous blade.

Sam said with a touch of stiffness. "I might ask the same of you."

"You don't need to ask."

"Don't I?" said Sam thoughtfully. He took an apparently absent-minded step.

"Stand still," said Baby Hohenbaum. "You heard him."

"Excuse me, Baby. Sorry." Sam looked bored with the convention. "Still nervous, eh?"

Ambielli walked closer to Kay. Now the big one, too, came closer. The beams of their inquiring attention crossed and she felt pin-pointed at that crossing. They were converging upon her. She could not stare them both down. She looked, she spoke, alarm. "Sam, who are these guys? Listen, I'm not gonna— What is this? If it's a holdup, give them your wallet. Get them out of here."

Sam said, smoothly, "Is it a holdup, Ambielli?"

Ambielli turned around. "You won't try to be witty, Sam. Will you?"

"I can see it's not your mood," said Sam quickly.

"Shall I put him quiet, boss?"

"No."

Baby said, "What about her?"

Ambielli's eyes raked her again. "Who is she, Sam?"

"A friend," said Sam. "A little friend. Miss Mae, this is Mr. Ambielli. And Mr. Hohenbaum." Nobody said how do you do. Sam shifted his weight. "What's on your mind, boss?"

Kay broke into the rhythm. She bounced up. "I couldn't care less what's on their minds. I'm telling you, Sam. Either they leave or I do."

"Aw, Bonnie . . ."

"All right," she said. "This isn't my idea of a quiet evening."

"Believe me, honey, it isn't mine."

"Well, get them out of here."

"Look into her bag," Ambielli said quietly. His eyes hadn't left her.

"You will not!" She flashed around and made a grab for the handbag that lay on a shelf. Baby's big hand took her arm and bent it away. She squealed and kicked at him. "Sam!"

"Sorry, honey. Look, relax." Sam's shoulders squirmed. "They've got something on their minds. Nothing to do with you. Just be patient, please."

She sat down and devoted herself to feeling resentfully patient. Baby's hands rifled her bag. He looked hurt. He whined, "She don't look right, boss. Listen to the way she talks."

Ambielli said, "Yes. I was listening. So this is Bonnie? A week end, Sam?"

"A delicate way to put it," Sam said irritably. "I realize you must be nervous about something. I wish—"

"Don't be stupid, Sam."

"Come out with it, then."

"You never talk, Sam?"

"What do you want me to talk about?" Sam stepped, and the step brought him nearer the table.

"I'm asking whether you've talked already, Sam?"

Sam didn't deny it. He simply looked lost in thought a moment. Then, as if he found a verifying idea of his own, he exclaimed, "I see what you mean."

"I thought," purred Ambielli, "that you would."

"You were up there in Salisbury's apartment." Sam's voice was eager with curiosity. "How *was* that?"

"You were up there, Sam."

Sam said, "For questioning. You too?" He managed to exude curiosity.

Ambielli said, "If you talked to them, Sam, you know I'll kill you?" The voice was thin steel.

Sam's voice had a tremor. "Personally?"

"Perhaps even personally," said the little man. The big man pouted.

"Be an honor," Sam said grimly.

For the first time, Kay believed. There was no doubt that this little man would do as he said. Once he was sure, he would kill Sam Lynch. Something shimmered and quivered and vibrated inside the small shell of his body. It would kill. It wanted to kill. It could hardly wait.

But she made herself put forth curiosity. She pushed it out of her, generated it within her mind. She said inside, over and over, What is this about? What is this about?

Sam said, irritably, "Well?"

"See whether that's a wig," the little man said, and Kay felt the big hand in her hair and there was a tug and a yank and a frightful pain, and she raised her hands to her scalp as she was dragged forward.

He let her go and she fell on her hands and knees, and she couldn't see because of the tears of pain, but the big man took no interest in her hurt. He said, "It's hair."

She scrambled to her feet, drying her eyes on her wrist, and let the simplicity of pure rage take her completely. She cried out and with her fists she tried to pound the big man, and he grabbed her as she fought him. Words kept coming out of her throat.

Sam moved, naturally, away from the struggle. He sat down in the chair beside the table and he tilted it and he was laughing. His fingers caught at the table edge as if to keep the chair balanced on its two hind legs, and he kept laughing. Struggling with the big one, she thought surely it was time, but Ambielli never took his eyes off Sam so Sam kept laughing.

She twisted toward him. "And what's so funny?" she howled. "Tell me the joke. You, Sam!"

"Bonnie." Sam sobered. "Let her go, Baby. Bites, doesn't she? You want to ruin my private life?" His eyes crinkled to laugh.

Ambielli said, "Let her go."

"Aw," said Baby in profound disgust, "this ain't Katherine Salisbury."

It was as if a stick cracked on something, as if a sharp rap sounded, commanding silence. And there was silence except for her panting breath.

Then Sam's body stiffened, and his two feet crashed on the floor, and his whole body jerked forward and then back. "*You're looking* for Katherine Salisbury?" he said as if he were strangling and the flesh of his cheeks rose up to narrow the wild mirth rising in his eyes. It was perfect, Sam's astonishment. The perfect reaction, including, as it honestly must, to be perfect, the joke of it. It shouldn't have been perfect. Ambielli said, "Shut up," and another brittle thing began to crack.

Sam put his head in his hands, "Sorry," he said quickly, apologetically, fearfully. "Sorry. Excuse me. I didn't mean— I thought—Sorry, boss." Kay thought, now he will die just for thinking it's funny. And she believed this, and the whole room rocked on the edge of that catastrophe.

Baby's big hands had released her. Baby was trembling. He waited for the boss to say. She tossed her hair away from her face. She thought, but we fooled him. We can't spoil it now. *No.* So she walked deliberately between Sam and Ambeielli and stood on the line of tension, the straight line between them. She leaned over the table. She said, "Give me the keys."

"Huh?"

"The keys to your car. I'm getting out of here. I'm leaving, Sam."

"Aw, Bonnie, look, just because there's been a little trouble, don't—"

"There's been too much as far as I'm concerned. Give me the keys. You boys can settle your troubles all alone."

"Going to walk out on me," Sam said bitterly.

"If there's going to be any killing," she managed to sound scornful.

"Nobody's going to do any killing."

"He looks like the type," she said, "this friend of yours. I don't think he's kidding. Where are the keys? In that drawer?" She began to lean over.

Sam put his hand on the table drawer. Their cold fingers touched. "I trust it's okay with you boys if Bonnie runs out on me. I guess the evening's disenchanted." He could snatch the drawer open. She was between him and Ambielli.

Baby growled something. But Ambielli spoke and his voice was soft again. It had been drawn back, the blade to the sheath. "Don't go, Bonnie. I'd like to talk to you, Sam. It won't be necessary for the young woman to leave."

Why, maybe they had fooled him! Their cold fingers winced and wondered, together. She thought it seemed too easy. Maybe they hadn't fooled him altogether, but given him doubt. Maybe he wasn't sure.

Ambielli said, "There seems to be a lock on that door. Put her in there, Baby. She's a distraction. No way out, is there?"

"You're not going to put me . . ." She whirled. She would fight and occupy the big one. But she was still on the line between Sam and Ambielli and before she could duck aside, Baby came and lifted her away. Then she saw, as she threshed in his grasp, that now, somehow easily and magically, it was Ambielli who had a gun in his hand.

"Take it easy, Bonnie." Sam was sober and stern. "Do what the man says. Good idea if we can clear this up. We can try." Sam wasn't laughing any more. His hands were in his pockets. He tilted the chair.

CHAPTER XIX

BABY carried her to the bathroom and dumped her on her feet inside. She didn't protest. He closed the door. He locked it. The room was black dark. She looked up at the strip of glass. There was faint light, out there, from the night sky. There were no faces. In all the vast night she could hear no sound of any car.

But she could hear Ambielli say, "Who sent Dulain after me, Sam?"

"That I don't know." Sam answered promptly.

"Why were you there?"

"Because they found out I ate with you on Wednesday."

"They did?"

"That's the way I got it."

"Why did they care?"

"I couldn't say."

"You don't say, Sam, as a rule. Break the rule."

"Is that a question?"

"That's advice."

"I'm talking," Sam said bitterly. "You listening?"

"Did you mention a newspaper picture?"

Sam hesitated. Then he said sharply, "I left that in Nick's." There was a beat of silence. "Nick have any two's to put together and make four, boss?"

Silence.

The big man growled.

"Do you think . . . ?" Sam began.

"I ask. You talk. What happened?"

"Where?"

"Up there."

"At Salisbury's place?" Kay could hear the creaking of the wooden chair. "Dulain asked how well I knew you."

"And?"

"I said, naturally, I knew who you are. Asked me did we

143

have lunch on Wednesday. I said, yes. Asked me had I planned to meet you. I said, no, happened to go into Nick's.

"Asked me if I knew where you went afterward. I said you left ahead of me. I didn't know. Asked me where is Katherine Salisbury. I said, isn't she here?"

"That's all, Sam?"

"No. Maybe this is something. Listen. They made me print some stuff. It was instructions. Part of a demand for money. You see what I thought?"

"Aw, we got the money," Baby said.

Ambielli hissed at him.

Sam said, in awe, "You never did!" His voice went on gathering reverence with the surprise. "Somebody else did the dirty work. You got the money. That's—that's . . ." The chair bumped the floor. "Marvelous! It's sweet. What a twist! Who . . . ?"

"Ah," said Ambielli, "how I wonder who."

"You care, eh?" Sam conceded this.

"I would like to know."

"I can see that you would. And yet . . . saved you trouble." The idea was delicately extended.

"I don't mind trouble, Sam. I do mind interference."

"Wait a minute. See what you mean. Somebody did more than talk." Sam spoke with lively interest. "If it was talk, the Salisburys would have locked her up. Nobody could have gotten her. And in that case, they'd never pay off."

Ambielli said smoothly. "It may have been that they didn't expect to pay off. There was an element of surprise, you see, Sam, as it was collected. It occurs to me that they may have had an ambush farther up the line."

"Real money?" Sam said quickly.

There was no answer.

"At least the numbers would be listed. That money must be hot."

"A test has been made," Ambielli said, dryly.

"It passed?" Sam sounded startled.

There was no immediate answer. Then Baby said, "It sure did," and laughed in a high whinny.

"You know a little too much for my best comfort, Sam. You can see how that is?"

"I don't know much more than I knew last Wednesday." Sam said tartly. "I remember, you said then, you never worried."

"Unless and until, I said, Sam."

"Make up your mind." Sam sounded weary. "Don't let me influence you. I'll tell you this much. I wish I'd never gone to Nick's. The trouble you can get into in fifteen minutes. So your whole damn future takes a zig or else a zag. I wish I'd had settled for tea and toast. You're not the only one thinks I had something to do with it."

"Who else, Sam?"

"That Dulain."

"We know. He put a tail on you."

"So he did," said Sam smoothly. "But I lost them."

"Oh, yes, you lost them, Sam. We helped a little. We rather got in the way."

"You were there, boss?"

"Now, come, Sam," Ambielli chided. "You know we were there."

"I do?" said Sam. "Well, if you say so."

"Could I help wondering, Sam?"

"No. You couldn't help wondering. Followed me all the way up here, eh, boss?"

Then Ambielli must have laughed, although Kay heard no laughter except the afternote in his voice as it went on. "It was unnecessary. Since Wednesday, we had asked around. Heard you had this little place. Naturally, I wondered." The voice sharpened. "I'd have stopped wondering, if they hadn't so obviously put a tail on you, Sam. I'd have been quite sure about you. I'd have been convinced that you were the one . . ."

"Is that right?" Sam said. "The one who . . . ?"

"Who took Katherine Salisbury, on Wednesday, and hid her somewhere. Who is working with that Dulain. Who let the father follow instructions. Who kept him in the dark, to make it convincing. He was convincing. Who set up an ambush that failed. Who went in, today, for another little conference. To plan how to trick me . . ."

Kneeling on the floor in the dark behind the door, Kay saw through the little man's eyes how she was nothing. She was a checker, a wooden piece, to be moved from square to square in a game he played for blood and money and for a lust to win. And so Ambielli thought she must be to Sam, too. And so Ambielli thought Sam was moving the piece as an enemy, for the other side.

But she could see that Sam was on no side so much as that

of the pawn itself, the little piece, which was not wood, but Katherine.

Then she heard Sam say, steadily, "Yet they put a tail on me. Doesn't fit, does it?"

"I wonder if you were that clever . . ."

"That devious," murmured Sam. "The credit is nice. Don't give me too much credit. Tell me, why would I do all this, boss? I don't seem to me to be the type."

"I hadn't thought so, Sam."

"I've got a reputation, too, you know."

"A reputation for not talking. But tonight you are talking. Aren't you, Sam?"

"I'm telling what I know," Sam said slowly. "It's possible, I could look around. I might turn up Katherine Salisbury for you."

"Are you sure she isn't in that bathroom?" Ambielli said softly. "Because I'm not, Sam. Not sure at all. Clever little girl, if she's Katherine Salisbury. But her vocabulary was literary, I thought. Didn't you?"

Silence.

"Keep your hands still, Sam. I'd rather you didn't move at all."

Silence.

"How shall we make sure?" Ambielli purred.

Then, in the vast night, a sound began. At last, again, there was a car approaching.

Kay knelt on the floor and listened to that noise. In the outer room, the shack's door whined on its hinges. She had a vision, painted on the dark that pressed against her eyeballs, of the finger flick that had sent the big man out to see. For she could still hear the car and Ambielli was still there. "Sit still, Sam."

She could barely catch Sam's muttering. ". . . sake, Bonnie's going to love this. Probably that damn Dulain." Then loudly, "Who is it, Baby?"

"Looks like Dulain. And the old man."

"What?" That was Sam.

"Alone?" drawled Ambielli.

"Yeah, boss."

"Another conference, Sam?"

"How do I know what the hell they want now?" Sam exploded. "Boss, if they find you and me, when they already think . . ."

"Would you like me to leave, Sam?" Ambielli was amused. Sam had no answer.

Kay's fingers and her teeth ached. She couldn't make her mind inquire into the future. Her imagination hit a blank wall.

"Step outside, Baby. Keep dark." Ambielli was moving around out there. "What's this place? Oh, the kitchen. This will do, I think."

Now, astonishing her, the key clicked near her ear. She almost fell out into the light.

Ambielli said, "In here, please." She got clumsily to her feet. Sam was still in the chair. But everything seemed blank. Ambielli now swiftly locked the door of the empty bathroom and took the key out of the lock. She couldn't understand.

He said, softly, "I am curious to see what they want of you, Sam." He was smiling. He held the gun in his hand. "I am very curious to see what their reaction is to your little friend who will stay in this room, to be seen. Do you know, I have an idea that their reaction will resolve all my uncertainties about you, Sam. Don't you think so?"

He smiled. He went into the kitchen and closed the door.

Kay looked at Sam. She understood now. She couldn't hide. She was there to be seen and recognized. Then came another thought. Ambielli must believe that cupboard door led outside. But it did not. There was no way out of that kitchen. She thought, Why, he's caught. He's caught in there.

Then, she thought, And I'm caught in here. I can't hide. No place to hide. The minute they see me, Ambielli will be made sure.

Then she thought, it is Sam who is caught. Then, wildly. Everybody's caught! *Somebody's going to die!*

It was too late for her to run out of doors. There were feet on the wooden porch already. And the big one was out there, anyhow. Keeping dark. There was no way to warn them. Sam said he'd told them so they *expected* to see her. She couldn't fool her own father with her streaked hair. Everybody was caught.

The kitchen door was a plywood slab. No lock, no key, no keyhole. Ambielli could hear, but he could not see. She said shrilly, "Sam, I don't like it. Feels to me somebody's going to get hurt. I don't want to get mixed up . . ."

He already had the gun in his hand. He nodded. He said soothingly, "Take it easy. Just take it easy. We'll see what this bunch wants." But his eyes had already left her face to fasten not on the door of the shack, but on the kitchen door.

Somebody was going to die.

"I'm saying I don't want to get mixed up," she shrilled. "You got no business dragging me out here into this kind of mess . . ."

Her own father's voice was crying, on the porch outside, "Katherine? Katherine?" And she could not be glad.

"Oh, no," groaned Sam. "Not them, too!"

"I'll give you Katherine," Katherine screeched. "All of you. Everybody. Go ahead. Open the damn door. Let them in."

Sam didn't move. His eyes didn't swerve. The gun didn't shake in his hand. It was she who opened the door.

CHAPTER XX

LIGHT fell on her father's face, and she reached up and touched his opening lips with one finger. She leaned against him and felt the pain of his hands on her shoulders. But his reaction was quick and his control quickly taken. He understood that he must not speak, that something here forbad it. She felt surprised that he was so flexible and understood so soon.

Alan had pushed past them and was moving toward Sam. Sam did not turn, not even his head, or his hand, or so much as an eyeball. He kept facing the kitchen door and Alan couldn't see the gun. If only she could keep Alan quiet, too. She flew after him.

Sam said in a tired, disgusted voice, "All right, Dulain. What is it now?"

Kay reached up from behind and put her hands on Alan's mouth. "You get the funniest company, Sam," she jeered. "Look at him, looking at me. Say, who is this Katherine everybody's looking for?" Alan tore her hands away. "The woods are full of people looking for Katherine. What's *she* got, Sam?"

"Aw, Bonnie, sit down." Sam hadn't moved.

Her father now stepped near her again, and she had her hands fluttering, trying to tell them, when Alan, leaning on the table, said, "You actually told the truth, Lynch."

Sam snarled, "Yeah. Surprise."

It couldn't hold. It wasn't going to work. Something was going to give. Somebody was going to die.

"I didn't believe you," Alan said. And then, calmly, "Are you all right, Kay darling?"

She felt as if she could see straight through the plywood door, through the dark in there. She could see Ambielli opening the cupboard. The cans of food would move under his groping hand. She listened for one to fall. And she

149

thought, then what? Then what? When he knows he is caught and he can't get out, then what?

She was standing there, dismayed, pulling her cheeks down with the flat of her fingers, when Sam shoved her. Sam had moved. He shoved her father, too. They reeled and wobbled, clutching each other. They fell together against the corner of two walls. Alan made an angry sound, and Sam shoved him, too.

The plywood door was shivering. *Don't wait! Sam, don't wait!* But she had not yelled it aloud. Alan, scrambling for balance, with one hand on the floor, was doing the yelling. "You in there, look out! He's got a gun!"

Kay cried with all her might, "No, Alan! No."

Ambielli kicked open the door.

She had one glimpse of his face before Sam's gun went off twice. Twice seemed to be enough.

Sam watched the thing on the floor closely for a moment or two. Then he put the gun on the table, lifted his hand away from it as if it stung, touched it once again, quickly, lifted his hand, walked away, as far away as he could, back into the far corner. There he set down with his back against the wall.

Alan, who had lost balance, was sitting on the floor. He began, all over again, in a new way, to get up.

Salisbury pushed himself off the wall. "Katherine, I'm going to take you out of this. You mustn't . . . Don't look . . ." He was trembling with the joy of finding her. She pressed her head against his arm.

Watching Alan, she spoke to Sam. "Sam?" Her voice was all right. "The big one? That Baby?"

Sam said, "I'm tired. Some other hero can go get Baby Hohenbaum." He had his eyes closed. She could tell that he was shaking as if he had a chill. "I'm through," he said. "This ain't for me. I'm a bystander by trade."

Then they heard, outside, rather distantly, the sound of yet another car.

She thought, that must be the big one, going away. We never heard their car. Heard nothing, only saw the face. But they must have had a car. *She* was shaking.

She said, "I'm tired, too." She was still looking at Alan. She couldn't see him very well. She said, plaintively, "Alan, why haven't you come and kissed me?" She stretched her eyes and forced a focus. He was on his feet, standing rather tensely between the table and Sam Lynch. "Alan, don't be silly . . ." she began feebly.

Then there were feet pounding on the porch and in the open door were two men she had never seen.

Alan said, "Well, what delayed you?" in anger and relief.

"Lost him. We got rammed. Hey!"

"Hi ya, boys," Sam said. "Warner. Reilly."

"Was that Ambielli fixed to have us rammed? Hey, Sam?"

"I wouldn't be surprised," said Alan.

"Don't be surprised, Dulain," Sam closed his eyes again. "It was."

The stouter one of the newcomers grunted, having noticed. The thinner one's voice changed and cried, "*That's* Ambielli? There?"

"It was," Sam said. He opened his eyes. "You boys see Hohenbaum?"

"Not since—" Warner looked quickly behind him.

"I mean here? Around here?"

"Not around here, Sam."

"See his car, then?"

"No car but Mr. Dulain's. Parked up above."

"Who got Ambielli like this?" Reilly asked in some awe.

"Lynch," said Alan.

"Self-defense?"

"Murder," said Alan.

Kay stirred on the bunk where her father had gently guided her.

"And that's her? She's okay?"

"She's okay," said Salisbury vibrantly.

"Who had her? Ambielli?"

"Lynch had her." Alan licked his lip. Then he became a commander. "Reilly, get out on the porch. Watch out. Although if Hohenbaum was here he's run off by now, I'm sure."

"You're sure," Sam murmured.

"He'll save his own skin if he can," snapped Alan. "Don't worry. We'll get him. We'll get you all."

"Alan," Kay tried to sit up.

"We must get *you* home, dear," her father said. "My dear. Get you home."

"Warner, go back to the nearest phone and get some authority out here. They'll know about it by now. You may meet them. Tell them we've got Ambielli dead and Lynch alive."

"Alan," Kay said in alarm. Sam only sunk his chin on his breast.

"Lie back, dear. Please, Katherine. Ah, your pretty hair."

"Just lie back, sister," Sam said without looking. "Please."

Salisbury said, "Wait a minute, Warner. Alan, let me take her home."

"Wait for me, sir."

"But this . . ." Kay thought, Daddy means the body on the floor. How funny. It's not dangerous now.

"I can't let her out of my sight. It won't be long. Just until the police take over."

"Then call Martha. Let Martha know." Salisbury darted after the man Warner. "I can't leave Katherine. You must call Mrs. Salisbury." He and both the strange men mumbled in the doorway.

"I can't leave Katherine, either," Alan said, "ever again." Now he was near. He held her. He kissed her. "You're all right? Truly?"

"I'm fine," she said, still shaking. "Don't leave me."

"No, darling. We must get this straightened around. Won't take long."

"Alan, I don't think you realize . . ."

"He realizes," Sam's voice stabbed the whole width of the shack. "I snatched you, sister. I killed Ambielli. He's right."

"But, Sam! Alan, he *had* to."

"Had to?"

"Of course, he had to. Somebody had to die."

Alan touched her forehead. "Have you had any food?"

"Of course, I've had food. Alan, didn't you see his face?"

"Whose face, darling?"

"That man's. Ambielli's."

"Hush, Kay. He can't hurt you, now."

"I know what I'm saying." She struggled to sit higher. "You weren't here. You don't know. He was going to kill Sam and me and probably you and Dad . . ."

"I was here, Kay," Alan said, pityingly. "Lie back."

"Alan, *listen* . . ."

"Tell it to the judge," said Sam gloomily, distantly. "Write a letter to the editor."

"Tell it to the—! I won't! There isn't going to be any." She was thoroughly alarmed.

Salisbury had turned back and was inside, again. Now he raised both his fists and held them against his breast as if to keep his furious feeling in. "Lynch, I will make you suffer as nobody ever suffered." She had never heard such a voice, seen such a face.

"None of you understand!" Kay cried. "*Listen!* Ambielli was after me. That man." She didn't look where he lay. "And the big one. They would have killed me. Don't you know that? Sam hid me from them." Their faces looked blank to her. What she said bounced back to her. As if it were unheard, unused by their ears.

"You can't do this, darling," Alan said gently. "It's impossible. You cannot protect—"

"He's so right," Sam said.

"He's so wrong. Sam, you know it. It wasn't like a real— It was a freakish thing." She had her feet to the floor now and she tossed her hair back. "You'll have to do this for me, Alan. And Daddy, you, too. There's no time to argue. This is the time. Now, before we get mixed up with the police. No, no, *listen!* You and Sam together saved me from Ambielli."

"Kay, I'm afraid—"

"You've got to put it that way."

"It isn't true," Alan said stiffly.

"It's true enough. It's truer than you—"

"Truth is an absolute," Sam said. "And he's so right. Let it go, sister."

"Sam, do you *want* to be tried for kidnaping and murder?"

"No, not especially." He shrugged.

"Then . . ."

"Take it easy," he said. "Don't excite yourself. Nothing you can do. This will have to take its course."

"Why?"

"Because Dulain is right about it. Don't get female, now, sister. Don't you know what I did has to be passed on by society?"

"Society," she scoffed. "Aren't you the one to be talking about society."

"Let it go, sister," Sam sounded just terribly tired. "Let's us be glad we're living. Anyhow, save your strength. He can't listen."

Salisbury said, sharply, "*I'm* listening. Kay, tell me the truth. What did Lynch do?"

She struggled to use this chance and quickly make it clear.

"He didn't think you believed his warning. He was terribly afraid for me. That Baby didn't want to bother with me alive. The minute after they'd got me . . ." The faces were blank. "Have you *seen* Baby Hohenbaum?"

Reilly, out on the porch, strained into the darkness and saw no person. Warner drove past the deep dark tunnel in the trees and missed, again, the car that was hidden there. Where Baby Hohenbaum lay, on the bank above the shack, he was hidden. He kept dark. He knew what had happened. He knew who did it. He knew what to do. He laid his pouting baby face to the ground.

"Yes, I—" Salisbury faltered. "I've seen him. Like a big dog." His eyes fled from her face to Sam's bent head and back.

"Have you seen Ambielli, alive?" she insisted.

"Yes, I—"

"Well, they didn't get me. Don't you know they were here looking for me?"

Alan said, "Who got the money?"

"They did."

"Then, it's absurd," he scoffed. "Why look for you?"

"Because—because . . . Sam, tell them."

"Not me," Sam said. "Let it go."

"He would have killed Sam for interfering. Because of his pride, his—his kind of honor."

Alan sighed and looked patient. "Ambielli died for his honor? Ah, Kay. . . ."

"Sam, please. You tell them." He didn't move his head or open his black eyes.

"But, if what you say . . ." Her father at least looked less angry and more troubled now, "Surely Lynch could have spared us."

"There were better ways," Sam said. "Lots of better ways. I made a fine mess of it. Shouldn't have left my seat on the aisle. Come on, put me in jail. Glad to go. Quiet place. Just don't excite yourself, Katherine."

"Don't call me Katherine." She nearly wept.

"Excuse me, Miss Salisbury."

She wailed.

Alan said, "Kay, I *can* listen and I've *been* listening. And what I hear simply does not add up. Suppose he feared for you, as you say? And risked his life for you, as *he* says? *Why* a man like Lynch—"

"A man of my type," Sam muttered.

"Shut up, Sam Lynch. Yes, go on, Alan."

"Why would he do that for you, Kay?"

Alan really asked. Surely he would listen to the answer. She considered carefully. "Why, because he loves me," she said slowly. "It's the only word I can—" Alan's chin jerked up. "I'm not using it the usual way, not the ordinary sense, Alan!"

"What other sense is there?" Dulain said, white in the face. "I thought you had met just once. I must be wrong."

Sam had his head on his hands. "Do you give up, sister?"

"No," she blazed.

"Pray do." Sam rocked in the chair. "Spare us. Spare *me*, and let it go."

"One human being," Kay began slowly, "can just . . . care for another."

"Certainly," Alan said.

"No," she cried. "Alan! Dad?"

"I think," Salisbury was deeply troubled, "I think *you believe* he was your friend, Kay. Whether I do . . ."

"Thank you for that much respect, Dad." She forced Alan's eyes to hers. "Will you put this whole thing the way I suggest?"

He was stony-eyed. "Too late," he said stiffly.

"Will you enjoy hearing all this in some courtroom?"

"Kay, please. Naturally, you are . . ."—she listened for the word to fall—"overwrought," said Alan.

She stood up and she was very angry. She knew she looked glittery and dangerous. "Perhaps it was more what you think than you thought," she said coldly. "Sam is a pretty glamorous figure to a romantic young thing, an innocent fun-loving child like me. Perhaps I wasn't fetched. I came. Perhaps it was . . . oh, a week end. Any courtroom would catch on quite quickly, as quickly as you, Alan. Are we going to let it go at that?"

Alan said, turning from white to red, "Why? *Why* are you fighting for him?"

"For Sam? Why, because I love him," she said quietly, "although not quite as you understand it."

Sam said in a matter-of-fact voice, "I'd rather be in jail than listen to any more of this stuff. Thanks just the same.

Good try, sister. We'd crucify you if you tried that. Me and Dulain."

"W-would you?"

"Just be quiet," he said. "We've all got our reputations. Let some of us keep some of them." He got off that chair. "You're a cute kid."

She exploded into tears, and Alan caught her to him.

CHAPTER XXI

"Let me go?" Sam said, low voiced. "Don't you think it would be better, if I go?"

Alan snapped, "You're not cleared of any of it."

"Let me take Kay home." The father was distressed. "She mustn't cry so. She's not herself."

Sam said, "She's overwrought." His head hung.

"Alan, for her sake," Salisbury pleaded, "let him go."

"I *can't.*"

"I'd be available to the Law," Sam said. "I'm not good for her." His mouth twisted. "Naturally, she's overwrought."

Salisbury's face turned. "She's been so . . . frightened, so terribly scared."

Sam looked across where she wept, and Alan held her. "Put it that she was scared," he said. "It's understandable, isn't it? What do you expect from a young thing?" His hands were shaking, and he hid the fact in his pockets. "She's a cute kid, though. A man could die for her, you know it? Some hero type."

"She's so young," the father said, "and confused. Dreadful experience."

"Sure. Sure. Sure. And romantic, too. And I upset her. She thinks she owes me something. Better let me go."

"Kay, darling." She was tearing her heart out. Alan looked over her head. "A reaction," he grimaced. "Lynch, you can be found."

"Why, sure," Sam straightened. "That'll be easy. I won't be far. You'll find me. And about where you want me."

"Then, get out!" snarled Alan.

Sam's head turned to look at the door behind him. Reilly thrust his head in. "Lynch wants to leave," said Alan Dulain. "I think it's safe to let him go." A strange expression crossed Sam's face.

157

Baby Hohenbaum wiggled on the bank closer to the roof of the car shelter. From here he could see the shack's exit door. He lay quietly on the cold ground. He didn't feel the cold. He felt little of anything. The boss was gone, but he knew what to do.

All Kay could hear was her own stormy weeping, although she knew Alan spoke. She knew that he had nodded.

"Then I'll say so long," Sam said, too softly to be heard by her. "So long, sister. You've been marvelous."

The father's hand lifted, uncertainly. But Sam went quickly through the door and quickly closing it shut the light off behind him. The dark heap, high in the darkness, all attention now, lay still. Reilly said, "Sam, I don't get this."

"Oh, you'll see," Sam said. He started for his car.

Katherine wept.

"Hush. It's all right. I understand. Hush, darling." Alan stroked her hair. "It's all over now."

"He's gone, Kay." Her father crooned. "Now, soon, we'll go too. You'll be better. Mother will . . ."

"Gone?"

She stopped her weeping. She stopped hearing even their voices. Her ears examined the world outside. The night sounds boiled up. Something slid on the roof. The lake was chuckling in the dark. Her hair stirred of itself.

"Somebody is going to die," she said.

She wrenched away from Alan. "Gone? Sam's gone? But he mustn't go. Not until the police come. You don't understand." She ran out, eluding her father's hands, passing the man on the porch. She knew Sam mustn't go alone. There was the big one, loose somewhere.

Somebody was going to die!

She knew it as she had known it before. Death was around and about. Sam's gun was back there on the table. He had no weapon. Death waited for him. Somewhere.

No, no. He must stay. He must keep within, wait for protection. *She* would keep him. Somehow. Although she had no means, nothing to use. Words were no good. Too slow, too thickened, battered by a million tongues. She had her bare hands, her quick feet, running in the dark toward the car shelter, the wild folly of her heart that had no fear for herself, but could not tolerate his dying.

158

She caught him as he was opening the car. The only thing she had, the only instrument, was her own body. Well, she would put one hundred and fifteen pounds of girl's flesh against the death in the air. If it would not keep him, she had nothing else.

So she threw herself against him in the deep darkness and her arms embraced his hard tense shoulders and the impact of her softness and sweetness, hurtling out of the dark, astonished and defeated his stiff defenses. He touched her. She felt his arms softening around her and the bitter alien identity going, and a healing tenderness clasped them both. She thought, this is what it is to be safe. All it is. Ever. Don't want each other hurt . . . ever . . .

But Alan Dulain came running to the rescue. His heels jarred on the earthy path, and he switched on his flashlight. The bold beam hunted them and found them and they, embracing, were spotlighted, and the safe dark fell away.

The blob on the roof shifted. The muzzle of Baby's gun sneaked like a snake's tongue through a gap in the ragged shingles and steadied.

Below, as the dark armor was peeled off, danger sung around them like a blade flashing, and Sam's breath sucked in. He pulled her arms down, fastening them at her sides with his own. He turned her. He made a shelter all around her as tall and as wide as his bones, as thick as his flesh, as frail as his life.

As the gun cracked, a cry tore out of a husky throat and the beam of light, shocked, flew away. Reilly, husky with excitement, yelled, "Roof! Roof!"

Baby scrambled, but the nervous light pursued. Reilly winged him the first time. The second time, he stopped him.

But in darkness Kay was slowly pressed on the cold metal of the car in which the door handle scraped cruelly on her sliding back, as the whole warm weight of Sam's body slackened and bore her down.

CHAPTER XXII

WHEN she woke she said, angrily, at once, "You drugged me. You doped me."

Her mother said, "We had to, sweetie. You're home. It's morning."

Kay sat up and a great woe possessed her. "Did he die?"

"Not . . . yet, darling."

Kay seized her mother's little hand. "Where is he, mother?"

"Hush, he's in the hospital. Up there."

"Up there? So far?"

"Katherine." Her mother's face was pinched and different. "Sweetie, he's going to die. At least, it's terribly possible."

"I know, Mother. I know. I know that." She looked at her room. "So strange here. Not the same."

"It'll be strange a little while. It's strange to me, too."

"Yes, must be. Do I look strange? Mother, do *you* understand?"

"Some of it," Martha said wanly. "The detective who came to talk to me found a note. I don't understand . . . all of it."

"Sam . . . Sam said to tell you . . ." She didn't go on.

"I . . . rather liked him," her mother said.

Katherine kissed her. "What time—?"

"It's not late. Alan's here. You look all right, sweetie. Not too strange."

"I want to get up. Mother, have you called?"

"Just now. Your father just called."

She dressed herself in a suit because she would be going out.

Alan was in the big room with her father. "Feeling better?" Alan was tender. He was concerned. "You look more like yourself," he approved.

"Sam isn't dead?" He winced as she asked, as she looked at him. "What will happen if he lives, Alan?"

"I don't know, dear. Let's not—"

161

"There'll be no trouble about Ambielli," Salisbury said, hovering. "It was self-defense, and I'll so testify."

"Hohenbaum could talk a little," Alan admitted.

"But he is dead?" Alan nodded. She shivered.

"Kay, if Lynch lives, we are going to try to save you as much embarrassment as we can," her father said. "But it's a sensation. Don't look at the papers."

"No, I won't." Their eyes met, as if they were both grown up, she and her father. There would be embarrassment, they knew.

"So far . . ." Alan twitched.

"You told it my way?" she asked sharply.

"We haven't told much at all to any reporters. We're besieged, of course."

She sat down to her breakfast. Her parents, although their lingering hands patted their love to her, withdrew. Left her with Alan. She tried to eat her breakfast. She couldn't taste it. The cup nearly slipped from her hand.

"Waiting to see which way the cat jumps? Whether he lives or dies?" She pressed both hands on her mouth.

"Kay, darling," Alan was gently, "we all realize you were a bit hysterical last night. We'll just forget about it. Just don't, please . . . not any more. You're home, dear. You're safe now."

She thought, *safe?* "You'll forgive it, too, Alan? My hysteria?"

"Of course."

"And understand it?"

"Of course, I understand," he chided. "Sam Lynch did kill the man who had been frightening you so. You saw him do it. Of course, you were grateful to him."

"That's a . . . neat pattern," she said slowly, "but it isn't so. You see, he killed the man who was frightening *him,* and *I* made him do it, and he was grateful to *me.*" She looked at him. Alan was troubled. "Am I still hysterical?"

"You were, last night. The way you ran out so recklessly. That really proves it."

"It's hysterical to take a notion you don't want somebody else to die. Then, I guess Sam was hysterical?"

"Whatever he tried to do, he made a mess of it," Alan said lightly.

"Yet here I am," she said thoughtfully. "Weren't you hysterical in that sense, Alan? About me?"

"You're sounding rather bitter, Kay. I did the best I could. Tried to keep my head."

"Didn't . . . blunder?"

He said, "What makes you angry with *me*, Kay? Why do you want to hurt *me*?"

"Ah, no. I don't. I may. Because I can't marry you and I'd better say so." He looked as if he'd felt a whip on his face. "You have no respect," she explained gravely. "You don't respect me. I don't feel that you do."

"I'm sorry. I feel that I do."

"You'll forgive me my foolish hysterical gratitude? You never listened at all."

He said crisply, "I know it was more than gratitude. And I understand that, too. After all, I saw the two of you." She looked at him with widening eyes. "And I could have believed it was your extreme youth and your romantic impulses and the heightened emotional atmosphere. In fact, I still believe it." He lifted his chin. "I'll wait."

"Don't wait," she said.

"But I will say this. If Lynch recovers, before you leap, *you* wait, Katherine. Consider his age and his background. A more unsuitable match—"

"*Match!*" she cried. "Did you think we'd *marry*? Sam and I? I wouldn't think of it. Neither would he. It isn't . . . That isn't it."

Alan said, "Don't be a fool. That's *always* it. Putting it nicely. Whatever innocent girlish idea you may now have . . . of a platonic type of thing . . ."

Her face flushed. "You have a name for all types of things, don't you, Alan?" She looked at her hands. "I don't especially want you to be right. Nor would he. It would certainly be a crazy match. A perfectly wild thing. But you may be right. Sam says you always are."

He said, very gently, "I'm sorry. I shouldn't try to talk, today. You've been upset. I don't blame you. You can't help it, of course.

She thought, a wooden piece.

"Pretend I haven't spoken. Nothing was said. Just try to wait, and think . . ."

She said, gravely, "Yes, I'm waiting. I'm thinking. I have been upset. But I won't marry you, Alan. Did you *hear* me?"

"I would say we had all better wait and see," he murmured. "And so I will, dear." He went away. She watched him go.

Charles Salisbury drove her, himself. He insisted that Reilly must go along, too. He declared she must not be without protection.

They passed through a group of men, downstairs, to the car. "Good morning, Mr. Reilly. Daddy, aren't you locking the barn door?" Kay tried to smile.

"Never mind." Her father looked stubborn. "It's a slippery world."

"You're looking good, Miss Salisbury," Reilly said.

"Mr. Reilly, if he lives, what will happen?"

"He'll be all right. He could write a book."

Salisbury said, "You know he may not. You are prepared for that?"

"I just must go."

"I won't go in," he said, "but Reilly must walk with you. I think I understand. You feel you must go. He did a brave thing for you."

"He isn't brave," she said. "He's not a hero. That made it harder."

Salisbury said, "I see. I see."

It was just a big old house, this private hospital, painted white, charming among green trees. Three men with cameras took her picture, but she walked in, and Reilly followed, and inside there was only one woman in white behind a desk.

"I came to see Mr. Lynch."

The woman looked serene, but grave. "No visitors, I'm sorry. Mr. Lynch is on the critical list. We can't allow him any visitors."

"You can't tell me whether . . . ?"

"No one can tell."

"Or how long?" The woman shook her head. Kay stood still, and her senses examined the air. "Is he awake?"

"I don't believe he's been conscious at all."

"Is the doctor . . . ?"

"He isn't here, at the moment. Everything is being done."

"Will Mr. Lynch . . . wake before he dies?"

"No one can tell, my dear." The woman was gentle and serene. "Are you a relation?"

"There's a relationship," Kay said.

"It's not wise to wait here. We can call you. It would be better." The woman's eyes were kind.

"Please. Do call me." Kay gave her number. "If he should wake, can you give him a message? Say, Katherine . . ."

"Katherine . . ." She had a pencil.

"No. Don't say Katherine. Say . . ." Her throat hurt, her eyes stung. "Put it this way. Say, sister . . ."

Pencil wrote *Mr. L's young sister*.

"It's very important. Will you please give him my respects?"

"We'll give him your love," the woman said soothingly.

Kay began to correct her. But then she murmured, "Maybe it's all the same."

She turned. The place was so clean and serene. She sent her senses out again to examine this air. She couldn't feel death around. Not here. Not in the morning. She said to herself, we must wait and see. Alan is right about that, too. Wait and see, about everything. It's a slippery world.

She began to walk toward the door. Reilly joined her with the question on his face. Kay shook her head in the motion that means *unknown*.

She walked out into the sun.

Top-rating mystery novels by top-rated writers

ACE BOOKS

G-523 HOURS TO KILL by Ursula Curtiss
"Unusually fine thriller-romance."
—Anthony Boucher
and **THE FORBIDDEN GARDEN by Ursula Curtiss**
"Excellent!" — Miami News

G-525 THE TENTACLES by Dana Lyon
"Packs a terrific punch." — Boston Post
and **SPIN THE WEB TIGHT by Dana Lyon**
Never before published sequel to her best novel.

G-526 THE DREAM WALKER by Charlotte Armstrong
"Quite the best since her MISCHIEF."
—New York Herald Tribune
and **THE MARK OF THE HAND**
by Charlotte Armstrong
"A major name in American mystery."
—Los Angeles News

G-528 CERTAIN SLEEP by Helen Reilly
"Quality." — Atlantic Journal
and **DING DONG BELL by Helen Reilly**
"A very pleasurable thriller." — Harper's

G-529 MRS. MEEKER'S MONEY by Doris Miles Disney
"A beautiful job." — New York Times
and **UNAPPOINTED ROUNDS**
by Doris Miles Disney
"Fast-moving . . . excellent." — Saturday Review

50¢

Any of the above double books may be ordered directly from
ACE BOOKS, INC. (Dept. MW), 1120 Ave. of the Americas,
New York 36, N. Y. Enclose 50¢ per book, plus 5¢ handling
fee.